Mia Faces an Unexpected Enemy . . .

I believe in judging people by their faces, myself. This one looked mean, and that was why I kept riding. He made me feel nervous. . . .

The hard man said to the others, "This one will be riding along with us to Midland for protection." He smiled, and the impression I had of a cat, a predatory cat, was increased. . . .

I shook my head. "I don't think so."

What the man did then surprised me. He said, "I do think so," and reached for the gun in his saddle boot.

I whipped my sonic pistol out from under my coat so fast that he was caught leaning over with the rifle half out. His jaw dropped. He recognized the pistol for what it was and he had no desire to be fried.

I said, "Ease your guns out and drop them gently to the ground."

They did, watching me all the while with wary expressions. When all the rifles were on the ground, I said, "All right, let's go."

RITE OF PASSAGE

RITE OF PASSAGE

ALEXEI PANSHIN

A TIMESCAPE BOOK
PUBLISHED BY POCKET BOOKS NEW YORK

A portion of Part III appeared in substantially different form in the July 1963 issue of *If* under the title *Down to the Worlds of Men* and is copyright © 1963 by Galaxy Publishing Co., Inc.

A Timescape Book published by
POCKET BOOKS, a Simon & Schuster division of
GULF & WESTERN CORPORATION
1230 Avenue of the Americas, New York, N.Y. 10020

Library of Congress Catalog Card Number: 76-10808

ISBN: 0-671-44068-3

First Timescape Books printing March, 1982

10 9 8 7 6 5 4 3 2 1

Printed in the U.S.A.

This book is for Charles and Marsha Brown

He kissed my breast, moved his tongue experimentally over the nipple, and it swelled without my willing it. I thought my heart would become too large and break with the surge it made. We moved tightly into each other's arms

Contents

RITE OF PASSAGE

They that have power to hurt and will do none,
That do not do the thing they most do show,
Who, moving others, are themselves as stone,
Unmoved, cold and to temptation slow;
They rightly do inherit heaven's graces
And husband nature's riches from expense;
They are the lords and owners of their faces,
Others but stewards of their excellence.
The summer's flower is to the summer sweet,
Though to itself it only live and die,
But if that flower with base infection meet,
The basest weed outbraves his dignity:
    For sweetest things turn sourest by their deeds;
    Lilies that fester smell far worse than weeds.

William Shakespeare
SONNET XCIV

1

To be honest, I haven't been able to remember clearly everything that happened to me before and during Trial, so where necessary I've filled in with possibilities—lies, if you want.

There is no doubt that I never said things half as smoothly as I set them down here, and probably no one else did either. Some of the incidents are wholly made up. It doesn't matter, though. Everything here is near enough to what happened, and the important part of this story is not the events so much as the changes that started taking place in me seven years ago. The changes are the things to keep your eye on. Without them, I wouldn't be studying to be an ordinologist, I wouldn't be married to the same man, and I wouldn't even be alive. The changes are given exactly—no lies.

I remember that it was a long time before I started to grow. That was important to me. When I was twelve, I was a little black-haired, black-eyed girl, short, small, and without even the promise of a figure. My friends had started to change while I continued to be the same as I had always been, and I had begun to lose hope. For one thing, according to Daddy I was frozen the way I was. He hit upon that when I was ten, one day when he was in a teasing mood.

"Mia," he said. "I like you the way you are right now. It would be a real shame if you were to grow up and change."

I said, "But I want to grow up."

"No," Daddy said thoughtfully. "I think I'll just freeze you the way you are right now." He waved a hand. "Consider yourself frozen."

I was so obviously annoyed that Daddy continued to play the game. By the time that I was twelve I was doing my best to ignore it, but it was hard sometimes just because

I hadn't done any real growing since I was ten. I was just as short, just as small, and just as flat. When he started teasing, the only thing I could say was that it simply wasn't true. After awhile, I stopped saying anything.

Just before we left Alfing Quad, I walked in with a black eye. Daddy looked at me and the only thing he said was, "Well, did you win or did you lose?"

"I won," I said.

"In that case," Daddy said, "I suppose I won't have to unfreeze you. Not as long as you can hold your own."

That was when I was twelve. I didn't answer because I didn't have anything to say. And besides, I was mad at Daddy anyway.

Not growing was part of my obvious problem. The other part was that I was standing on a tightrope. I didn't want to go forward—I didn't like what I saw there. But I couldn't go back, either, because I tried that and it didn't work. And you can't spend your life on a tightrope. I didn't know what to do.

There are three major holidays here in the Ship, as well as several minor ones. On August 14, we celebrate the launching of the Ship—last August it was one hundred and sixty-four years ago. Then, between December 30 and January 1, we celebrate Year End. Five days of no school, no tutoring, no work. Dinners, decorations hung everywhere, friends visiting, presents, parties. Every fourth year we tack on one more day. These are the two fun holidays.

March 9th is something different. That's the day that Earth was destroyed and it isn't the sort of thing you celebrate. It's just something you remember.

From what I learned in school, population pressure is the ultimate cause of every war. In 2041, there were eight billion people on Earth alone, and nobody even had free room to sneeze. There were not enough houses, not enough schools or teachers, inadequate roads and impossible traffic, natural resources were going or gone, and everybody was a little bit hungry all the time, although nobody was actually starving. Nobody dared to raise his voice because if he did he might disturb a hundred other people, and they had laws and ordinances to bring the point home—it must have been like being in a library with a stuffy librarian twenty-four hours a day. And the population continued to rise. There was a limit to how long all this could go on, and that end was reached one hundred and sixty-four years ago.

I'm lucky, I know, even to be alive at all. My great-great-grandparents were among those who saw it coming and that's the only reason I'm here.

It wasn't a case of moving elsewhere in the Solar System. Not only was Earth the only good real estate in the vicinity, but when Earth was destroyed so was every colony in the system. The first of the Great Ships was finished in 2025. One of the eight that were in service as well as two more that were uncompleted went up with everything else in 2041. Between those two years we Ships planted 112 colonies on planets in as many star systems. (There were 112 at the beginning, but a fair number simply failed and at least seven acted badly and had to be morally disciplined, so around ninety still exist.)

We in the Ships learned our lesson, and though our Ship has only a small, closed population, we won't degenerate. We won't become overpopulated, either. We have a safety valve. Within three months of the day you turn fourteen, they take you from the ship and drop you on one of the colony planets to survive as best you can for thirty days. There are no exceptions and a reasonably high percentage of deaths. If you are stupid, foolish, immature, or simply unlucky, you won't live through the month. If you do come home, you are an adult. My problem was that at twelve I wasn't afraid to die, but I was afraid to leave the Ship. I couldn't even face leaving the quad we lived in.

We call that month of survival "Trial," and I don't think there was a day from the time I was eleven that it wasn't in my thoughts at least once. When I was eleven, a man named Chatterji had a son due to go on Trial, and he had serious doubts that the boy would make it. So he went to a great deal of trouble to try to ease the boy through. He found out where his son was to be dropped and then he coached him on every danger that he knew the planet had to offer. Then, before the boy left, he slipped him a whole range of weapons that are not allowed to be carried on Trial, and he advised him to find a protected spot as soon as he landed and to hole up there for a month, not stirring at all, thinking the boy might have more of a chance that way.

The boy still didn't make it. He wasn't very bright. I don't know how he died—he may not have been able to cope with one of the dangers he knew was there; he may have run into something unexpected; he may accidentally have blown his head off with one of those weapons he wasn't supposed to have; or he may simply have tripped over his own feet and broken his neck—but he didn't live to come home.

And Mr. Chatterji was expelled from the Ship. He may have died, too.

This may sound harsh—I can't judge. It doesn't really matter whether or not it's harsh, because it was necessary and I knew that it was necessary long before I was even eleven. At the time, however, this made a great impression on me, and if I had been able to force myself to face things outside the confines of the quad in which I lived I would have rested much easier.

There may have been other reasons, but I suspect that all this is why when Daddy became Chairman of the Ship's Council he decided that we had to move.

Boys and girls, all of us in the Ship grew up playing soccer. I'm sure I knew how to play by the time I was four or five, and I was certainly kicking the ball around earlier than that. We used to play every chance we got, so it wasn't surprising that I was playing soccer in the quad yard—Alfing Quad, Fourth Level—when I got word to come home. The yard stretches three floors high and two hundred yards in each direction. There's a regulation-sized soccer field, green and beautifully kept, in the yard, but some older kids newly come back from their month of Trial and feeling twice as tall because of it had exercised their privileges and taken the field for themselves. We had moved down to the smaller field set up in the far end and were playing there.

In soccer you have a five-man front line, three halfbacks who serve as the first line of defense and who bring the ball up so the forward line can take it and score, two fullbacks who play defense only, and a goalie who guards the nets. It's a game of constant motion that stops only when a penalty is called or when a ball goes out of bounds or when a score is made, and then stops only for a moment.

I was playing the inside left position on the forward line because I have a strong left-footed kick. It's my natural kicking foot.

From midfield, trying to catch my breath after running hard, I watched our goalie dive on a hard boot at the nets.

He was up almost instantly, bounced the ball once, then held it and kicked it high and long. The goalies are the only players on the field who are allowed to touch the ball with their hands. The rest of us have to use our heads, elbows, knees and feet. That's what makes the game interesting.

Our right halfback knocked the ball down and trapped it with his foot. The instant he had control, he passed the ball over to Mary Carpentier at center halfback and we all started ahead on a rush for the goal.

The ball criss-crossed between our halfbacks running behind us up the field almost as though it had a life of its own, a round brown shape that darted and dodged and leaped in the air, but always was caught and controlled, never quite getting away.

Once the other team intercepted the ball and it went back past midfield, but Jay Widner picked off a bad pass and we began to rush again. Finally Mary Carpentier headed a pass to me when I was in the clear for a moment. I had a step on Venie Morlock, who was playing fullback against me. She was big, but slow. Even having to concentrate on keeping the ball moving in front of me, I was faster than she was. I had a good opening for a shot at the goal when Venie saw she couldn't get the ball. She swerved into me, gave me a neat hip, and sent me skidding onto my face. I was running full tilt and couldn't help myself. I went flying and hit hard. My kick went bouncing out-of-bounds wide of the white posts and the net of the goal.

I looked up, sputtering mad. "Soccer is *not* a contact sport!" I said.

It was like Venie to pull something like that if she saw no other way to keep from losing, and especially to me. We were confirmed old enemies, though I think it was more of a deliberate policy on her part than on mine. Just as I scrambled up from the floor the wall-speakers whistled twice for attention.

There were always announcements coming over the speakers. This time they were calling for me. They said, "Mia Havero is wanted at home. Mia Havero is wanted at home."

Ordinarily Daddy didn't have me paged and let me come home when I was good and ready. There was a woman named Mrs. Farmer who used to tell Daddy that I was undisciplined, but that wasn't true. When Daddy did call for me, he only had to call once.

"Time for you to go home," Venie said. "Run along."

The immediate flash of anger I had felt when I was skidding along had passed, but I was still smoldering.

"I'm not ready to go yet," I said. "I have a fresh kick coming."

"What for?" Venie demanded. "It's not my fault that you ran into me."

If it was my own fault that I'd wound up on the ground, I had no reason for complaint. If it was Venie's fault, then I had a shot at the goal coming on a major penalty. That's soccer. I guess Venie thought if she denied doing anything long enough and loudly enough somebody would take her seriously.

Mary Carpentier, my best friend, spoke up then. "Oh, come off it, Venie," she said. "We all saw what happened. Let Mia take her shot so she can go home."

After some fruitless argument on Venie's part, everybody agreed I had a free kick coming. I set the ball on the X-mark on the ground in front of the goal.

The goalie was Mrs. Farmer's son, Peter, who was younger than I and slow enough to be put in the goal. He poised himself with his hands on his knees and waited. The goal is eight feet high and twenty-four feet wide, and the ball is set down thirty-six feet away. The goalie has a big area to cover but in two quick steps he can reach any ball aimed at the goal. It takes a good shot to get by him.

Both teams stood behind and watched as I backed off a step or two from the ball. After a moment I ran, faked a kick with my good left foot, and put a weak right-footed kick dribbling just past the goalie's outstretched fingers into the corner of the nets. Then I left.

I dodged into the outside corridor and made straight for my shortcut. I unclipped a wall grate that provided an entrance to the air ducts, lifted it off and skinnied through the hole into the dark, and then from the inside pulled the grate back into position. That was always the hardest part, clipping the grate in place from inside. I had to stick a finger through, then turn my elbow out and up so my finger could reach the clip, then wiggle the clip until it caught. My fingers just weren't long enough, so it was always a frustrating moment or two until I succeeded. When I had the grate in place, I turned and walked through the dark with a light steady breeze tickling my cheek. I concentrated on counting the inlets as I passed them.

Changing the Ship from a colony transport into a city was as big a job as turning my mother into an artist—her project ever since I could remember. And they had this much in common: neither was completely successful, so far as I'm concerned. In both cases there were a lot of loose ends dangling that should have been tied into neat square knots.

As an example, the point where our quad left off and the ones on either side began was completely a matter of administration, not walls. The quad itself, and they're all this way, was a maze of blank walls, blind alleys, endless corridors, and staircases leading in odd directions. This was done on purpose—it keeps people from getting either bored or lazy, and that's important on a Ship like ours.

In any case, there are very few straight lines, so in order to save yourself distances, you have to know which way to go. In a strange quad it's quite possible to get lost if you don't have a guide, and every so often they broadcast a general appeal to be on the lookout for some straying three-year-old.

I was in a hurry to make up lost time when I left the quad yard, so I had gone straight to my shortcut. If the Ship were a person, the air ducts would be the circulatory system. Your blood travels from your heart to your lungs, where it passes off carbon dioxide and picks up oxygen; back to the heart; into the body, where the oxygen is used and carbon dioxide is picked up; and then back to the heart again. The air in the Ship goes through the ducts to the Third Level, where it picks up oxygen; then through the ducts and into the Ship, where the air is breathed; then back into the ducts and down to Engineers, where water and dirt, carbon dioxide, and germs are removed, and a touch of clean water is added. They kick it around a little more, and then they blow it back up to the Third Level.

The ducts moved in straight lines, and walking within them you could move through walls and arrive almost anywhere faster than you could through the halls. Anybody bigger than I was was too big to squeeze through the grate openings—there were larger openings for repairmen, but they were kept locked—and all the other kids I knew were too frightened to follow me, so the shortcut remained my own private route. They all thought I was foolish to go where I did, and for the sake of prestige I liked to pretend that they were right, though they weren't. As long as you avoided the giant fans you were all right. It was simply that it was people, not things, that frightened me.

When I got to our corridor, I slipped the grate out and pulled myself up and out on the floor. I reset the grate and gave a swipe to my hair to teach it to behave and lie down flat again. I inherit my hair and eyes, my straight nose and my complexion from my Spanish and Indian ancestors on Daddy's side of the family, and though I wear my black hair short, it *will* misbehave.

"Hi, Daddy," I said as I came into our apartment. "Am I late?"

The living room was in a real mess. Books and papers were all in piles on the floor and the furniture was all shoved to one side. Our home ordinarily had a lived-in look, but this was far worse than usual.

Daddy was sitting in one of the chairs, sorting books. Daddy is Miles Havero. He is a small man just into middle age with a face that is hard to read, and a very sharp mind. He is mainly a mathematician, though he sits on the Ship's Council and has for years. He and I had lived in this apartment since I left the dormitory when I was nine.

He gave me an inquiring look. "What happened to you?"

"I didn't mean to be late," I said.

"I didn't mean that," he said. "I'm talking about your clothes."

I looked down. I had on a white shirt and yellow shorts. Across the front of both were streaks of dust and grime.

The Ship is a place where it is almost impossible to get dirty. The ground in the quad yards isn't real dirt-and-grass, for one thing. It's a cellulose product set in a milled fiber and plastic base—when a square gets worn they rip it out and put in a new one, just like in your living room floor. The only place there is dirt in any quantity is the Third Level, where there isn't anything else but. A certain amount of dirt does get carried out of the Third Level and spread and tracked around the Ship. Eventually it gets sucked into the collecting chutes and blown down to Engineers on the First Level, where it is used to feed the Convertors to produce heat, light and power inside the Ship. But you can see that ordinarily there isn't much opportunity to get filthy.

I once asked Daddy why they didn't work out a system

to keep the dirt at its only source—the Third Level—instead of going to the trouble of cleaning the Ship after it gets dirty. It wouldn't be hard to do.

He said, "You know what the Ship was built for, don't you?"

"Yes," I said. Everybody knows that. It was built to carry Mudeaters out to settle the Colonies—I don't call them that in Daddy's presence, by the way; though it may seem surprising, he doesn't like the word.

Daddy went on to explain. The Mudeaters—Colons, rather—were packed in at very close quarters. They weren't clean people—try to convince a peasant to wash—and people packed in as close as they were are going to sweat and stink anyway. For that reason, mainly, the Ship was built with a very efficient cleaning and air-distribution system. The Ship is used now for a completely different purpose, so we no longer need that system.

Daddy said my suggestion wasn't completely out of line.

"Why doesn't the Council do something about it, then?" I asked.

"Figure it out yourself, Mia," Daddy said. He was always after me to try to figure things out myself before I looked them up or asked him for the answers.

I did figure it out. Simply, it would be just too much trouble for too little result to scrap a complicated existing system that worked well at no present cost in favor of another system whose only virtue was its simplicity.

I brushed at my shirt and most of the dirt went its own way.

"I took a shortcut home," I said.

Daddy just nodded absently and didn't say anything. He's impossible to figure. I was once taken aside and pumped to find out how Daddy was going to vote on a Council Question. They weren't very nice people, so instead of telling them politely that I didn't have the least idea, I lied. I can't guess what Daddy is thinking—he has to tell me what's on his mind.

He set down the book he had been looking at and said, "Mia, I have some good news for you. We're going to move into a new place."

I gave a whoop and threw my arms around his dear neck. This was news I had wanted to hear. In spite of all the empty space in the Ship, we were crowded in our apartment. Somehow after I left the dorm and moved in with

Daddy we just had never gotten around to trading in his small apartment for a larger one. We were too busy living in the one we had. The one thing I had disliked most when I was living in the dormitory was the lack of space—they feel they have to keep an eye on you there. Moving now meant that I would have a larger room for myself. Daddy had promised I could.

"Oh, Daddy," I said. "Which apartment are we going to move into?"

The population of the Ship is about 30,000 now, but once we had transported thirty times that many and cargo besides. The truth is that I don't see where they had fit them all. But now, even though we've spread out to fill up some of the extra space, all the quads have empty apartments. If we had wanted to, we could have moved next door.

Then Daddy said, as though it made no difference, "It's a big place in Geo Quad," and the bottom fell out of my elation.

I turned away from him abruptly, feeling dizzy, and sat down. Daddy didn't just want me to leave home. He wanted me to leave the precarious stability I had worked out for myself. Until I was nine, I had nothing, and now Daddy wanted me to give up everything I had gained since then.

Even now, it isn't easy for me to talk about it. If it were not important, I would skip right over it and never say a word. I was very lonely when I was nine. I was living in a dormitory with fourteen other kids, being watched and told what to do, seeing a procession of dorm mothers come and go, feeling abandoned. That's the way it had been for me for five years, and finally there came a time when I couldn't stay there any longer, and so I ran away. I got on the shuttle, though I don't know quite how I knew where to go, and I went to see Daddy.

I kept thinking about what I'd say and what *he'd* say and worrying about it all the distance, so that when I finally got in to see him I was crying and hiccuping and I couldn't stop.

"What's the matter?" Daddy kept asking me, but I couldn't answer.

He took out a handkerchief and wiped my face and he finally got me calmed down enough to find out what I was trying to tell him. It took awhile, but finally I was finished and had stopped crying, and was only hiccuping occasionally.

"I'm truly sorry, Mia," he said gravely. "I hadn't really understood how things were. I thought I was doing the best thing for you. I thought you'd be better off in a dormitory with other children than living here alone with me."

"No," I said. "I want to live with you, Daddy."

He looked thoughtful for a long moment, and then he gave a little nod and said, "All right. I'll call up the dorm and let them know so they won't think you're lost."

Alfing Quad then became one of the two certain things in my life. You can't count on a dorm or a dorm mother, but a quad and a father are sure. But now Daddy wanted us to leave one of my two sureties. And Geo Quad wasn't even on the Fourth Level—it was on the Fifth.

The Ship is divided into five separate levels. First Level is mainly Technical—Engineers, Salvage, Drive, Conversion, and so on. Second is mainly Administration. Third has dirt and hills, real trees and grass, sand, animals and weeds—it's where they instruct us kids before they drop us on a planet to live or die. Fourth and Fifth are Residential, where we all live. Of these five, the Fifth is the last. All of us kids knew that if you lived way out on the Fifth Level you weren't much better than a Mudeater. If you lived on the Fifth Level you were giving up one of your claims to being human.

I sat in my chair thinking for a long time, trying to recover myself. "You can't be serious about moving to the Fifth Level?" I asked, hoping Daddy might be joking—not really hoping; more just trying to keep from facing the situation for a moment longer.

"Certainly I am," he said, as though it were nothing. "I had to hunt for a long time before I found this apartment. I've already started getting us ready to move. You'll like it there, I think. I understand there's a boy your age in the school there who's somewhat ahead of you. It will give you a chance to scratch for awhile instead of coasting along with no competition the way you do here."

I was afraid, and so I started to argue desperately, naming all the places we could move into inside Alfing. I even cried—and I didn't do that often anymore—but Daddy was unshakable. Finally I dragged my sleeve across my face to dry my eyes and folded my arms and said, "I'm not going to go."

That wasn't the right tack to take with Daddy. It just convinced him that I was being stubborn, but it wasn't stubbornness now. I was truly frightened. I was sure that if we moved things would never be the same for me again. They couldn't be.

But I couldn't say that to Daddy. I couldn't admit to him that I was afraid.

He came to the chair where I was sitting defiantly with my arms crossed and fresh tears lurking in the corners of my eyes, and he put both of his hands on my shoulders.

"Mia," he said. "I realize that it isn't easy for you, but in less than two years you will be your own master and then you can live where you please and do as you like. If you can't take an unpleasant decision now, what kind of an adult will you make then? Right now—no arguments—I am moving. You have a choice. Move with me, or move into the dormitory here in Alfing Quad."

I'd lived in a dormitory and I had no desire ever to go back. I did want to stay with Daddy, but it was still a hard decision for me to make. It was a question of which of my two certainties I wanted to give up. In the end, I made my decision.

After I wiped my eyes once again with the lower edge of my shirt, I walked slowly back down to the quad yard. When I got there, both soccer games had broken up and the whole yard was a turning kaleidoscope of colored shirts and shorts. I didn't see Venie Morlock anywhere in the mass of playing kids, so I asked a boy I knew if he had seen her.

He pointed. "She's right over there."

"Thank you," I said.

I got her down. I rubbed her nose in the ground. Then I made her beg to be let up. I got a black eye for my trouble, but it was worth it to make her remember who was who, even if I did live on the Fifth Level now.

After that, Daddy and I moved.

2

The people who run our schools are very conservative—that probably holds true just about everywhere, not just on our Ship. In any case, usually once you get assigned to a tutor you don't change to another for years. In fact, I knew a boy in Alfing Quad who hated his tutor and got along so badly with him that they could both show scars, and it took him *three* years to change to another.

Compared to that, anything less has to seem frivolous.

Monday morning, two days after we moved, I reported to my new school supervisor in Geo Quad. He was thin, officious, prim and exact, and his name was Mr. Quince. He looked at me standing in front of his desk, raised his eyebrows as he took in my black eye, finished examining me, and said, "Sit down."

The supervisor is in charge of all the school's administrative work—he assigns tutors, handles class movements, programs the teaching machines, breaks up fights, if there are any, and so on. It's a job with only a minimum of appeal for most people so they don't make anybody stay with it for longer than three years.

After looking through all my papers with pursed lips, and making a painstaking entry in a file, Mr. Quince said, "Mr. Wickersham."

"I'm sorry," I said, puzzled.

"Mr. Wickersham will be your tutor. He lives at Geo C/15/37. You're to meet him at his home at two o'clock Wednesday afternoon, and thereafter three times a week at your mutual convenience. And please, let's not be late on Wednesday. Now come along and I'll show you your room for first hour."

School is for kids between the age of four and fifteen. After fourteen, if you survive, they let you give up all the nonsensical parts. You simply work with a tutor or a craft master and follow your interests toward some goal.

I was due to make a decision on that in about two years. The trouble is that except for math and reading old novels I had a completely different set of interests than I had had a year before, and since I didn't really have a solid talent for math and reading old novels isn't much use for anything, I had to find something definite. I didn't really want to specialize. I wanted to be a synthesist, knowing a little about everything and seeing enough to put the pieces together. It's a job that had appeal for me, but I never talked about wanting it because I suspected I wasn't smart enough to handle it and I wanted room to back down in if I had to.

At my moments of depression I thought I might well wind up as a dorm mother or something equally daring.

At some point between fourteen and twenty everybody finishes his normal training. You pick something you like and start doing it. Later, after twenty, if you're not already in research, you may apply for educational leave and work on a project of some sort. That's what my mother keeps herself busy with.

I followed Mr. Quince to the room I was scheduled to be in first hour. I wasn't anxious to be there at all, and I was half-scared and half-belligerent with no way of knowing which part would dominate at any given moment. When we arrived, there was a lot of sudden moving around. When the people unsorted themselves, I saw there were four kids in the room, two boys and two girls.

Mr. Quince said, "What's going on here?"

Nobody said anything—nobody ever does to a supervisor if they can avoid it.

He said, "You, Dentremont. What are you up to?"

The boy was red-headed and even smaller than I, with very prominent ears. He looked very young, though he couldn't have been since he was in the same class as I.

He said, "Nothing, sir."

After a moment of sharp gazing around, Mr. Quince accepted that and unbent sufficiently to introduce me. He didn't introduce anybody else, apparently assuming I could catch on to the names soon enough on my own. The buzzer for the first hour sounded then and he said, "All right. Let's set to work."

When he left, the red-headed boy went behind one of the teaching machines and busied himself in tightening down the back plate.

The girl nearest me said, "'One of these days Mr. Quince

is going to catch you, Jimmy, and then there really will be trouble."

"I'm just curious," Jimmy said.

Everybody more or less ignored me, probably no more knowing how to take me than I knew how to take them. They did watch me and I have no doubt they took their first opportunity to tell everyone their idea of what that new girl from the Fourth Level was like. It was soon clear to me that they eyed us as suspiciously as we on the Fourth Level regarded them, with the added note that in our case it was justified while in theirs it was not. I took no pleasure in having girls look at me and then put their heads together and whisper and giggle and if I had been a little more sure of myself I would have challenged them. As it was, I just dug into my work and pretended I didn't notice.

After first hour, three of the kids left. Jimmy Dentremont stayed where he was, and since my schedule card called for me to stay here second hour, I didn't move, either. He looked closer at me than I could like. I didn't know quite what to say. But then people had been staring and prying and even prodding from the moment we arrived in Geo Quad.

Our furniture had been moved over on Saturday morning—the pieces we wanted to keep—and Daddy and I came up on Saturday afternoon bringing everything else that we owned. I had four cartons full of boxes, clothes, and my personal things. I also had a pennywhistle that I'd salvaged. It was about eight inches long and had brass ends and finger holes. It turned up when we were going through our things, in some old box of Daddy's, and he had put it on his "to throw" pile, from which I immediately rescued it. Sometimes I don't understand my father at all.

The cartons went in my new room, which *was* larger than my old one. Larger, plus having more book shelves, which pleased me because I like my books out where I can use them, not piled away for lack of space.

I stood looking at the cartons, and not having the courage to attack them immediately, I began experimenting to see what sounds I could get out of the pennywhistle. Three minutes—that was the time we had in peace before the door rang.

First it was our neighbors. They crowded in and said, Oh, Mr. Havero, it's a thrill to have you here on *our* corridor, we hope you love it here as much as we do, and some of us men get together once in awhile, you know, for a little evening, keep it in mind, and oh, so that's your daughter, she's sweet, she's adorable, Mr. Havero, I mean that, I really do, and you know, Havero, there are some things I've been meaning to talk over with our rep on the Council, but now that you're here, well, I might as well say it right to you, go right to the top, so to speak . . .

After that came the sightseers and the favor askers. A lot of favor askers. I could tell them from the neighbors because they tried to butter me up, as well as Daddy. The neighbors just buttered up Daddy.

I don't know why it is, but in a case like this, the very people you'd enjoy meeting are the ones who have the good taste to stay home and not bother you. I think it may be an unsolvable problem.

Within minutes, Daddy retreated to his office and the people took over our living room while they waited to talk to him. The new apartment had two wings with the living room in between like the meat in a sandwich. One wing had three bedrooms, a bath and a kitchen-dining room. The other had a study for Daddy and an office. Adjoining the office on the far side was another smaller, empty apartment. Eventually, this was supposed to be a waiting room, but it wasn't ready yet and so the people were camping themselves inside our house.

I watched the people for awhile, and then I pushed my way through the crowd and went into the bedroom wing. I called up Mary Carpentier from there.

"Hello, Mia," she said. "Seeing you on the vid like this, you might still be home."

"I *am* still home," I said. "I haven't moved yet."

"Oh," she said, and her face fell. She must have had her heart set on a call from a distance.

"I was just fooling," I said. "I have moved."

That brightened her up again and we talked for awhile. I told her about all the people who were squatting in our living room, and we got giggling like madmen about all the imaginary errands we made up for them to have come about. We also swore again that we would be true-blue friends forever and ever.

When I was done, I went out in the hall just in time to see a heavy-set man coming out of my bedroom. I knew I'd never seen him before.

"What are you doing in there?" I asked.

Before he answered, he stuck his head into the next room for a moment to take a good look around in there. Then he said, "I'm just poking around, same as you."

"I'm not poking around," I said quietly. "I live here."

He realized then that he'd made a mistake. He didn't say anything. He just turned red and pushed by me hastily. And that's the way things had been ever since.

Now, Jimmy Dentremont, looking closely at my face, asked, "What happened to your eye?"

I don't believe in answering leading questions if I can avoid them, but even beyond that I had no intention of telling anybody what had happened to my eye.

"How old are you?" I asked in an even voice.

"Why?"

"If you're as young as I think you are, you have no business asking me anything. Children should be seen and not heard."

"Well, I'm older than you are," he said. "I was born November 8, 2185."

If he was telling the truth, then he was right by three weeks to the day.

"How do you know how old I am?" I asked.

"I asked about it when I found you were moving here," he said quite openly.

See what I mean? Staring and prying.

The buzzer in the schoolroom sounded to signal the start of the second hour.

"Is this First Room?" I asked.

"I don't know," Jimmy Dentremont said. "They don't tell you that."

Well, I knew they didn't. They don't want anybody feeling bad about what level he's studying at—or feeling too good, either—but since it's simply a matter of comparing notes, everybody knows just exactly what level his room is.

Jimmy Dentremont was simply being contrary. So far we had been feeling each other out, and I had no idea of how to take him or even whether or not we could get along. I thought not.

Mr. Quince called me in again after lunch, raised his eyebrows once more at my black eye—I had the feeling that he didn't approve of it—and informed me that he had a change to make in my schedule.

"Mr. Mbele," he said, handing me an address.

"Excuse me," I said.

"Mr. Mbele is your tutor now. Not Mr. Wickersham as I told you this morning. I assume everything else I told you this morning will apply. Show up at two o'clock on Wednesday and please remember what I said about being late. I don't want the students in my charge being late. A bad reputation always gets back and I'm the one who has to think up explanations."

"Can you tell me why I'm being switched?" I asked.

Mr. Quince raised his eyebrows. With acerbity, he said, "That doesn't seem to be any of my business. I was informed of the change, and I am informing you. You may believe that it wasn't my idea. I'm going to have to alter two assignments now, and I do not deliberately make work for myself. So don't expect any answers from me. I don't have any."

It seemed like an odd business to me—switching me from one tutor to another before we'd even had a chance to inflict scars on one another. Almost frivolous.

In spite of myself, I was glad to meet Jimmy Dentremont on Wednesday afternoon. I was having trouble finding Mr. Mbele's apartment and he helped me find my way.

"That's where I'm going, as a matter of fact," he said. Standing there in the hall with a slip with the address in his hand, he seemed almost friendly, perhaps because there weren't any other kids around.

So far, I hadn't won any friends in Geo Quad, and by being quick-tongued had made one or two enemies, so I didn't object to somebody being pleasant.

"Is Mr. Mbele your tutor, too?"

"Well, only since yesterday. I called Mr. Wickersham to find out why I was being switched around, and he'd only just been told about it by Mr. Quince, himself."

"You didn't ask to be switched?"

"No."

"That does seem funny," I said.

Mr. Mbele opened his door to our ring. "Hello," he said, and smiled. "I thought you two would be showing up about now."

He was white-haired and old—certainly well over a hundred—but tall and straight for his age. His face was dark and lined, with a broad nose and white eyebrows like dashes.

Jimmy said, "How do you do, sir."

I didn't say anything because I recognized him.

No name on the Ship is completely uncommon and I knew as many Mbeles as I knew Haveros. I just didn't expect my tutor to be Joseph L. H. Mbele.

When he sat on the Ship's Council, he and my father were generally in disagreement. Daddy led the opposition to his pet plan for miniaturized libraries to be distributed to all the colonies. The third time it was defeated, Mr. Mbele resigned.

When I was in the dorm, I once got into a name-calling, hair-yanking fight with another girl. She said that if Mr. Mbele wanted something to be passed, all he had to do was introduce a resolution against it, and then sit back. My father would immediately come out in favor of the proposal and ram it through for him.

I don't think this girl knew what the joke meant, and I know I didn't, but she intended it to be slighting, and I knew she did, so I started fighting. I didn't know Daddy very well in those days, but I was full to the brim with family loyalty.

Assigning me Mr. Mbele as a tutor seemed like another poor joke, and I wondered who had thought of it. Not Mr. Quince, certainly—it had cost him extra work and his time was precious.

"Come inside," Mr. Mbele said. Jimmy prodded me and we moved forward. Mr. Mbele tapped the door button and the door slid shut behind us.

He motioned us toward the living room and said, "I thought today we'd simply get acquainted, arrange times that are convenient for all of us to meet, and then have something to eat. We can save our work for next time."

We sat down in the living room, and though there wasn't much doubt as to who was who amongst the three of us, at least in my mind, we all introduced ourselves.

"Yes, I think I've met both of your parents, Jimmy," Mr. Mbele said, "and, of course, I knew your grandfather. As a matter of interest to me, what do you think you might like to specialize in eventually?"

Jimmy looked away. "I'm not positive yet."

"Well, what are the possibilities?"

For a long moment, Jimmy didn't speak, and then in a low and unconfident voice, he said, "I think I'd like to be an ordinologist."

If you think of the limits of what we know as a great suite of rooms inhabited by vast numbers of incredibly busy, incredibly messy, nearsighted people, all of whom are eccentric recluses, then an ordinologist is somebody who comes in every so often to clean up. He picks up the books around the room and puts them where they belong. He straightens everything up. He throws away the junk that the recluses have kept and cherished, but for which they have no use. And then he leaves the room in condition for outsiders to visit while he's busy cleaning up next door. He bears about the same resemblance to the middle-aged woman who checks out books in the quad library as one of our agriculturists does to a primitive Mudeater farmer, but if you stretched a point, you might call him a librarian.

A synthesist, which is what I wanted to be, is a person who comes in and admires the neatened room, and recognizes how nice a copy of a certain piece of furniture would look in the next room over and how *useful* it would be there, and points the fact out. Without the ordinologists, a synthesist wouldn't be able to begin work. Of course, without the synthesists, there wouldn't be much reason for the ordinologists to set to work in the first place, because nobody would have any use for what they do.

At no time are there very many people who are successful at either one job or the other. Ordering information and assembling odd scraps of information takes brains, memory, instinct, and luck. Not many people have all that.

"How much do you know about ordinology?" Mr. Mbele asked.

"Well, not very much at first hand," Jimmy said. And then, with a touch of pride, "My grandfather was an ordinologist."

"He was, indeed. And one of the best. You shouldn't feel apologetic about trying to follow him unless you're a complete failure, and you won't be that," Mr. Mbele said. "I'm not in favor of following ordinary practice simply because it's done. If you don't tell anybody, we'll see if we can't arrange to give you a detailed look at ordinology, and some basis for you to decide whether you want it or not. All right?"

It was plain that Mr. Mbele was going to be an unorthodox tutor. What he was proposing was something you don't ordinarily have the chance to do until you're past fourteen and back from Trial.

Jimmy grinned. "Yes," he said. "Thank you."

Then Mr. Mbele turned to me. "Well, how do you like living in Geo Quad?"

"I don't think I'm going to like it," I said.

Jimmy Dentremont shot a look at me. I don't think he'd expected me to say that.

"What's the matter?" asked Mr. Mbele.

I said, "There hasn't been one moment since we arrived here in this quad that we haven't had strangers all over the house. They don't leave us any privacy at all. It was never like this back in Alfing Quad, believe me."

Mr. Mbele smiled openly. "It isn't Geo Quad that's to blame," he said. "This always happens when somebody becomes Chairman. The novelty will wear off in a few weeks and things will be back to normal again. Wait and see."

After a few more minutes of talk, Mrs. Mbele brought us something to eat. She was somewhat younger than her husband, though she wasn't young. She was a large woman with a round face and light brown hair. She seemed pleasant enough.

While we ate, we decided that we would meet on Monday and Thursday afternoons and on Friday night, with the possibility of changes from week to week if something came up to interfere with that schedule.

Mr. Mbele wound up our meeting by saying, "I want to make it clear before we begin that I think your purpose is to learn and mine is to help you learn, or to make you learn, though I doubt either of you has to be made. I have very little interest in writing out progress reports on you, or sticking to form charts, or anything else that interferes with our basic purposes. If there is anything you want to learn and have the necessary background to handle, I'll be ready to help you, whether or not it is something that formally falls among the things I'm supposed to teach you. If you don't have the background, I'll help you get it. In return, I want you to do something for me. It's been many years since I was last a tutor, so I expect you to point out to me when I fail to observe some ritual that Mr. Quince holds essential. Fair enough?"

In spite of my basic loyalties, and contrary to them, I found myself liking Mr. Mbele and being very pleased that I had been lucky enough to be assigned to him, even though I couldn't admit it publicly.

When we were in the halls again and on our way back home, Jimmy said suddenly, "Hold on."

We stopped and he faced me.

"I want you to promise me one thing," he said. "Promise not to tell anybody about my grandfather or about me wanting to be an ordinologist."

"That's two things," I said.

"Don't joke!" he said pleadingly. "The other kids would make it hard for me if they knew I wanted to be an odd thing like that."

"I want to be a synthesist," I said. "I won't say anything about you if you don't say anything about me."

We took it as a solemn agreement, and after that anything that was ever said in Mr. Mbele's apartment was kept between us and never brought out in public. It was, if you like, an oasis in the general desert of childish and adult ignorance where we could safely bring out our thoughts and not have them denigrated, laughed at, or trampled upon, even when they deserved it. A place like that is precious.

Jimmy said, "You know, I'm glad now that I was switched. I think I'm going to enjoy studying under Mr. Mbele."

Cautiously, I said, "Well, I have to admit he's different."

And that was about all that we ever said to anybody who ever asked us about our tutor.

I saw Daddy after he closed his office for the day. That is, he closed our living room to new people at five o'clock, and by almost eleven he'd seen the last person who was waiting.

Excitedly, I said, "Daddy, you know my new tutor is Mr. Joseph Mbele!"

"Mmm, yes, I know," Daddy said, matter-of-factly, stacking papers on his desk and straightening up.

"You do?" I asked in surprise. I sat down in a chair next to him.

"Yes. As a matter of fact, he agreed to take you on as a personal favor to me. I asked him to do it."

"But I thought you two were against each other," I said. As I have said before, I don't fully understand my father. I am not a charitable person—when I decide I'm against somebody, I'm *against* him. When Daddy's against somebody, he asks him to serve as my tutor.

"Well, we do disagree on some points," Daddy said. "I happen to think his attitude toward the colonies is very wrong. But just because a man disagrees with me doesn't make him a villain or a fool, and I sincerely doubt that any of his attitudes will damage you in any way. They didn't hurt me when I studied Social Philosophy under him sixty years ago."

"Social Philosophy?" I asked.

"Yes," Daddy said. "That's Mr. Mbele's major interest." He smiled. "I wouldn't have you study under a man who didn't have something to teach you. I think you could stand a very healthy dose of Social Philosophy."

"Oh," I said.

Well, there was one thing I could say for Mr. Mbele. He hadn't done any eyebrow raising over my black eye. Neither had his wife, for that matter. I did appreciate that.

Still, I wished that Daddy had warned me beforehand. Even though I had liked Mr. Mbele, it would have saved me a few uncharitable thoughts right at the beginning.

3

Two weeks after we moved, I came into Daddy's study to tell him that I had dinner ready. He was talking on the vid to Mr. Persson, another Council member.

Mr. Persson's image sighed and said, "I know, I know. But I don't like making an example of anybody. If she wanted another child so badly, why couldn't she have become a dorm mother?"

"It's a little late to convince her of that with the baby on the way," Daddy said dryly.

"I suppose so. Still, we might abort the baby and give her a warning. Well, we can hash it all out tomorrow," Mr. Persson said, and he signed off.

"Dinner's ready," I said. "What was all that about?"

Daddy said, "Oh, it's a woman named MacReady. She's had four children and none of them have made it through Trial. She wanted one more try and the Ship's Eugenist said no. She went ahead anyway."

It put a bad taste in my mouth.

"She must be crazy," I said. "Only a crazy woman would do a thing like that. Why don't you examine her? What are you going to do with her, anyway?"

"I'm not sure how the Council will vote," Daddy said, "but I imagine she will be allowed to pick out a colony planet and be dropped there."

There are two points—one is population and the other is Trial—on which we cannot compromise at all. The Ship couldn't survive if we did. Imagine what would happen if we allowed people to have children every time the notion occurred to them. There is a limit to the amount of food that we have space to grow. There is a limit to the amount of room that we have in which people could live. It may seem that we are not very close to these limits now, but they couldn't last even fifty years of unlimited growth.

This woman had four children, not one of which turned out well enough to survive. Four chances is enough.

What Daddy was suggesting for the woman sounded over-generous to me, and I said so.

"It's not generosity," Daddy said. "It's simply that we have to have rules in the Ship in order to live at all. You play by the rules or you go elsewhere."

"I still think you're being too easy," I said. It wasn't a light matter to me at all.

Somewhat abruptly, Daddy changed the subject. He said, "Hold still there. How's your eye today? It's looking much better, I think. Yes, definitely better."

When Daddy doesn't agree with me and he doesn't want to argue, he slips out by teasing.

I turned my head away. "My eye's all right," I said. It was, too, since the bruise had faded away almost completely.

At dinner, Daddy asked, "Well, after two weeks, how do you like Geo Quad? Has it turned out as badly as you thought it would?"

I shrugged, and turned my attention to my food. "It's all right, I guess," I mumbled.

That's all I could say. It just wasn't possible for me to admit that I was both unhappy and unpopular, both of which were true. There are two reasons I started off wrong in Geo Quad, one big one and one small one.

The small one was school. As I've said, the only kids who are supposed to know how you stand are the others at the same level in each subject, people just like you. In practice, though, everybody has a pretty good idea of just where everybody else is and those at the top and bottom are expected to blush accordingly. I've never been able to blush on command, and, as a newcomer, it was all the harder for me because of it. It's not good to start by being singled out.

The big reason, on the other hand, was completely my fault. When we moved, I knew I wasn't going to like Geo Quad, and it mattered not at all what anybody there thought of me. By the time it sank through to me that I was really and truly stuck in Geo Quad and that I'd better step a little more lightly, my heel marks were already plain to see on more than one face.

As it turned out, my position and my conduct interacted to bring me trouble. This is how things go wrong—and this is just a sample:

At the beginning of the week, the whole school went down to the Third Level on an educational jaunt. The afternoon was really more in the nature of a holiday because we older ones had seen the rows of broad-leaf plants they raise for carbon dioxide/oxygen exchange more than once before. At the end of the day we were coming back home to Geo Quad by shuttle and to pass the time some of us girls were playing a hand game. I was included because I was there and they needed everybody present to make a good game of it.

The game goes like this: Everybody has three numbers to remember. At a signal, everybody claps their hands on their knees, claps their hands, then the person starting the game calls a number. Knees, hands, then the person whose number was called calls someone else's number. Knees, hands, number. Knees, hands, number. It goes on, the speed of the beat picking up, until somebody claps wrong or misses when one of her numbers is called. When that happens, everybody gets licks with stiffened fingers on her wrist.

The game is simple enough. It's just that when the pace picks up, it's easy to make a mistake. We girls stood in a group in the aisle, one or two lucky ones sitting down, near the front of the shuttle car.

We started out—*clap, clap,* "Twelve," said the girl starting.

Clap on knees, *clap* together, "Seven."

Clap, clap, "Seventeen."

Clap, clap, "Six." Six was one of my numbers.

I clapped hands on knees, hands together, and "Twenty," I said.

Clap, clap. "Two."

Clap, clap, "———."

Somebody missed.

It was a plump eleven-year-old named Zena Andrus. She kept missing and kept suffering for it. There were seven of us girls playing and she had missed five or six times. When you've had licks taken on your wrist thirty or thirty-five times, you're likely to have a pretty sore wrist. Zena had both a sore wrist and the idea that she was being persecuted.

"You call me too often," she said as we lined up to rap. "It's not fair!"

She was so whiney about it that we stopped calling her number almost entirely—just often enough that she didn't get the idea that she was being excluded. I went along with this, though I didn't agree. I may be wrong, but I don't see any point in playing a game with anybody who isn't just as ready to face losing as to face winning. It's not a game if there's no risk.

A moment later when somebody else lost I noticed that Zena was right up there in line and happy to have the chance to do a little damage of her own.

We seven weren't the whole class, of course. Some were talking, some were reading, Jimmy Dentremont and another boy were playing chess, some were just sitting, and three or four boys were chasing each other up and down the aisles. Mr. Marberry, who was in charge of us for the afternoon, said, "Sit down until we get to Geo Quad," to them in a resigned voice every time they started to get too loud or to make too much of a nuisance of themselves. Mr. Marberry is one of those people who talk and talk and talk, and never follow through, so they weren't paying too much attention to him.

As we reached the last station before Geo Quad, somebody noticed and we decided to play just one last round. Since we were so close to home, the boys were out of their seats and starting up the aisle past us to be first out of the shuttle. They were bouncing around, swatting one another, and when they got up by us and saw what we were playing they began to try to distract us so that we would make mistakes and suffer for it. We did our best to ignore them.

One of the boys, Thorin Luomela, was paying close attention to our numbers so he could distract the right person when that number was called again. By chance, the first number he heard repeated was one of mine.

"Fourteen."

Thorin waited until the right moment and smacked me across the behind. He put plenty of sting into it, too.

I said, "Fifteen," and clouted him back. I brought my hand back hard and set him back on his heels. In those days, I was small and hard and I could hit. For a moment I thought he might do something about it, but then his resolve wilted.

"What did you do that for?" he asked. "I was only fooling."

I turned back to the game. "Fifteen" happened to be Zena Andrus and she had missed as usual, so we started to take licks.

When I stepped up for my turn, Zena glared at me as though I had deliberately caused her to miss and was personally to blame for her sore wrist. I hadn't intended to hit her hard at all because she was so completely hapless, but that look of hers just made me mad, it was so chock full of malice. I took a tight grip on her arm, stiffened the first two fingers of my left hand, and whacked her across the reddened area of her wrist as hard as I could. It hurt my fingers.

The shuttle was just coming to a stop then, and I turned away from Zena and said, "Well, here we are," ignoring her whimper of self-pity as she nursed her wrist.

We were free to go our own way after the shuttle dropped us at Geo Quad, so I started for home, but Zena caught up with me before I'd gone very far.

She said, "Your father's being Chairman of the Ship's Council doesn't make any difference to me. In spite of what you think, you're no better than anybody else."

I looked at her and said, "I don't claim that I'm better than everybody else, but I don't walk around telling everybody that I'm not, the way you do."

I saw immediately that I'd made a mistake. Every so often I meet somebody with whom I just can't communicate. Sometimes it is an adult. More often it is somebody my own age. Sometimes it is somebody who thinks in a different way than I do so that the words we use don't mean the same things to both of us. More often it is somebody like Zena who just doesn't listen.

What I'd said seemed obvious to me, but Zena missed the point completely. There were lots of times when I didn't think well of myself at all, but even when I had cause to whisper *mea culpas* to myself under my breath, I would not concede that I was inferior to other people. I knew that I was smarter than most people, smaller than most people, clumsier than most, untalented in art (I inherited that), less pretty than most, and that I could play the pennywhistle a little bit—at least, I owned one, and most people didn't. I was what I was. Why should I crawl, or cry, or be humble about it? I really didn't understand.

Zena either didn't hear what I said the way I said it or she simply wasn't able to understand anything that complicated.

"That's what I thought," she said. "You do think you're better than everybody else! I didn't think you'd admit it. I've been saying that's the way you are. You're stuck-up."

I started to protest, but she'd already turned away, as pleased as though she'd been handed a cookie. I knew it was my fault, too. Not for what I'd said, but for losing my temper and being unpleasant in the first place. You can't stamp on people and not get hurt in return.

It didn't end there, though. Zena spread what she thought I'd said, plus some interpolations, plus some liberal commentary that demonstrated just how thoroughly noble she was, and how objective, all over the quad and there were kids willing to listen and to believe. Why not? They didn't know me. And I didn't care. Geo Quad meant nothing to me.

By the time that I realized that it did matter, I'd backed myself neatly into a corner. I had a few enemies—perhaps even more than a few—and a fair number of neutral acquaintances. I had no friends.

The major reason that I found it hard to think of leaving the Ship is that the Mudeaters, the Colons, are so different from us. They are peasants, farmers mostly, because that sort of person was best equipped to stay alive on a colony planet, some of which are pretty rough places. On the other hand, we people on the Ship mostly have technical training.

We could have joined them, I suppose, when Earth was destroyed—as, in fact, it was planned that we would—but if we had it would have meant dropping the better part of 5000 years of advance. You see, you have to have *time* for science, and working every minute through the day just to stay alive in order to be able to do the same thing tomorrow leaves no free time at all. So we never left the Ship, and none of the other Ships were abandoned, either.

Now when we need something from one of the colonies, we trade some of the knowledge we have preserved all these years, or some of the products our science has worked out, and in exchange we get raw materials—what we have for what they have. It's a fair trade.

The truth is, I guess, I just find it easier to cope with things than with people. When I came to Alfing Quad, I got to know everybody. I thought I was settled for good and I set down roots. Or, you might say, I dug in my fingernails and held on for dear life. But then we came to Geo Quad and I had to face all these new people. I might not have done it very well, but I could do it because they were *Ship* people. People-type people. But they aren't like us on the planets.

I really think I could have faced Earth. I think I could understand anybody who could take an asteroid roughly thirty miles by twenty by ten and turn it into a Ship. They split it into two halves, carved out forty or fifty percent of the rock in the two parts, leaving matching projections, and then put them back together again and restuffed the interior with all the fittings needed to make a Ship. All in one year.

To me, these people were fantastic and wonderful and it still hurts me to think that they had to cap it all by blowing themselves to pieces. But that was Earth. Not the Mudeaters.

On the second Sunday after we finished moving to Geo Quad, I was reading a book in my room when Daddy knocked on my door. I put the book aside when he came in.

"Did you have any plans for next weekend, Mia?" he asked.

"No," I said. "Why?"

"I had an idea I thought you might like."

"Oh?"

"I've just finished talking with the Supply Steward. We're going to have to make a barter stop, so we're laying by Grainau this weekend. The Council has given me the job of dealing with them. I thought you might enjoy coming along with us."

He ought to have known better than that. I shook my head and said, "I don't think I want to see the Mudeaters."

"Don't use that word," Daddy said. "They may be primitive, but they're still people. You might be surprised at what you could learn from them. The world doesn't end with a quad. It doesn't end with a Ship, either."

My heart pounding, I said, "Thank you, but I don't think I'm interested," and picked up my book again.

"You might think about this," Daddy said. "In twenty months you're going to be alone on a planet with people like these, doing your best to live with them and stay alive. If you can't stand to be near them now, what are you going to do then? I think you ought to be interested."

I shook my head, but then I suddenly couldn't pretend to be indifferent any longer. With tears in my eyes, I said, "I am interested. But I'm scared."

"Is that all?"

"What do you mean, 'Is that all?' "

Daddy said, "I'm sorry. I didn't mean that the way it sounded. I can see how the thought might frighten you. Most of the colony planets are pretty unpleasant places by any civilized standard. What I meant was, is that your only reason for not wanting to come along?"

"Yes," I said. "But it's not the planets that scare me. It's the people."

"Oh," Daddy said. He sighed. "You know, I was afraid of something like this. One of the reasons I had for moving was that I thought you were too dependent on Alfing Quad. You were living in too small a world. The trouble is that you don't *know* that there is anything real beyond the things you are familiar with at first hand. If I could take you down on Grainau and show you something new, and show you that it isn't all that bad, I think you'd get over this fear of yours."

My stomach lurched with fear. "You're not going to make me go, are you?" I asked desperately.

"No. I won't make you go. I won't ever force you to do anything, Mia. I'll tell you what, though," he said, his manner changing abruptly. "If you come along, if you go down to Grainau with me this weekend, I promise I'll unfreeze you. How about that?"

I had to smile, but I shook my head.

"Think about it," Daddy said. "You may change your mind."

When he went out, I had the feeling he was disappointed, and suddenly I felt depressed and even more unhappy. It was as though having my fingers dug in and holding on as best I could to my security, suddenly I wasn't to be allowed it anymore, and Daddy was prying my fingers loose one-by-one. That wouldn't have been so bad if he weren't disappointed that I wouldn't let go.

So, not quite knowing why, I went back to Alfing Quad. Perhaps it was because it was the one place where I knew that they were satisfied with me as I was. I took the shuttle to the Fourth Level and then the cross-level shuttle to Alfing Quad.

First I went to our old apartment and let myself in with the key I should have turned in and hadn't. There wasn't a bit of furniture there. No books, no book shelves. I wandered through the rooms and they all seemed identical. It didn't seem like home anymore, because all the things that had made it home were gone. It was just another empty corner of my life and I left very shortly.

Mrs. Farmer was standing in the hall when I went out, looking at me and noting, no doubt, that I had a key that I shouldn't have had. She and I had never cared too much for each other. She always had made it a point of honor to tell Daddy when I did something that she would never have let her Peter do, in some cases things that Daddy had told me specifically that I could do. Daddy always listened politely to her, then closed the door behind her and forgot about the whole thing. She just looked at me; she didn't say anything.

I went to the quad yard next, and nobody was there, so I went to the Common Room. It was odd, but I felt like a stranger here in these familiar halls, as though I ought to tiptoe and duck around corners to avoid meeting somebody who might recognize me. I felt like an intruder. That isn't the feeling that you ought to have when you go home, but somehow in the process of our moving Alfing Quad had become an uneasy place for me.

I could hear the kids making noise in the Common Room before I even got there, and I hesitated to wind up my courage before I went in. The Common Room was not just one room, actually. It was a complex of rooms: a lounge, a library, two game rooms, study rooms, a music practice room, a music listening room, a small theater, and a snackery. The snackery was where I expected to see my friends.

It seemed to be my day for meeting Farmers, because Peter Farmer came out as I was hesitating. He isn't one of my favorite people and his mother keeps him on a very short leash, but I saw no reason not to be friendly.

I said, "Hello."

Peter stared frankly at me, and then he said, "What are you doing back here? My mother said that she was glad you were gone because you're such a bad example."

So I looked straight at him and lied. "How can you say such a thing, Peter Farmer? I just saw your mother and she was perfectly sweet. She said if I ran into you I was to tell you it was time to run along home."

"Oh, you never met my mother."

"Of course I did," I said, and went into the Common Room.

There is a firm social line drawn between kids over fourteen and kids under. As adults and citizens, they have rights that the younger ones don't have and they are not slow to let the younger ones know it. In a place like the Common Room where both come, the older ones have their area, and the younger ones their area. Though there isn't any real difference between them, somehow the adult area has a mystique and attraction that the younger area lacks. I went over to the corner where my friends gathered.

Mary Carpentier was sitting at a table with Venie Morlock and two or three of the other kids, and I headed over to them.

When she saw me, Mary said, "Well, hi, Mia. Come on and sit down. What are you doing here?"

"I just thought I'd visit and see how you were doing," I said, sitting down at the table. I wasn't going to say how unhappy I was in Geo Quad—not with Venie sitting there listening to every word and ready to shout hallelujah.

I said, "Hi," and everybody at the table said, "Hi, Mia," back.

Mary said, "Gee, Mia. I didn't expect you to turn up back here. Why didn't you call and tell me you were coming?"

"It was a sort of a spur-of-the-moment thing," I said.

"Well, it's good to see you. Hey, how do you like it where you are now?"

"It's all right, I guess," I said. "I'm still getting used to things. I haven't met everybody or been everywhere yet."

"Hey, do you still do that crazy business of walking

around in the collecting chutes over there?" one of the others asked.

"No," I said. "I haven't gotten around to it, but I expect I will."

"Which quad did you move to, now?"

"Geo Quad," Mary answered for me.

"That's on the Fifth Level, isn't it?" another of the kids asked.

"Yes," I said.

"Oh, yes," Venie broke in. "I remember. I've heard of Geo Quad. That's where all the oddballs live."

"Oh, you know that isn't so, Venie," I said sweetly. "You haven't moved there yet. By the way, why don't you? We've got a place on our third-string soccer team waiting for you."

"I may not be very good," Venie said, stung, "but I can outplay you any day of the week with both eyes closed."

"Mary," I said, "how has your family been?"

"All right, I guess," she said unhappily.

"At least my parents didn't dump me in a dormitory to get rid of me while they were still married," Venie said.

Without turning to look at her, I said, "Venie, if you want another punch in the nose, keep saying those things. Mary, why don't we go over to your place? Then we won't have any interruptions."

"Oh, don't leave on my account," Venie said. "I'm going myself. The air is getting a little close in here. You kids coming with me?"

She pushed back her chair and the other three girls got up and started after her as she eased her way out between the red, yellow, green, and blue topped tables.

I said, "Shall we go over to your place, Mary?"

Unhappily, she said, "Gee, Mia, I can't. We were just about to go over and play soccer."

"Well, that's good," I said and stood up. "Let's go play."

Mary said, "I don't think Venie would like that."

I asked, "What's the matter with you? Since when did it ever matter what Venie thinks?"

Mary stood there looking at me, and finally she said, "Mia, I love you dearly, but you just don't live here anymore. I do. Can you understand that? I've got to go now. Will you call me up sometime?"

"Yes," I said, and watched her hurry out after Venie Morlock. "I will," I said softly, but I knew I wouldn't. I knew, too, that one more finger had just been pried loose.

4

Lacking anything else to do, I left the Common Room and went back to Geo Quad. I may have seemed outwardly calm—I think I did—but inside I was frantic. Once, when I was about ten, I had been on an outing on the Third Level and gotten into a patch of nettles. I didn't discover what they were until I was well into them, and I had no choice but to continue pushing my way through. By the time I came out on the other side my legs and arms were itching furiously and I was dancing up and down, driven almost into a frenzy by the fiery prickling, wishing for anything that would make it stop. What I was feeling mentally now was something very similar. I had an itch I couldn't stop and couldn't locate, I was jumpy and unhappy, and very depressed.

I wanted to get away. I wanted someplace dark to hide. I wanted something to do to occupy my mind. When I got back to our apartment—a place that held the furniture but not the feel of home—I hunted up a piece of chalk and one of those small lights that dorm mothers use to count heads with after lights-out. Then I went out again. It was about two o'clock in the afternoon then, and though I hadn't eaten for hours I was far too agitated to think of food.

I didn't just pick the nearest grate to our apartment and pop into it. I wandered a little until I found a quiet bywater of a hall not too far away. I was in no mood at all to try to explain myself to some uncomprehending adult, so I did some looking around before I decided on a particular grate to use as my entrance into the Fifth Level collecting chutes.

I knelt down by the grate and began to take it off. It was hung by clips on both sides and they hadn't been worked for such a long time that they were stiff and unmoving. Once I started to use them regularly they wouldn't be any problem, but right now they refused to yield to my prying fingers. I worked at it in a very slow-paced way, not feeling up to much more, and it was fully five minutes before my judicious wiggling of the left-hand clip unfroze it. I was about to start on the other when a voice asked, "What are you doing?"

I had my face in my hand at the moment, and I jumped guiltily at the sudden sound. I composed myself as best I could before I looked around. It was Zena Andrus standing there.

I said, "What are *you* doing?"

She said, "I live back there," pointing to a door not so far down the way. "What are you doing?"

I pointed through the grate at the collecting chute. "I'm going down in there."

"You mean down in the ducts?"

"Yes," I said. "Why not? Does the idea scare you?"

She bristled. "I'm not scared. I can do anything you can."

With deliberate malice, I said, "In that case, come on along with me."

She swallowed a little bit hard, then knelt down beside me and looked through the grate, feeling the indraft and becoming conscious of the distant sound of fans. "It's awfully dark down there."

"I have a light," I said. "We won't need it much, though. It's more fun running along in the dark."

"*Running?*"

"Well, walking."

Uncertainly, she looked back at the grate again. They say that misery loves company, and I was bound to make someone else miserable.

"Oh, well," I said. "If you're afraid to come along . . ."

Zena stood up. "I am *not.*"

"All right," I said. "If you're coming, stand aside and let me get the grate off."

In a minute I had the other clip pulled to the side. I set the grate on the floor and pointed to the black hole. "After you."

"You're not going to shut me up in there?"

"No," I said. "No, I'll be right behind you. Go through feet first."

Since she was a butterball, it was a tight fit for her, but after she did some earnest wriggling, she popped through. I handed the chalk and the light down to her and then I slid through myself. When I was standing on the floor of the duct, I took the chalk and light back.

"Put the grate on," I said, and while she was doing that I made an X-mark and put a neat circle around it, the chalk squeaking lightly on the metal.

"That's the mark for home," I said. The ducts corresponding to arteries have pushing fans, the ducts corresponding to veins have sucking fans. Between the chalk marks I make and the direction and feel of the wind, I always have a good enough idea where I am, even in a strange place like this one, to at least find my way home again. There was certainly more similarity here to the ducts at home than there was in the layouts of Alfing and Geo Quads proper. I didn't think it would take me long to get my bearings.

When Zena had the grate in place, we set off.

I walked first down the metal corridor. Zena followed uncertainly behind me, tripping once and skidding, though there was nothing there to trip on except her feet. The duct itself, fully six feet wide and six feet high, was made of smooth metal. The darkness was complete except for the occasional grille of light cast into the dust at a grate opening, and the beam cast by my little light. As we passed them, I numbered the grates and the cross-corridors to give me a ready idea of how far from home I was.

As we passed the grates, occasionally noises penetrated from the outside world, but it was clearly another world than the one that we were in. The sounds of our world were the metallic echoes of our whispers, the sound of our sandals padding dully, and the constant sound of the fans.

I had read more than one novel set in the American West two hundred years before Earth was destroyed, where conditions were almost as primitive as on one of the colony planets. I remembered reading of the scouts who even in strange territory had the feel of the country, and I felt much the same way myself. The feel of the air, the sounds, all meant something to me. To Zena they meant nothing and she was scared. She didn't like the dark at all.

At those points where the corridors joined there were sometimes fans to be ducked. The corridors also sloped at the junctions so that there were no straight corners, and this was disconcerting when the corridor you were meeting ran up-and-down, even when it was the equivalent of a capillary and could be gotten over with one good jump.

Zena balked at the first of these that we encountered and had to be prodded before she would cross it.

"I don't *want* to," she said. "I can't jump that far."

"All right," I said. "But if you don't come along, you'll just be left here all alone in the dark."

That made her mind up for her and she found that she could jump it, and with very little effort, either.

But I'll have to admit that old-collecting-chute-hand or not, I wasn't prepared for what we found next. In the darkness, there was no floor in front of us. Above us, no ceiling. My light showed our own corridor resuming on the far side of the gap, fully six feet away. The floor sloped sharply down and the air rushed strongly along. I had never encountered an up-and-down duct of this size before.

"Well, what is it?" Zena asked.

There were handholds at the side on which to cross the gap, and holding onto one of these, I leaned over and dropped a piece of broken chalk in a futile attempt to gauge the depth of the cross-duct. I listened, but I never heard a sound.

"It must connect one level with the next," I said. "A main line. I bet it goes straight down to the First Level."

"Well, don't you *know?*"

"No, I don't," I said. "I've never been here before."

I wasn't about to jump that distance, so I examined the hand- and footholds carefully. If you slipped and fell, and it was as far down as I suspected, all that would be left of you would be jam. I shone my light up and down, and the beam only managed to nibble at the blackness. The holds went up-and-down, too, as well as across, a ladder that went much farther than I could see.

"Maybe it connects with the Fourth Level down there," Zena said, "but where does it go to up there?" She pointed straight up the duct.

I didn't know. The Fifth Level was the very last, the outside, but this duct went beyond the Fifth. Air chutes don't lead into blind corners and air doesn't come from nowhere.

"I don't know," I said. "But as long as we're here, why don't we see where it goes?"

I reached over and put my toe in the inset in the wall. Then I grabbed the first handhold I could reach and swung out. They were good firm holds and while the distance straight down bothered me a little, as long as I couldn't see how far down it was I wasn't really scared. I once had the experience of walking along a board three inches wide while it was set on the ground—I went the whole length and probably could have walked on for a mile and never fallen off. Then the board was raised into the air and I was challenged to try again. When it was set on posts ten feet high, I wouldn't even try it because I knew I couldn't make it. This was something of a similar situation, and as long as I couldn't see I knew I wouldn't worry.

I grabbed the next hold and started up. Before I could get anywhere, Zena leaned over and held me by the foot. "Hey, wait up," she said, and gave my foot a tug.

"Watch it!" I said sharply. "You'll make me fall." I tried to jerk my foot loose, but she wouldn't let go.

"Come on back down," Zena pleaded.

Reluctantly I came down. I said, "What is it?"

"You can't go and just leave me."

"I'm not leaving you," I said. "Just follow me and you can't be left behind."

"But I'm scared," she said.

That was really the time for her to finally admit it. We had both known that from the beginning, but she had refused to admit it until things were getting interesting.

"It's not going to hurt you," I said. "All we have to do is climb until we find out what's up there." I could see she was wavering, caught between the fear of climbing the ladder and the fear of being left behind. "Come on," I said. "You first." I wanted her to go first. That way she couldn't grab me again.

After a moment, I edged her down the beginning of the slope to the first handhold. I got her onto the ladder and actually moving again. I followed her. I had the light clipped at my waist, pointing upward and giving both of us some idea of what and where to grab as we continued to climb.

I could hear Zena whimpering as she climbed, making scared noises in her throat. To get her mind off her troubles, I said, "Can you see anything up there?"

She was clinging tightly to the ladder as we went up, and now she stopped, flipped her head up for just the shortest instant and then brought it down again.

"No," she said. "Nothing."

I should have known better, I told myself as we continued to climb. You don't bring somebody who has a habit of choking up into a situation like this.

Suddenly, without any warning, Zena stopped moving. Before I could help myself, my head rammed so hard into her foot that a shock of pain ran through my neck. If I'd had my head up, I would have seen that she'd stopped, but you can't climb indefinitely with your head thrown back without getting a crick in your neck. I stopped immediately and went down one step.

"What's the matter?" I asked.

"I just can't go any farther. I can't."

I lifted my head and peered upward. I couldn't see anything beyond Zena that would hold her up. She was just clinging to the ladder, her face pressed close to the metal. I could hear her breath rasp in her throat.

"Did you run into something?"

"No. I just can't go any farther," she said tearfully. "I'm scared."

I reached up and put my hand on her leg. It was rock-hard and trembling. I said, "Move ahead, Zena," in a firm but gentle tone—I didn't want to frighten her—and pushed at the calf of her leg, but she didn't move.

I could see that it had been a mistake to be in the lower position on the ladder. If Zena let go and fell, I would be swept along no matter how hard I tried to hold on. That would save me trying to explain what had happened—and it might be difficult to explain if I came back by myself without Zena: "Oh, she fell down one of the air chutes"—but that wasn't anything to be happy about. I was genuinely frightened. My heart was beginning to speed up and I could feel a trickle of sweat running down my back.

"Don't let go, Zena," I said carefully.

"I won't," she said. "I won't move."

I unclipped the light at my belt and then I leaned back as far as I could until I could see beyond her. It would take twenty minutes to go down the ladder—in her state, probably longer—and even if I could start her moving, I doubted she could hold on that long. I held the light up at arm's length over my head. About forty or fifty feet above us I could see something black at the side of the duct. A cross-corridor, perhaps, but I couldn't be sure. All I could do was hope that it was.

"I want to go *down*," Zena said.

We couldn't go down. We certainly couldn't stay where we were. I didn't know what was ahead of us, but it was the only direction in which we could go.

"You're going to have to climb a little more," I said.

"But I'm *scared,*" Zena said. "I'm going to fall."

I could feel sweat on my forehead now. A runnelet ran down and caught in my eyebrow. I wiped my brow.

"No, you're not going to fall," I said confidently. "I just looked up above, Zena, and there's a cross-corridor just thirty feet or so over your head. That's all you have to climb. You can do that."

Zena just screwed her face in against the metal even harder. "I can't."

"Yes, you can. I'll help you. Keep your eyes closed. That's right. Now, move your foot up one step. Just one step." I pushed at her leg. "That's right. One step. All right, now reach your hand up—no, keep your eyes closed. Now move your other foot."

One foot, one hand at a time, I got her moving again. For the first time since I could remember, the darkness seemed oppressive, a place where anything could happen. It was the way it must have seemed to Zena all along.

In a minute, I said, "It's not more than twenty feet or so now," but Zena was blocking my view and I couldn't do anything but hope I was right. "You're doing fine. It's only a little bit farther."

I continued to urge her on, and she went up slowly, a rung at a time. It was more than twenty feet, but not too much more than that, when Zena gave a little cry and was suddenly no longer above me. I looked up, and in the beam of the light clipped at my waist I could see the cross-corridor just over my head.

All I could do, sitting on its floor, was try to catch my breath and calm my heart. My heart was thumping away, sweat was continuing to drip from my forehead, and now that I was safe my mind was thinking of all that could have happened in full detail. Beside me, Zena was sobbing soundlessly.

After a minute, in a voice filled with wonder, Zena said, "I did make it."

I breathed through my open mouth, trying not to pant. Then I said, "I told you that you would, didn't I? Now all we have to do is get you back down again."

Zena said, in a determined tone that surprised me, "I can make it back down again."

I said, "Well, as long as we're here, we may as well have a look around."

In a minute or two, we walked down the corridor until we came to the first grate opening. The opening was there, but not the grate, and there was no light shining into the duct from outside as there would have been in Geo Quad or Alfing. I snaked through the hole and then gave a hand up to Zena. And we were standing in a hall on the Sixth Level, the level that shouldn't have been there.

I shone my light around and all was silent, and dark, and deserted. The corridor was bare. All the fixtures were gone. Anything that could be removed was gone, only the holes remaining after. There was a doorway showing in the beam of my light.

"Let's go look at that," I said.

There was no door—that was gone, too. Nothing had been yanked ruthlessly or broken off. Everything had simply been removed.

The room into which the doorway led was bare, too. It was a very long room, longer than anything else I had seen in any quad, short of a quad yard. Its closest resemblance was to a dormitory, but it was as though somebody had taken all the rooms in a dormitory and torn out all the walls in order to make one long room. There were holes bored in the walls at regular intervals, columns of holes. But the room was bare.

"What is it?" Zena asked.

"I'm not sure," I said.

We went back into the hall. It was long and straight, without any of the dead ends, stairs, or sudden turns that you ordinarily expect to see in any normal hallway. It was straight as a string. That was strange and different, too.

I noticed the numbers 44-2 painted neatly on the wall by the door of the room. There was a red line that started at the doorway, moved to the center of the hall and made a sharp right turn to run beside green, yellow, blue, orange and purple lines that continued past, running down the center of the hall.

"Let's see where the lines go," I said, and set off down the corridor.

* * *

It was late, past dinner time, when we got back to Geo Quad. We came out of the ducts from our original opening just down the hall from Zena's home. My stomach was starting to notice how long it had been since I had eaten and I had a healthy appetite.

Zena hesitated for a minute outside her door, and then she said, "You're much nicer than I thought you were at first." And then, rapidly, as though to cover that statement up, she said, "Good night," and went quickly into her apartment.

When I walked in, Daddy was just getting ready to go out for the evening. He and some of his friends used to get together regularly and build scale models and talk. Models of machines, animals (bones and all), almost anything imaginable. This group had met on Sunday nights for as long as I had lived with Daddy, and he had a whole collection of the models he had made, though they hadn't yet been unpacked since we had moved here from Alfing.

Actually, I had no fault to pick with his models. Daddy used to say that everybody needs to have at least one mindless hobby to occupy himself with, and I had several.

Daddy asked, "Where have you been?"

"Up on the Sixth Level," I said. "What do we have on hand to eat?"

"There's some Ham-IV in the kitchen, if you want that," Daddy said.

"That sounds good," I said.

I liked Ham-IV very much. It comes from one of the two or three best meat vats in the Ship, though some people find it too strong for their taste. Gamey, I think they say. Still they have to put up with it, because it's one of the best producing meat cultures on the Ship. It doesn't hurt to like the inevitable.

I started for the kitchen and Daddy followed.

"Isn't the Sixth Level completely shut up?" he asked. "I didn't know you could still get up there."

"It's not that hard," I said, and started getting food out. "Just why did they tear everything out the way they did?"

"Nobody has ever told you why they closed it down?"

I said, "Before today, I didn't even know that there *was* a Sixth Level."

"Oh," Daddy said. "Well, it's simple enough. At the time they converted the Ship it was pretty Spartan living here. We had more space than we needed with all the colonists gone, but not enough of everything else. They stripped the Third and Sixth Levels and used the materials to fix up the rest of the Ship more comfortably. They changed the Third to as near an approximation of Earth as they could, and closed the Sixth down as unnecessary."

"Oh," I said. That seemed to make sense out of the tomb that we had seen.

Daddy said, "I guess I'd forgotten how barren the Sixth Level is. If you want to find out more about it, I can tell you where to look it up. Right now, though, I have to be on my way or I'll be late."

Before he got out of the kitchen, I said, "Daddy?"

He turned around.

I said, "I changed my mind today. I think I'd like to go with you next weekend after all."

Daddy smiled. "I was hoping you'd change your mind if I gave you a little time. You make your share of mistakes, but most of the time you show good sense. I think you did this time."

Daddy is nice, so he wouldn't say, "I told you so," but I was certain that he thought that it was seeing the Sixth Level and not getting stricken dead for it that had changed my mind. It wasn't, though. I think I changed my mind on the ladder—there are times when you have to go forward whether you like it or not, and if Zena Andrus could do it, as scared as she was, so could I. That's all.

I smiled and said, "Do I get unfrozen?" I was at least half-serious. For some reason, getting Daddy to say so was important to me.

Daddy nodded. "I guess you do. I guess you do."

I was still smiling as I sat down to eat. It was just about time I started to do a little growing. It was then that the thought struck me that if I did start to grow, in not very long at all I wouldn't be able to squeeze my way into the ducts.

Well, you can't have everything.

5

While I think of it, I want to excuse myself in advance. From time to time, I'm going to say terribly ignorant things. For instance, when I come to speak of boats shortly, anybody who has ever sailed will probably find reason to laugh and shake his head at my description. Please forgive me. I'm not writing technical descriptions, I'm simply trying to tell what I saw and did. When I felt the need to grab onto something, I didn't grab onto a "gunwale," I grabbed onto the plain old side of the boat. That's what it was to me.

In any case, through the week before we went to Grainau, my spirits slid down again. Having decided to go on Sunday, if I had left on Monday I wouldn't have felt bad at all, but unfortunately I had a whole week to mull things over, worry and imagine. Friday night, the night before we were to leave, I lay awake for hours, unable to sleep. I tried to sleep on my stomach, but bleak possibilities came into my head, one after another. Then onto my side, and imaginary conversations. Onto my back, and thoughts of all the things I might be doing tomorrow instead, if only I could. Finally I did go to sleep, but I didn't sleep well.

At breakfast, Daddy advised me to eat up, but I couldn't. My stomach was nervous. After breakfast, we got on the shuttle and traveled down to the First Level, and then over to the bay in which the scoutships sit waiting to take damned fools places they'd rather not go.

We arrived in the scout bay fifteen minutes before we were supposed to leave for Grainau. Daddy said, "Wait here, Mia. I'll be right back." He went over to a cluster of men standing by the nearest scoutship.

I stood there in a great entranceway carved in the rock, feeling just a little abandoned. Daddy had brought me here, and now he was just going off and leaving me. I was nervous and scared. If I could legitimately have gone back home and crawled in bed, I would have—and not gotten up again for two days, either. If I could have done it without losing face. Unfortunately, it was now harder to back out than to go on, so I was going on, carried by the momentum of my Sunday night decision.

It was the first time I'd ever been in the scout bay. Hesitantly, I looked around. The rock roof arched over the long single line of ships, all squatting over their tubes, waiting for the catch bars that ringed their rims to be released so they could drop out of sight. Scoutships are used for any errands planetside where the Ship can't go itself because of its size. These include delivering and picking up traded items, tooting off on joyrides, carrying diplomatic missions like ours, and dropping kids on Trial. The scoutships are pigeons that nest in a cote that hoves between the stars, and some are out and away at almost any time. To keep my mind off my unhappy stomach, which was growling sourly, I counted the ships that were home, and there were a dozen. The ships are disc-shaped, with bulges top and bottom in the center. Each of them had at least one of its four ramps lowered.

In a moment, Daddy came back with one of the men he'd been speaking with—a young giant. He was at least a foot taller than Daddy. He was very ugly, unpleasant-looking and formidable. I don't think I'd have cared to meet him at any time.

"This is George Fuhonin," Daddy said. "He's going to be our pilot."

I didn't say anything, just looked at him. Daddy prodded me. "Hello," I said, in a small distant voice.

"Hello," he said, in a voice I'd have to call a bass growl. It was deep and it rumbled. "Your father tells me that this is going to be your first trip outside the Ship."

I looked at Daddy out of the corner of my eye, and then I looked up at the big, ugly man. I nodded warily, the least little dip. He scared me.

"Would you like to take a look around the scout before we take off?" he asked. "As your pilot and your father's regular chauffeur, I guarantee I'll leave out nothing."

I wanted to say a definite no, and was just about to when Daddy pushed me forward and said, "Go ahead and enjoy yourself, Mia." He motioned toward the other men. "I've got some things to settle before we leave."

So this man, this monster, George Whatever-His-Name-Was, and I walked up the scoutship ramp, me feeling totally betrayed. I sometimes think that parents enjoy putting their children in uncomfortable situations, maybe as a way of getting back without admitting it. I don't say that is what Daddy was doing, but I certainly thought so at the time.

The top of my head came to about the bottom of this George's ribcage, and he was so big that one of his steps was worth two and a half of mine, so that even when he was walking slowly that half-step kept me either ahead or behind him. If I'd been feeling better, it would have seemed like playing tag around a dinosaur. As it was, I'd just have enjoyed a hole to hide in. Black, deep, and secret.

The main part of the scoutship was at the level we entered. In the center, surrounded by a circular separating partition about four feet high, were lounge beds with sides that stuck up a foot or more like a baby's bed, comfortable chairs, magnetized straight chairs that could be moved, and two tables. In the exact center was a spiral stairway that led both up and down. Around the edge of the ship were storerooms, racks, a kitchen, a toilet, and a number of horse stalls with straw-covered floors. Two horses were being led into place as we came up the ramp and into the ship.

The monster said, "Those are for your father and his assistant after we land."

I didn't say anything. I just looked stonily around.

When the colonies were settled, they took horses to work and ride, because tractors and heli-pacs have such a low reproductive rate. There weren't any opportunities to set up industries on the colonies, simply time enough to drop people and enough supplies to give them a fair chance to survive. Then the Ships would head back to Earth for another load and another destination. Those supplies included very little in the way of machines because machines wear out in a few years. They did include horses. Nowadays when we land on a planet where they haven't made any progress in the last 170 years, we ride horseback, too.

At that time, of course, I hadn't learned to ride yet and I was a little shy of horses. When one was led past me and wrinkled its lips and snorted, I jumped back.

I noticed the toilet then. We were only a few feet away

from it. I looked up at the giant and said, "I have to go to the bathroom."

Before he could say anything, I was inside with the door locked. Escaped, for the moment. I didn't have to go to the bathroom at all. I just wanted to be left alone.

I looked around at the bare-walled room. I ran the water and washed my hands. Altogether, I managed to stay inside for a full five minutes before being alone in the little empty room with my nervousness got to be too much for me. I kept imagining that Daddy was on board by now, and I even thought I could almost hear his voice. Finally I was driven outside to see.

When I opened the door, the giant was standing exactly where I had left him, obviously waiting for me. There were people moving things on board, the horses were locked in their stalls and moving around, and Daddy was still outside somewhere.

Exactly as though I'd never been gone, the giant said, "Come on upstairs," in his deep voice. "I'll show you my buttons. I keep a collection of them there."

Resignedly, I preceded him up the flight of metal stairs that led upstairs, winding around a vertical handpole like threads winding around a screw. It was obvious that he was determined to keep me in his charge, and I wasn't feeling up to arguing, even if I'd dared to. At the top we came out in a bubble-dome in which were two seats hung on swivel pivots, a slanting panel directly in front of them with inset vision screens, dials and meters—the slant of the panel low enough so as not to obscure vision out the dome—and beside these, perhaps enough room to turn around twice.

The giant waved a paw at the console at the base of the panel. "My button collection," he said, and smiled. "I'll bet you didn't think I had any."

They were there. Enough buttons to keep a two-year-old or a pilot occupied for hours. It was obvious that in his way this George was trying to be friendly, but I wasn't in the mood to be friendly with any large, ugly stranger. After one brief glance at the panel and console I turned away to look outside.

Through the dome I could see the rock roof glowing gently all above us. The ring of the scoutship's body cut off the view directly beneath us and I couldn't see Daddy or the men with him at all. It's no fun to be deserted. It's a miserable feeling.

This George said, "Your father will be a little while yet." Feeling caught, I stopped looking for him and turned back around.

"Sit down," the giant said, and somewhat warily I did. The chair bobbed on its pivot as I sat down. I kept my eyes on George.

He leaned carelessly against his panel and after a moment he said, "Since you don't seem to want to talk and we have to be here together for awhile yet, let me tell you a story. It was told to me by my mother the night before I went on Trial."

And with that, he launched full into it, ignoring the fact that I was too old for such things:

Once upon a time (he said) there was a king who had two sons, and they twins, the first ever born in the country. One was named Enegan and the other Britoval, and though one was older than the other, I don't remember which it was, and I doubt anyone else does, either. The two boys were so alike that not even their dear mother's heart could tell one from the other, and before their first month was out they were so thoroughly mixed that no one could be sure which to call Britoval and which Enegan. Finally, they gave the whole thing up as a bad lot, used their heads and hung tags on the boys and called them Ned and Sam.

They grew up tall and strong and as like each other as two warts on the same toad. If one was an inch taller or a pound heavier at the beginning of the month, by the end of it they were all even again. It was all even between them in wrestling, running, swimming, riding, and spitting. By the time they were grown-up young men, there was only one way to mark them apart. It was universally agreed that Sam was bright and Ned was charming, and the people of the country even called them Bright Sam and Charming Ned.

"Hark," they would say as a horse went by on the road. "There goes Prince Charming Ned." Or, alternatively, "Hey, mark old Bright Sam thinking under yon spreading oak."

The boys did earn their names, and honestly. Ask Sam to do a sum, parse a sentence, or figure a puzzle and he could do it in a trice, whereas Ned just wasn't handy at that sort of thing. On the other hand, if you like charm and heart, courtesy and good humor, Ned was a really swell fellow, a delight to his dear mother, and a merry ray of sunshine to his subjects, while Sam at his best was a trifle sour.

Then one day the Old King, their father, died and the question arose as to which son should inherit, for the kingdom was small and the treasury was empty, and there simply was not enough for both.

The Great Council of the Kingdom met to consider the problem. They met and considered, considered and voted, voted and tied. At first they said it was obvious that the elder son should inherit, but they found that no one at all could say which was the elder. Then an exasperated soul proposed that the younger should inherit, and all agreed that was a fine way out until they discovered that it was equally problematic which was the younger. It was at this point that they decided to vote to settle the question—but the vote turned out a tie, for half said, "A king should be bright so as to be able to rule intelligently and deal wisely with the friends and the enemies of the kingdom. Nobody really has to like him," and the other half said, "A king should be beloved by his subjects and well thought of by his neighbors and peers. The Council can always provide the brains needed to run things if brains are ever required."

At last, finally, and in the end, it was decided by all that there was only one way to settle the matter. Charming Ned and Bright Sam must undertake a Quest and whichever of them was successful would become King of the Realm, and take his fine old father's place. If neither was successful, they could always bring in a poor second cousin who was waiting in the wings, hat in hand. Kingdoms always have second cousins around to fill in when they're needed.

The Quest decided upon was this: it seems that many miles away—or so the story had come to them in the kingdom—there was a small cavern in which lived a moderate-sized ogre with a fine large treasure, big enough to handle the kingdom's budget problem for some years to come. It was agreed that whichever of the two boys could bring the treasure home where it belonged would have proved to the satisfaction of everybody his overwhelming right to be king.

* * *

At this point the story was interrupted. One of the three crewmen stuck his head up through the stairwell and said, "We're all tight, George. Miles says we can leave any time now."

George said to me, "Strap yourself in there," and pushed the button that locked himself into his own seat. Humming slightly to himself, he rapped a switch with the back of his hand and rumbled, "Ten seconds to drop. Mind your stomachs."

In ten seconds, the rim bars pulled back and we dropped slowly into our tube and then out of the Ship. I was leaving home for the first time. Geo Quad, even at its worst, was still "Us" rather than "Them." As we dropped into the tube, the dome went opaque around us and lights came on. There was none of the stomach-upsetting moment of transition as we shifted from the artificial gravity of the Ship to the artificial gravity of the scoutship of which George had just warned us, though there might have been. Which meant that whatever else he might be, this George creature was a relatively effective pilot.

I still didn't know how to take him. I have that problem when I first meet people—I have to get used to them slowly. For the moment, too young for me or not, I was content to have him go on with his story, because it gave me something to think about instead of Grainau and whatever I would find there.

He punched buttons for a minute, and then said, "Well, that ought to hold us for awhile. Now where was I?"

"The ogre and the treasure."

"Oh, yes," he said, and continued with his story:

Well, the two young men set off the very next morning, when the sun was up and the air was warm. Sam, intelligent as always, had loaded food and supplies into a knapsack and put it on his back, and buckled a great sword about his waist. Ned took nothing—too heavy, you know—but simply put his red cap on his head and walked on down the road, whistling. Everybody in the kingdom came down to the road to wave and see them off. They waved until the boys were around the first bend in the road, and then, like sensible folk, they all went home to breakfast.

Sam was loaded so heavily that he couldn't walk as fast as his dear brother, and Ned was soon out of sight ahead of him. This didn't seriously bother Bright Sam, because he was sure that preparation and foresight would in the end more than make up for Ned's initial brisk pace. When he got hungry, not having any food would slow him down.

But Sam walked a long time, day and night, and never saw his brother. Then he came on the skinniest man he'd ever seen, sitting by a great pile of animal bones.

"Hello," Sam said. "I'm looking for an ogre who lives in a cave and owns a treasure. Do you know where I can find him?"

At the question, the man began to cry. Sam asked him what the trouble was, since sour or not, he hated to see people cry. The man said, "A young fellow stopped a day or two ago and asked me the same question exactly. And he brought nothing but trouble on me. I had a flock of sheep, and fine ones, too, and I was roasting one for my dinner when he stopped, and he was such a nice, pleasant fellow that I asked him to eat with me. He was still hungry after the first sheep, so I killed another, and then another, and then another. He was so friendly and charming, and so grateful, that I never noticed until he had gone that he had eaten every last one of my animals. Now I have nothing at all. And I'm starting to get hungry myself."

Sam said, "If you will tell me where the ogre lives I will give you some of the food that I have with me."

The man said, "Give me some of your food and I will tell you just what I told that other young fellow."

So Sam gave him food and when the hungry man was done eating, he said, "The answer is that I don't know. I don't have any truck with ogres. I just mind my own business."

Sam went on down the road with his pack a little lighter than before. He walked a long time, day and night, and never saw his brother. Then he came on a little castle in which lived a princess—well, perhaps not a princess as most people reckon it, but since she lived there alone there wasn't a single person to say she wasn't. That is how royal families are founded.

This little castle was being besieged by a very rude and unpleasant giant. As a passing courtesy, Sam drew his sword and slew the giant, lopping off his great hairy head. The princess, and pretty indeed she was, came out of her castle and thanked him.

"It was very nice of you," said she, "but I'm afraid that

the giant here," and she nudged his head with the toe of her dainty slipper, "has seven brothers and the whole lot take turns besieging my castle. This will no doubt make them a bit angry. I used to have a charm that kept my land protected from all such creatures, but alas no longer. A young man with a red cap came whistling down the road last week looking for an ogre and he was so sweet and charming that I gave him the charm to protect himself with and keep him from harm, and ever since these horrid giants have been attacking my castle."

"Well, why don't you move?" said Sam. "There aren't any giants where I live, though we do have a dragon or two, and we have some very nice castles looking to be bought."

The princess said that sounded like a very nice idea, and she just might take his advice.

"By the way," said Sam, "do you know, by chance, where I can find the ogre you were speaking of just a minute ago?"

"Oh, certainly," she said. "It's not far at all. Just follow your nose for three days and nights and you'll be there."

Sam thanked her, slew a second giant come to look for his brother, and went on his way. He followed his nose, and after three days and nights it told him that he had found the ogre's cave. He knocked politely and the ogre came out. The cave was a bit small for him. He was covered with hair, and he had three red eyes and two great yellow fangs. Other than his appearance, he seemed friendly enough.

Sam drew his sword and said, "Excuse me, but I've come for your treasure."

"Well, if you can tell me a riddle I can't guess," said the ogre, "I'll give all I have to you. But if I do answer it, I want your money and all that you have."

Sam agreed. It is common knowledge that ogres are not bright as a rule, and Sam knew some very hard riddles indeed.

He thought, he did, and finally he said, "What is it that is not, and never will be?"

The ogre turned the question over in his mind. Then he sat down to really think about it. For three whole days and three whole nights they sat there, and nobody thought it odd of them because nobody lived nearby. The ogre tried a dozen answers one by one, but each time Sam said, "I'm sorry, but that's not it."

Finally, the ogre said, "I can't think of any more answers. You win. But don't tell me the answer. Write it on a piece of paper. I can think about it after you're gone."

So Sam wrote his answer down on a piece of paper and gave it to the ogre. Then he said, "And now, could I trouble you for your treasure?"

The ogre said, "You won all that I have fair and square. Just a minute." He went inside the cave and in just a moment he was back with a single brass farthing. "I'm sorry, but that's all there is. There used to be more, but I gave it to a nice young man who was here just a week ago. I had to start all over again after he left, and now that you've beaten me, I'll have to start even another time."

Because he knew his brother well, Sam asked disbelievingly, "This young fellow didn't ask you any riddles you couldn't answer, did he?"

The ogre drew himself up and said in a wounded tone, "Of course not. But he was such a nice young fellow that I couldn't bear to let him go away empty-handed."

Well, that left Sam with something of a problem. He'd beaten the ogre and won his treasure, but nobody was likely to take a single brass farthing as proof of that. So he thought for a minute, and then he said, "And how do you find your cave for size, my friend?"

"Cramped," said the ogre. "But good caves are hard to find."

"And do you have much company here?"

"No," said the ogre. "I think on my riddles to pass the time."

"Well," said Sam, "how would you like to come along home with me? When I'm king at home I can provide you with a fine large cave and pleasant neighbors, and send people with riddles to you from time to time. How about that?"

The ogre could hardly turn an offer like that down, so he agreed readily and they set out together. When they got near home, it was apparent to Sam that a celebration was going on in the kingdom.

He said to his ogre friend, "How would you like to go to a party?"

"Oh, fine," said the ogre. "I'm sure I'd like a party, though I've never been to one."

"Well, I'll go in first, and then I'll come out for you in a minute," said Sam.

He went inside to find that there was a double celebration in progress. His brother Ned was about to be crowned king and to marry the sweet princess that Sam had sent home. Sam thought that was most unkind.

"Stop the wedding," said Sam. They stopped the wedding and looked around at him. He said, "I succeeded at the Quest, and I claim the right to be king."

Everybody laughed at him. They said, "Charming Ned brought home the ogre's treasure. What did you bring?"

Sam showed them his single brass farthing. "I brought this," he said and they all laughed the more. "And I brought one more thing," he said, and threw open the doors. In walked the ogre, looking for the party he'd been promised.

Sam explained to the ogre that the party would begin straight away the moment he became king. Since the ogre was standing in the only doorway, Sam was made king in no time at all.

Well, after that, Sam set the ogre up in a cave of his very own, and after the neighbors found he wasn't a bad sort he got on quite well. The ogre became a regular tourist attraction, one of the finest in the kingdom, and brought in a nice regular bit of revenue. Sam opened a charm school with his brother Ned in charge, and that brought in even more money. Sam married the princess himself and everybody lived happily from then on. If they haven't moved away, and I don't know why they would, they'll be living there still.

Oh, yes. It took the ogre a full ten years to decide he couldn't answer Sam's riddle. Every week he would bundle the answers he'd thought of together and send them to Sam and Sam would send them back. Finally the ogre decided he would never find the right answer to the question, "What is it that is not and never will be?" He opened the paper Sam had given him so long before and took a look. The answer was, "A mouse's nest in a cat's ear." (And that, my little friend, is the only real, true answer there is.)

"Oh, hell," said the ogre. "I was just about to guess that."

"There's a moral, too," George said. "My mother told it to me and I'll tell it to you: If you're bright and use your head, you'll never go too far wrong. Just keep it in mind, and you'll get along."

Right after that, we reached the atmosphere of Grainau. George was busy with his buttons. I was thinking that he meant well enough and I was feeling a bit more friendly toward him.

I had gathered that entering a planet's atmosphere was a tricky business, but George didn't seem particularly concerned. The main problem was the same as when leaving the Ship: to strike a balance between one gravity field and the other, so that the people aboard were not plastered against the floor or left suddenly without any feeling of weight at all. Besides that, he had to take us to the point on the planet to which we were going, and how he did that, I couldn't tell. Apparently he got bearings from his instruments. The dials and meters said incomprehensible things to me, but by some strange gift of tongues, he understood them. He switched on the vision screens and they showed nothing but a billowy gray blankness beneath us. Without any coaxing from George, the dome above our heads became first translucent and then gradually transparent, our interior lights fading in correspondence to the increasing light from outside.

As we descended, I looked all around through the dome. I was still feeling apprehensive, but my curiosity was getting the better of me. I freed myself from my chair and strained to see all I could, but it wasn't heartening. In every direction the view was the same, a slightly rolling gray-whiteness that looked soft and bouncy, lit uniformly by the red-orange sun that was low in the sky ahead of us as we traveled, and gradually rose higher. It was the first sun I had seen at close range and I didn't like the glare it gave off. The automatic polarizer in the dome reduced the brightness until it was bearable to look at the bright disk, but I could see its light was unpleasant. The vision screens showed the same bouncy amorphous whiteness directly beneath us as we moved.

I said, "That isn't what a planet looks like, is it?"

George laughed and said, "Those are clouds. The planet's down underneath. It's like frosting with cake under it."

He reached to rap at the same switch he'd turned on before and saw it was on. He frowned and then made an announcement to the people below: "We'll be setting down in about ten minutes." He hit the switch and it popped up.

"I'm going downstairs," I said.

"All right," George said. "I'll see you later."

He turned his attention back to his job and we suddenly sliced down into the gray-white clouds and were surrounded by the sick, smothering mass. The lights came up a little in the dome to restore the life that was missing in the grayness outside. It was the most frightening stuff to be lost in that I could imagine and I didn't want to look at it. I went down the spiral stairs and in the warm haven of the room below I looked for Daddy. He was sitting in an easy chair by himself in the center section. Mr. Tubman, Daddy's assistant, was watching while the horses were saddled. Men were bustling around doing those last-minute things that people always discover five minutes before it will be too late to do them. Daddy had a book and was reading quite calmly, as I might have expected. Daddy ignores confusion.

I sat down in a heavy brown chair beside him and waited until he looked up. He said, "Hello, Mia. We're just about there. How are you doing?"

"All right, I guess." Meaning I was nervous.

"Good. And how are you gttting on with George?"

I shrugged. "All right, I guess."

"I've asked him to keep an eye on you today while I'm in conference. He'll show you around the town. He's been here before."

"Are you going to be busy all day long?" I asked.

"I think so. If I wind things up before dark, I'll find the two of you."

I had to be satisfied with that. A few moments later we touched down smoothly for a landing. Grainau had heavier gravity than home—that was the first thing I was certain of after all our motion had ceased. I could feel the extra weight as a strain on my calves and arches when I stood up. Something that would take getting used to.

George came downstairs and walked over to us. Daddy stood up and said, "Well, all ready to take over, George?" Meaning me.

George towered over both of us. He nodded.

Daddy smiled and said, "That was a pretty good story, George. You have talents I never suspected you of having."

"Which story?" I asked.

"The story George was just telling you," Daddy said. "The speaker was on from the time we left the Ship."

George grinned. "I didn't notice that until just a minute ago."

"It was a *fine* story," Daddy said.

I flushed, thoroughly embarrassed. "Oh, no," I said. To listen to a story like that was one thing, but to have everybody else know it was something else and thoroughly disconcerting.

I shot George an accusing look and then ran for cover, heading for the toilet again. I didn't want to be seen by anybody.

Daddy was after me and caught me before I got to the separating partition. He grasped my arm and brought me to a stop.

"Hold on, Mia," he said.

I struggled to get loose. "Let me *go*."

"Don't make a scene, Mia," he said.

"Let go of me. I don't want to stay here."

"Quiet!" he said sharply. "I'm sorry I made the mistake of telling you, but George didn't do it intentionally. Besides, I enjoyed his story and I'm more than six times your age."

"That's different," I said.

"You may be right, but whether you're right or not doesn't make any difference right now. It's time to go outside. I want you to put yourself together and walk outside with me. When we face these Colons, I want you to be somebody I can be proud of. You don't want to show up badly in front of these people, do you?"

I shook my head.

"All right," he said, and let go of me. "Put yourself together."

Keeping my head averted, I did my best to get a grip on myself. I straightened my blouse and hitched my shorts, and when I was ready, I faced around.

The ramp was down on the far side of the ship, and I could hear noise from outside. People shouting.

"Come along," Daddy said and we walked across the center area. George was still standing there and I gave him a hostile glance as we passed, but he didn't seem to notice. He fell in behind us.

We paused for a moment at the top of the ramp, and that seemed to be taken as a signal for a band to start playing and for people to yell even louder.

6

The horses had already been led outside and were being held there by Mr. Tubman. Standing beside him was an officious-looking man in a tall hat in which was placed a great wilted white feather. At another time he might have been funny. There were two children with him, a boy and a girl, both somewhere near my age. We had set down in what must have been the main square of the town, and there were ranks of people yelling and staring up at us from either hand. It made me feel on display. The sky was low and gray above us, the yellow bricks of the square were wet and shining, and there was a warm, damp breeze. The band was directly in front of us, all of the band members dressed in dark green uniforms. They played enthusiastically—loudly, that is—but badly.

I was looking all around at this, but Daddy took my arm and said, "Come on. You can gawk later."

We started down the ramp and all the people in the square increased the volume of their noise. I didn't like it and started to feel very nervous. I wouldn't like being yelled at by large numbers of people in any case, but this was all the more discomfiting because I couldn't tell from the noise whether they were friendly or not. Whatever tune the band was playing became indistinguishable and simply added a small contribution to the general hubbub.

Daddy and the officious-looking man shook hands. Daddy said, "Mr. Gennaro. It's good to see you again."

The man said, "You timed things well, Mr. Havero. The rain stopped here less than an hour ago, though I won't guarantee that it will stay stopped."

Daddy nudged me forward. "This is my daughter, Mia. I believe you've already met Mr. Tubman and George Fuhonin, my pilot." As I shook hands, I took a good look at him. He had an eager-to-please manner that I didn't know how to take, and I couldn't get any clue from Daddy's face or tone.

Gennaro indicated the boy and the girl with him. "These are my children, Ralph and Helga. When you said you were bringing your daughter, I thought she might like to meet some children of her own age." He turned on a smile and then turned it off again.

The boy had dirty-blond hair. He was just a shade taller than I, but much more squarely built. The girl was also squarely built, and about my size. They both said hello, but not in an overwhelmingly friendly way.

I said hello just as cautiously myself.

"That was very thoughtful," Daddy said to Mr. Gennaro.

The man said, "Glad to do it. Glad to do it. Anything to keep up good will. Ha, ha."

The people and the band continued to make noise. "Shall we be going?" Daddy said.

"Oh, yes," Mr. Gennaro said. "Children, mind your manners."

Daddy didn't say anything to me, but simply gave me a sharp look. Mr. Gennaro mounted his horse, and Daddy and Mr. Tubman swung up on theirs. The band, still playing, backed off enough for them to pass through, and they clattered off and out of the square. The band followed after, still playing loud and tinnily, and a good portion of the crowd trailed them.

I said, "Why is everybody following after Daddy?"

"Your father is a celebrity," George Fuhonin said in an ironic rumble, standing just behind me.

I hadn't been speaking to him, just voicing my thoughts, but I was reminded that I had determined not to speak to him, ever again. So I moved away a little.

A section of the remaining crowd pressed forward toward the scoutship, bent on getting a good close look at us. George looked out at them with no particular sign of pleasure, as though he'd like to shoo them away.

"Stay here," he said to me. "I'll be right back."

He walked up the ramp to the place where the three crewmembers were standing. They were lounging in the mouth of the ship and getting a big kick out of the crowd. When George came up, they said something that sounded like a joke, and laughed. George didn't laugh. He shook his head irritably and motioned them to go inside.

"What do we do now?" the boy, Ralph, said to his sister, and I turned back to look at them.

On the Ship we have such long lives and low population that you never see brothers and sisters closer than twenty years apart, never as close together as these two. All the kids I know are singletons. I don't know what I was expecting to see, but except for build, this brother and sister didn't look much alike at all. I had thought they would—in books they always do; either that or exactly like their long-lost Uncle Max, the one with all the money. Helga had dark hair, though not as dark as mine, and it was quite long, hanging down to her shoulders and tucked in place with combs. She wore a dress with a yoke front. Her brother wore long pants like those Daddy had put on to wear today, and a plain shirt. They had both obviously done some grooming for this little ceremony, and it made them look as stiff as their manners.

I suppose I looked just as odd to them as they did to me. I was a short, dark little thing with close-cut black hair, and I was wearing what I usually wore, a white blouse with loose sleeves, blue shorts, and high-backed sandals. It was a costume I would have felt comfortable in at almost any sort of gathering within the Ship. I wouldn't have worn exactly that to play soccer in—something a little less formal, actually, and harder shoes—but I was presentable. My clothes were clean and reasonably neat. However, after the glory of all those dark green uniforms, I could see that these kids might consider what I was wearing just a bit lacking in elegance.

We looked at each other for a long starchy moment. Then the boy unbent a little and said, "How old are you?"

"Twelve," I said.

"I'm fourteen," he said. "She's twelve."

Helga said, "Daddy told us to show you around." She said it tentatively.

I took a deep breath and said, "All right."

"What about him?" she said, pointing to the ramp. George was standing just inside the ship with his back to us. "He told you to stay here."

"He's supposed to watch me, but I don't have to pay any attention to him," I said. "Let's leave before he comes back."

"All right," Ralph said. "Come on then."

He ran under the high rim of the scoutship, in exactly

the opposite direction from Daddy and his own father. Helga and I followed him. George saw me as I started off, and yelled something, but I just kept on running. I'd be damned if I'd pay any attention to him.

Ralph made a slight detour to tag the lower bulge of the ship—maybe to be brave and have something to tell about afterward, maybe just to do it—and then dashed on. We went all the way under the rim of the ship and out the other side. There were a few people there, but a much smaller crowd than on the side where the ramp was lowered, possibly because there weren't any Ship people to stare at over here. We charged through them, and I noticed that they were all squarely built, too. We left them looking after us and dashed around the first corner we came to. I was feeling pretty daring in my own way, as though I were cutting loose on a great adventure.

We took a couple of quick turns from one street into another, and if George was following after, he was soon left behind. By that time, I had no idea of where we were. It was a street like the others we'd been in, made of rounded stones and about the width of a large hallway at home, with buildings of stone and wood, and a few of brick, on either side.

"Hold on," I said. "I can't run any more."

My legs were aching and I was out of breath. It took a lot more effort to get around here than it did at home, and I had no doubt that if I fell down it would hurt more. Grainau was a planet that was what they called "Earth-like to nine degrees," as were all the colony planets, but that one degree of difference offered a great deal of latitude for the odd or uncomfortable, including Grainau's slightly stronger gravity. That "slightly stronger" was enough to tire me in almost no time.

"What's the matter?" Ralph asked.

I said, "I'm tired. Let's just walk."

They exchanged looks, and then Ralph said, "Oh, all right."

The air was a little hard to catch your breath in, it seemed so thick and warm. It felt wet. Something like walking through stew, and about as pleasant as that.

"Is the air always like this?" I asked.

"Like what?" Helga asked, with the barest hint of a defensive edge in her voice.

"Well, thick." I could have added, "and smelly, too,"

since it carried an odd variety of odors I couldn't identify, but I didn't. They always prate about planetary fresh air, but if this was it, I didn't like it.

"It's just a little humid today," Ralph said. "This breeze that's coming up now should clear the air."

We started that afternoon by all being a little afraid of each other, I think. But very quickly Ralph and Helga found out how silly their fear was, and pretty soon, when they didn't think to mind their manners, the contempt that replaced the fear slipped out. It took me awhile to see what it was. All I knew was that they found a lot of what I said foolish, and made it clear that they found it foolish, and that they did a lot of exchanging of significant glances.

I found I didn't know *any*thing. I didn't even know what time it was. I said something about the morning, something that made it clear that I thought it was morning and they both turned on me. Turned out it was after lunch here. No matter that *I* had stared at my breakfast just before we left.

I pointed at a building and asked what it was.

"That's a store, silly. Haven't you ever seen a store?"

Well, I hadn't. I'd read about them, and that's all. We have such a small society on the Ship that buying and selling aren't really practicable. If you want something, you put in a requisition for it and in a little while it comes. You can live as simply or as lavishly as you want—there's a limit as to how much you can jam into one apartment, though some people do live up to the limit. In a society where anybody can have just about anything he wants, there's no real prestige in having things unless you use them or get some esthetic pleasure from them, so I would say the tendency in general is toward simple living.

I can think of only one regular program of exchange on the Ship. Kids under fourteen are given weekly allowance chits to draw against in the Common Room snack bars; that way none of them get a chance to ruin their health. After fourteen, they assume you know what you're about and leave you alone.

"Can I take a look?" I asked.

Ralph shrugged. "All right, I guess."

It was a clothing store, and most of the clothes looked very strange to me. There were even some items I couldn't figure out.

After a minute, the man who ran the place came up to

Ralph and said in a loud whisper, "What's he dressed like that for?"

"She's a girl," Helga said. "And she doesn't know any better."

My ears went red, but I pretended I didn't hear and just kept poking through the racks of cloaks I was looking at.

"She's down from that Ship," Ralph said in a whisper as good as a shout. "They don't wear clothes up there. She probably thought that junk she has on is what we wear."

The man sneered and quite deliberately turned away from me. I wasn't sure why and I was puzzled, because it was obviously meant to be offensive. He only stopped short of spitting on the floor at my feet. It seemed excessive if it was only because I didn't have the sense to dress like a proper girl in the horrible things he had to sell.

As we went out, the storekeeper muttered something about "grabbie" that I didn't catch. Ralph and Helga didn't seem to notice, or pretended they didn't, and I said nothing.

We had just left the store and turned the corner, starting on a long downhill slope, when I stopped still and said, "What's that?"

"What?"

I pointed at the dead gray mass tipped with white that stretched across the bottom of the street, blocks away downhill. "Is that water?"

They looked at each other, and then in an "any blockhead should know *that* much" tone of voice, Ralph said, "It's the ocean."

I'd always wanted to see an ocean, since they're even rarer on the Ship than stores. "Could I take a look?"

"Sure," Ralph said. "Why not?"

First there was a stone wharf and warehouses stretching away on either hand. The harbor stretched two great arms around to enclose a large expanse of water. At the sides were wooden docks on pilings running out like fingers into the harbor. Close at hand were boats of all sizes. Nearest were the great giants with several masts, big enough to have smaller boats tied on board. There were medium and small boats tied up at all the docks.

Even in the harbor, the water ran in white-crested peaks and slapped noisily at the stone and wood. There were birds of white, and gray, and brown, and black, and mixtures of all these colors, all wheeling around and crying overhead, and some of them diving down at the water. The air down here smelled strongly—of fish, I think. Outside the harbor the water was running in mountains that made the peaks inside look small, and it stretched away farther than I could see clearly, to join somewhere in the distance with the gray sky overhead.

I might have made comments about all the things I saw, the odors, the men working, but I didn't know what to say that wouldn't strike Ralph and Helga as amusing, and by that time I was starting to be a little cautious about exposing myself. I was seeing them as something less than the allies they had been when we were running from George. We walked along the waterfront and off the quay and onto the wooden docks. Ralph led us out onto a little spur and we stopped there.

He pointed down at a little craft tied alongside. It was about twelve feet long, with a mast that stood up high enough to reach above the dock. It had a boom that was lashed in place. It was painted a serviceable white with black trim, and had the odd name *Guacamole* painted on it.

"What do you think of her?" he asked.

"It's a very nice ship," I said.

"It isn't a ship. It's a boat, a sailing dinghy, and it's ours, Helga's and mine. We go sailing all the time. Want to go for a sail?"

Helga looked at him, obviously pleased. "Oh, can we?"

"If she'll go," Ralph said. "It's up to her. Otherwise we've got to do what Daddy said and stay with her."

"Oh, do come on," Helga said to me.

I looked at the water and tried to make up my mind. The water looked rough and the boat looked small. I really didn't want to go at all.

Helga said, "We'll just stay inside the harbor."

"It isn't dangerous," Ralph added, looking at me.

I didn't want him to think I was scared, so after a minute I shrugged and started down the wooden ladder that reached from the dock down to the rear of the boat. The ladder stood about two feet above the dock at its highest point, and I grabbed it and backed down. I seemed to be seeing more of ladders lately than I really cared to. Ralph and Helga started down after me.

The boat was rising and falling on the water as the swells came in to break on the docks and the quay. I waited until the boat was rising and then stepped in. I almost slipped, but I held my feet and then moved carefully to the front, grabbing on when I had to. When I got by the mast, I sat down on the seat that ran across the front. Helga dropped into the boat as I was sitting, and Ralph was right behind her.

I blinked a little as a trace of spray wet my cheek. "Aren't we going to get wet?" I asked.

They didn't hear, and I repeated my question in a louder voice.

"It's just spindrift," Helga said. "You've got to expect that. We won't get too wet."

Ralph said, "Besides, the water will get you clean. I know you don't see much water in your Ship."

That was another thing that irritated me about Ralph and Helga. They had all sorts of misconceptions about the Ship which they insisted on trotting out. Ralph was worse, because he was dogmatic. I thought at first he was being malicious until I realized he actually believed what he was saying, like that bit about going naked—that wasn't completely wrong; some people do go without clothes in the privacy of their own apartments, but I would like to see somebody trying to play soccer while completely bare. The point is that what he said wasn't quite right, either, and he wouldn't listen. He would just say his misconceptions flatly and expect you to agree with him.

Right at the beginning he'd said something about how it was too bad we had to live in crowded barracks—something along that line—and didn't I like all the space here? I tried to explain that that was only the way it used to be on the Ship, right at the beginning, but then I made the mistake of bringing in the dormitories, which are a little bit that way, trying to be honest, and that only confused the issue. Ralph finally said that everybody knew what things were like, and I didn't have to try to explain.

Helga was a little more bearable because she only asked questions.

"Is it true you don't eat food on your Ship?"

"What do you mean?"

"Well, they say you don't grow food like we do, that you eat dirt or something."

"No," I said.

And: "Is it true that you kill babies who are born looking wrong?"

"Do you?"

"Well, no. But everybody says you do."

The thing that really annoyed me about Ralph and his "water to get you clean" remark is that we on the Ship had very clear memories of how dirty the colonists had been. Ralph apparently wasn't even able to notice the horrid odors that clung to the whole harbor, which demonstrated how defective his sense of smell was, but I still didn't like the blithe, "of course" way he said it.

Ralph and Helga got the sail up in short order, while I watched, and then Helga came up by me, untied the bow, and sat down. Ralph untied the stern and we pushed off. He had a little stick tiller to steer with and held the boom by a line. He put the boom over and the breeze filled the sail with an audible *flap*.

We started from the right-hand curve of the harbor with the wind behind us, and sailed across the long width of the harbor. The chop of the waves and the spray were annoying, and the grayness of the day wasn't very nice, but I thought I could see how, given better weather and time to get used to this sort of thing, sailing could be fun.

Uncharitably, though, I couldn't help thinking that we handled weather much better on the Third Level than they did here. When we wanted rain, everybody knows it's coming ahead of time. We throw a switch and it rains until we want it to stop, and then it stops. None of this thick air with its clamminess.

As we were sailing, Helga started a conversation, trying to be friendly I think. She said, "Do you have any brothers and sisters?"

"No," I said. "I don't think so. I never heard of any."

"Well, wouldn't you know? I mean half-brothers and half-sisters, too."

"I don't know for sure, but I was never told of any. My parents have been married so long that if I had a brother he'd be all grown or dead years ago." This may seem strange, but it was an idea that I'd never entertained before. I just never thought in terms of brothers and sisters. It was an interesting notion, but I didn't really take it seriously even now.

Helga looked at me with a slightly puzzled look. "Married? I thought you didn't get married like regular people. I thought you just lived with anybody you wanted to."

I said, "My parents have been married more than fifty years. That's Earth years."

"Fifty years? Oh, you know that isn't so. I just saw your father and he isn't even as old as my dad."

"Well, how old is your dad?"

"Let's see," she said. She did some obvious figuring. "About fifty."

I said, "Well, my dad is eighty-one. Earth years."

She looked at me with an expression of total disbelief. "Oh, that's a lie."

"And my mother is seventy-four. Or seventy-five. I'm not sure which it is."

Helga gave me a disgusted look and turned away.

Well, it was true, and if she didn't want to believe it, too bad. I won't say it's usual for people to be married as long as fifty years. I get the impression that people tend to get tired of each other after twenty or thirty years, and split up, and there are some people who don't want anything as permanent as marriage and just live together. And people who don't even know each other who have children because the Ship's Eugenist advises it. Whatever Helga had heard, it had been a garbled or twisted version of this.

My parents were a strange pair. They'd been married for fifty years, which wasn't usual, and they hadn't lived together for eight years. When I was four, my mother got an opportunity she had been looking forward to for the study of art under Lemuel Carpentier, and she'd moved out. I guess that if you've been married as long as fifty years, and apparently expect it to go on for maybe fifty years more, that a vacation of eight years or so is hardly noticeable.

To tell the truth, I didn't know what my parents saw in each other. I liked and respected my father, but I didn't like my mother at all. I'd like to say that it was simply that we didn't understand each other, and that was partly true. I thought her "art" was plain bad. One of the few times I went to her apartment to visit, I looked at a sculpture she'd done and asked her about it.

"That's called 'The Bird,' " she said.

I could see that it was meant to be a bird. Mother was working directly from a picture and it looked just like it. But it was so stiff and formal that it had no feel of life at all. I said something about that, and she didn't like the remark. We got into an argument, and she finally put me out.

So part of it was misunderstanding, but not all. For one

thing, she made it quite clear to me that she'd had me as a duty and not because she particularly wanted to. I firmly believed that she was just waiting for me to go on Trial, and then she'd move back in with Daddy. As I say, I didn't like her.

When we got to the far side of the harbor, instead of coming directly back, as I somehow had thought we would, Ralph turned us so that we were traveling out at an angle toward the mouth of the harbor. Traveling that way, we were running at an angle through the waves, too, and the chop increased tremendously. We would go up in the air, and then quite suddenly down again, and after a few minutes of this, I was starting to feel queasy. It was a different sort of upset than I'd been suffering earlier in the day. This was nausea and accompanied by a whirling in the head.

I said to Helga, "Can't we go straight back? I'm starting to feel sick."

"This *is* the quickest way back," she said. "We can't sail directly into the wind. We have to tack, head into the wind at an angle."

"But we're going so slow," I said. It was the slow way we rammed into waves, surged high, and then pitched down on the other side that threw my stomach off stride.

Ralph yanked on the line that was attached to the boom, and swung it over from one side of the boat to the other, turning the tiller at the same time, and we headed back in toward the quay in another slow tack. By that time, I was feeling miserable.

"Don't throw up," Helga said cheerfully. "We'll be back soon enough." Then she raised her voice. "You've had it your fair turn, Ralph. Let me take over."

"Oh, all right," Ralph said, quite reluctantly.

Helga ducked back to the stern, taking the tiller and the boom line from Ralph. She nodded at me. "She's feeling sick," she said.

"Oh," Ralph said. He came forward and sat down beside me.

He looked at me and said, "It takes awhile to get your sea-legs. After you sail for awhile you get used to it."

He didn't say anything while we completed that leg and part of the next tack. He just watched Helga a little wistfully. I began to think that this sailing thing—provided first that you were feeling well enough to enjoy it at all—

was much more fun for the person actually doing the sailing than for the passengers. Helga and Ralph, at least, both seemed to be having much more fun when they were sailing than when they were sitting up front. Perhaps it was just that they felt they had to talk to me, and that was an effort for them.

Ralph said, "Uh, well, how do you think our fathers are getting along?"

I swallowed, trying to keep control of my stomach. I said, "I don't know. I don't even know what they were going to trade for."

He looked at me in surprise. "You don't even know that? We operate placer mines just to produce tungsten ore for you, we ship it all the way there, and you don't even know it!"

"Why don't . . ." I paused, and grabbed hard onto the side of the boat (gunwale) and fought hard to hold onto my composure as we dipped into a sudden trough. "Why don't you mine this stuff, whatever it is, just for yourselves?"

Somewhat bitterly he said, "We don't know how to reduce it. You Ship people won't tell us how. When we trade with you, all you give us is little bits and pieces of information."

We were heeling over into our last tack then, about to head down the last stretch to the dock.

I said, "And why not? We preserved all the knowledge through the years since Earth was destroyed. If we gave it all to you, what would we have left to trade with?"

"My dad says you're parasites," he said. "You live off our hard work. You're Grabbies, and that's no mistake."

"We are not parasites," I said.

"If things were the way they ought to be, we'd be the ones living like kings, not you."

"If we live like kings, why were you saying earlier that we had to live all crowded together in barracks?"

He was nonplussed for a moment and then he said, "Because you like to live like pigs, that's why. I can't help it if you like to live like pigs."

"If there are any pigs around here, it's you Mudeaters," I said.

"What?"

"Mudeaters!"

"Grabbie! Why don't you take a bath?" He put his

hand against my chest and gave a hard shove. In spite of our quarreling, he caught me unprepared, and I went tumbling overboard.

The feel of the water was shocking. It was colder than the air, though after the first moment not unpleasantly cold. I got a mouthful of water as I went under and it was very bad-tasting, dirty and bitter. I came up, coughing and spluttering, as the boat swung on past me. I got a glimpse of Helga with her head turned back toward me and a surprised look on her face. I treaded water while I coughed out the water that had gone down my windpipe, and some that had gone down the wrong way came up the wrong way and out my nose. It took several seconds before I was breathing properly. The shock and choking did settle my stomach, I found to my surprise, but it wasn't the way I'd have chosen to do it if I had had a choice.

Helga had spilled the air out of the canvas and turned the tiller. The *Guacamole* was just rocking on the water and drifting. She stood up, looking back at me.

"Do you need help?" she called.

We weren't really far from the dock, so I called, "No, I can swim in."

I had light clothing on. My wet, loose sleeves were a little of a problem, but I found I could manage. I'd never swum in anything but a pool before, but I found it wasn't really a problem to stay on top of the waves, though I had to be careful that I didn't swallow any more of that bitter water. I wasn't a fast swimmer, but I was built enough like a cork that all I had to do was keep at it and I had no trouble going where I wanted to.

As it was, we were close enough to the dock when I went overboard that I was able to reach a ladder by the time they had the *Guacamole* all tied up. I pulled myself up and then found that I was very tired, collapsed in a heap and dripped water all over the boards of the dock. I watched as thirty feet down the way, Ralph and Helga lowered the sail and lashed the boom.

As they finished, I got up and walked down the dock to the head of their ladder. The gravity had taken most of the energy out of me. Ralph caught on to the end of the ladder and started up. He had an apologetic look on his face as he saw me waiting. When he had gotten to the top and was just about to step out on the dock, I grabbed the ladder in both hands to brace myself, put a sandal lengthwise across his stomach, and pushed off as hard as I could.

He had a strong grip, but I caught him off balance. He let go of the ladder, waved his arms in an attempt to hold his balance but then saw he couldn't. He twisted to guide his fall and turned it into a dive. He entered the water cleanly just behind his little boat. I leaned over and waited until he came up. Then I gave a look at Helga.

She shook her head. "I didn't do anything," she said fearfully.

Ralph caught on to the stern of the *Guacamole*, and clung there. He looked up at me, hopping mad.

"I had a real swell time," I said. "Both of you will have to come up to the Ship sometime, and let me show *you* around."

Then I walked away, leaving a dripping trail. I pushed my wet hair back off my forehead, squeezed a little water out of my sleeves, and shook myself as dry as I could. Then I left the quay. I didn't look back at all. Let them solve their own problems.

I set off up the street that we'd come down. Some of the people on the street looked oddly at me as I passed. I suppose I was a strange sight, an odd little girl, dressed in funny clothes and wringing wet. I wasn't sure where I was and where I'd find the scoutship, but I wasn't worried about it. Somehow, during the course of the hours I'd been here, Grainau had lost its power to scare me.

As it turned out, it didn't matter that I didn't know my way around. Before I'd even gotten to the top of the hill I ran into the monster, the dinosaur, George Fuhonin. He'd been out looking for me, and surprisingly, I was almost glad to see him.

He said, "What happened to you?"

I wasn't dripping by that time, but I was still wet, looking, I'm quite sure, like a half-drowned kitten fished out of the water. Thoroughly bedraggled.

I said, "We went swimming."

"Oh. Well, come back to the ship and we'll get you dried out."

I fell into step beside him, as best I could. We walked on silently for a few minutes, and then he said, "You know, I really didn't intend to embarrass you. I wouldn't have done that intentionally."

"It doesn't matter," I said. "Just make sure the switch is off next time, please."

"All right," he said.

When we got back to the ship, I went into the toilet and turned on the hot air blower in the refresher. In a few minutes I was dry.

Then I discovered that in spite of my various stomach upsets, I was hungry. I ate heartily and felt much better. There's nothing like the feeling of being comfortably full.

It was near nightfall outside when Daddy came back, though it was still in the middle of the afternoon by Ship time. When it started to grow dark outside, the people who'd been coming to stare all day had gone, I suppose home to dinner. When Daddy came back, there was no band playing this time.

I heard the horses and I went outside. One of the crew went by me and down the ramp. Mr. Tubman and Daddy handed their horses over to him and then turned their attention back to Mr. Gennaro, who was standing by his own horse. They didn't see me standing near the top of the ramp.

In a very anxious voice, Mr. Gennaro said, "Now are you sure that this unfortunate business isn't going to make any difference to our agreement?"

"I'm quite sure," Daddy said, smiling. "You made your apology and I'm quite sure my daughter got whatever satisfaction she needed from pushing your boy into the water. Now let's drop the whole matter. Our ship will be down for the ore you have ready next week . . ."

I didn't wait to hear him finish. I just turned and went inside with a little glow warming me. He wasn't mad at me.

"What are you smirking about?" George asked.

"Oh, nothing," I said.

7

We took off shortly after Daddy came aboard. He and I and Mr. Tubman were sitting in the center of the downstairs lounge in easy chairs. The three crewmen were playing cards, and George Fuhonin was upstairs piloting.

I felt quietly pleased with myself. Viewed from one angle, my time on Grainau had been nothing but one long mistake. I wasn't bothering to view it that way, even though I did realize dimly that I had made a few errors in tact and simple good sense. It wasn't important to me, and even now I would say that it was comparatively unimportant in real terms.

I think I was deservedly elated. I was filled to the brim with the discovery that I could meet Mudeaters on their own grounds, and if not come off best, at least draw.

Like the girl who first found out how to make fire, like the girl who invented the principle of the lever, like the girl who first had the courage to eat moldy goat cheese and found Roquefort, I had discovered something absolutely new in the world. Self-confidence, perhaps.

My errors had been made. My self-confidence was still in the process of becoming. If Daddy had pointed out the errors, they would not have been mended, and the self-confidence might have been stillborn. But Daddy just smoked and smiled.

I was curious enough about the things that Ralph Gennaro had said that I repeated the comments to Daddy and asked about them.

"Don't worry about it," Daddy said.

"There's not much sense in even listening to a Mudeater," Mr. Tubman said. "They have no perspective. They live in such limited little worlds that they can't see what's going on."

"I wish you wouldn't use that word, Henry," Daddy

said. "It's just as thoughtless as that silly word that Mia picked up. What did that boy say?"

" 'Grabbie?' "

"Mm, yes. That one. There's no reason to trade insults. We have our way of life and they have theirs. I wouldn't live as they do, but disrespect seems pointless. I'm sure there are good people among them."

"It's their lack of perspective," Mr. Tubman said. "I'll bet Gennaro is complaining right now that you cheated him."

"He might be," Daddy said.

"You didn't cheat him, did you, Daddy? He seemed happy that you were willing to make a deal."

"When did you hear this?"

"When you rode up."

"Lack of perspective," Mr. Tubman said. "He doesn't bargain well and he was afraid that your dad had been offended by your adventure. He gave in more easily than he had to. He was happy at the time, but he's probably regretting it now."

Daddy nodded and filled his pipe again. "I don't see any reason to mind his interests for him. As far as I'm concerned, the less we do for the colonists, the sooner they'll learn to watch out for themselves. And all the better for them when they do. That's where Mr. Mbele and I disagree. He believes in exceptions to rules, in treating the colonists better than we treat ourselves. I'm not ready to accept that."

Mr. Tubman said, "I'll have to admit that I've learned things about bargaining from watching you, Miles."

"I hope so. You will be a poor trader if you underestimate the people you deal with. And you, Mia, will be making a mistake if you underestimate a man like Mr. Mbele. His principles are excellent—sometimes, however, he only sees one route to a goal."

After a few minutes, Mr. Tubman went over to make a fourth in the card game. I decided to go upstairs.

Daddy looked up as I left. He took the pipe from his mouth. It had gone out without his noticing. "Going to hear another story?" he asked.

"I don't know," I said. "Maybe." And I went up and spent the rest of the trip with George.

So, I went home to Geo Quad. In my own time, I thought about things and discovered at least some of my errors, and the discovery did not hurt me, as it might have.

Sometimes there is art of a subtle sort in not touching, in simply sitting and smoking and talking of other people. When I got back to the Ship, I was still feeling good. And it lasted until I went to sleep.

I sat in a large comfortable chair—uncomfortably—and waited for Jimmy Dentremont. I wasn't twitching; I merely had a definite feeling of unease. This was the living room of the Geo Quad dorm, and very similar to the one that I had once lived in. The similarity didn't bother me much, but I was a stranger here and a little hesitant because of it. If it hasn't become clear previously, perhaps I should say that I always prefer to feel in command of a situation.

The room was nicely-enough appointed, but very impersonal. Individuality in a room comes from personal touches, personal care, personal interest, and the more public a room is, the less individual it is bound to be. My own room at home was more personal and individual than our living room, our living room better than the sleeping quarters of this dorm—though I hadn't seen them, I remembered well enough what dorm sleeping quarters were like—and the quarters better than this room I was sitting in. To be a stranger in an impersonal room in which there are other people who are not strangers to one another or to the place is to have the feeling of strangeness compounded.

The dorm had a living room, where I was sitting, a kitchen and study rooms out of sight, and living quarters upstairs. When I came in I looked around, and then stopped one of the small kids who obviously belonged here, a little girl of about eight.

"Is Jimmy Dentremont around?"

"Upstairs, I imagine," she said.

Near the door there was a buzzer board for the use of people like me who didn't live here. I looked Jimmy's name up, then rang two longs and a short. Since it was not far out of his way, Jimmy usually stopped by for me on the way to Mr. Mbele's, rather than me coming after him, but I had something to talk with him about today.

He came on the screen by the buzzer and said, "Oh, hello Mia."

I said, "Hi."

"What are you doing here?"

"I came to talk to you about something. Get dressed and come on down."

"All right," he said. "I'll be down as soon as I get some clothes on." He rang off and his image faded.

So I picked a seat and waited for him. He hadn't been living in the dorm long, only a year or so. His birth had been a result of a suggestion by the Ship's Eugenist—his parents had barely known one another—but his mother had wanted him and raised him. When he was eleven, however, she had decided to get married, and on Jimmy's own suggestion he had moved into a dorm.

"I didn't want to be underfoot," he'd said to me. "I do go over there evenings sometimes. And I see my father, too, from time to time."

Perhaps it was because he could move back with his mother if he wanted that he didn't find living in the dorm painful. He seemed to view it as just a temporary situation to be lived with until he came back from Trial and could have an apartment of his own. In any case, I hadn't gone into the subject of dorm living too deeply with him, not because I hesitated to probe his tender spots but because I would have been probing my own. This is called tact, and is reputed to be a virtue.

There were kids playing a board game of some sort and I sat in my chair. I watched the game and I watched the people watching the game, and I watched people passing, but nobody watched me at all. Jimmy came down in a few minutes and I got out of my chair, quite ready to be gone.

By way of greeting, I said, "What I really want to know is whether you want to go over with me on Friday."

"Where?"

"What do you mean, 'where'?"

"Mia, you know I'd go anywhere you asked. Simply name a place and lead the way."

"You're lucky I'm not bigger than you are. If I were bigger, I'd hit you. You don't have to be smart."

"Well, where is it that you're going?"

"Don't you know what I'm talking about?"

He shook his head. "No."

I got out the note that had come for me yesterday and unfolded it. It said that I was to have a physical examination Wednesday, and on Friday I was to assemble with the others in my survival class at Gate 5, Third Level for our first meeting. I handed the note to Jimmy and he read it.

This first meeting of my survival class would be on Friday, June 3, 2198. My physical would be one year and six months to the day before we would be dropped on one colony planet or another to actually undergo Trial. There is no rule that says a child has to attend a survival class, but in actual practice everybody takes advantage of the training that is offered. Clear choices as to the best course to take in life are very rare, and this was one of those few. They don't drop us simply to die. They train us for a year and a half, and then they drop us and find out how much good the training has done us.

New classes are started every three or four months, and the last one had been in March, so this note was not unexpected. Since Jimmy had been born in November, too, as he had been so quick to point out when we first met, he was bound to be in the same class with me. Frankly, I wanted company on Friday.

"I didn't know about this," Jimmy said. "I should have a note, too. When did this come?"

"Yesterday. I thought you'd call me this morning about it but you didn't."

"I'd better check this out. Hold on here." He went off to find the dorm mother and came back in a few minutes with a note similar to mine. "It was here. I just never looked for it and she never thought to mention it."

There was one thing that irritated me about Jimmy, but that in a way I admired. Or, perhaps, something I marveled at. On at least two occasions, I had called Jimmy and left a message, once to call me back, once to say I wasn't going to be able to make our meeting with Mr. Mbele. Neither time did he get the message, because neither time did he stop to look for one. That irritates me. I also feel envious of anyone who can be so unanxious about who might have called. Jimmy simply says that he's so busy that he never stops to worry about things like that.

Jimmy liked the idea of going to the first meeting on Friday together. To this time, at least, we were not close friends—there was an element of antagonism—but we did know each other and we had Mr. Mbele in common. It seemed to make sense to both of us to face the new situation together.

As we were on our way to Mr. Mbele's, I said, "Do you remember when I got back from Grainau and I was talking about that boy and his sister to you and Mr. Mbele?"

"The one with the weird ideas of what we're like?"

"Yes. One of the things they said was that we went around naked all the time. I was objecting to all the things they were saying. I wonder what I would have said if they'd been here to see you on the vid without even your socks on."

"I suppose they would have thought they were right all along," Jimmy said reasonably.

"Yes. But they weren't."

"I don't know. I was naked, wasn't I?"

"Sure, but that was in your own room. I go naked at home, too. They thought we never wear clothes."

"Well," Jimmy said brightly, "there's no real reason we ought to, is there?" He started to pull his shirt off over his head. "We could be just what they think we are, and we wouldn't be worse because of it, would we?"

"Don't be perverse," I said.

"What's perverse about going naked?"

"I'm talking about your contrariness. Are you going to eat dirt just because they think we do? I shouldn't have brought the subject up in the first place. It just struck me as something incongruous."

"In*con*gruous," Jimmy corrected, putting the accent on the second syllable where it belonged.

"Well, however you pronounce it," I said. This comes of reading words and not having heard them pronounced. This also was a matter of talking about the wrong things to the wrong people. It seemed that I might do better just to leave Grainau out of my conversations completely. Just after I'd gotten back home, I'd made the mistake of saying what I really thought about the Mudeaters in front of Jimmy and Mr. Mbele.

"Do they really stink?" Mr. Mbele asked.

Jimmy and I were seated on the couch in Mr. Mbele's apartment. I had my notebook with notes on my reading, subjects I wanted to bring up, and some book titles that Mr. Mbele had suggested. I realized that I'd just said something I couldn't really defend, so I backtracked.

"I don't know if they do. Everybody *says* they do. What I meant is that I didn't like what I saw of them."

"Why not?" Jimmy asked.

"Is that a serious question, or are you just prodding?"

"I'm interested, too, Mia," Mr. Mbele said. In his case, I could tell that it was a seriously intended question, not just digging. Mr. Mbele never did any ganging up with either one of us against the other.

"I'm not sure," I said. "We didn't get along. Do I have to have a better reason than that?"

"Of course," Jimmy said.

"Well, if you think so," I said, "give me one good reason you have for being so antagonistic."

Jimmy half shrugged, looking uncomfortable.

"You don't have one," I said. "I just said something you didn't take to. Well, I didn't take to the Mudeaters. I can doggone well say they stink if I want to."

"I guess so," Jimmy said.

"Hmm," Mr. Mbele said. "What if it doesn't happen to be true? What if what you say damages the other person, or if you are just building yourself up by tearing another person down?"

"I don't know," I said.

"Would you agree that it isn't a good policy?"

"I suppose."

"Well, it's my personal opinion that saying the Colons stink is simply a self-justifying myth invented to make us feel morally superior and absolutely in the right. Your statement is likely to keep me from listening to any valid arguments that you might actually have. That certainly wouldn't do you any good."

Jimmy had been following the argument. He said, "How about this? It's all right to dislike people for poor reasons, but not to call them names. You don't have to justify your dislikes, but you have to justify your contentions."

"That's a little oversimplified," Mr. Mbele said.

For the moment I was off the hook, and since I was struck by a thought, I brought it forward. "What about the people whom you ought to like—only you don't? And the people you ought not to like that you do?"

"And what does all that mean?" Jimmy asked.

"Well, say you and I agree on everything, and I respect you, and you never do me any harm—like backbiting all the time for no good reason—and yet I can't stand you. Or say there were somebody I ought to dislike—a total rat, somebody who'll do anything if he sees advantage in it—and I like him. Can you separate liking from what a person does?"

Mr. Mbele smiled, as though the course of the conversation amused him. "Well, *do* you separate them?"

"I suppose I do," I said.

"Jimmy?"

Jimmy didn't say anything for a minute while he decided whether he did or whether he didn't. I already knew the answer, having just worked it out myself. Everybody does, or there wouldn't be charming socially-accepted bastards in the world.

Jimmy said, "I suppose I do, too."

I said, "What I think I mean was *should* you separate them?"

"Isn't it more to the point to ask whether it makes any difference if you do or not?"

"You mean, if you can't help it anyway?"

"No," Mr. Mbele said. "I meant do your emotions make a difference in your judgment of people that you like or dislike?"

Jimmy said, "Alicia MacReady? Everybody likes her, they say. Will that make any difference in what the Assembly decides?"

Alicia MacReady was the woman who was carrying an illegal baby. The question of what to do in the case had come up before the Council, but it hadn't stayed there. She had apparently thought that she would get more lenient treatment if the Ship's Assembly were to make the judgment, so before the Council could decide, she had opted to take the matter out of their hands. The Council had agreed, as in difficult or important cases they were likely to.

The Ship's Assembly was a meeting of all the adults in the Ship, coming together in the amphitheater on Second Level, and voting. Since she was a popular person—I'd heard this only; until this had come up I had never heard of her or met her—the MacReady woman wanted to face the Assembly, hoping her friendships would count for more than they would in Council.

"That's a good example," Mr. Mbele said. "I don't know if it will make a difference. I would suggest that since you can't attend, you watch what goes on on your video. Then perhaps we can discuss the decision next time. This is just part of a larger problem, however: what constitutes proper conduct? That is, ethics. This is something an ordinologist"—a nod to Jimmy—"or a synthesist"—a nod toward me—"should be thoroughly familiar with. I'll give you titles to start with. Take your time with them, and when you're ready to talk, let me know."

So he started us reading in ethics. He went to his book shelves and called off titles and authors for us to copy: Epicureans and Utilitarians; Stoics; Power Philosophers, both sophisticated and unsophisticated; and Humanists of several stripes. All these not to mention various religious ethical systems. If I'd known all this was to come out of my one simple, honestly prejudiced remark, I would never have opened my mouth. Maybe there is a lesson in that, but if there is, I've never learned it; I still have an unbecoming tendency to open my mouth and get myself in trouble.

I saw Dr. Jerome on Wednesday, June 1. I'd seen him once or twice a year ever since I could remember. He was of middle height, inclined to be portly, and like most doctors wore a beard. His was black. I'd asked him about it when I was much younger and he'd said, "It's either to give our patients confidence or to give ourselves confidence. I'm not sure which."

As he examined me, he talked as he always did, a constant flow of commentary directed half at me and half at himself, all given in an even, low-pitched voice. Its effect, and perhaps its intention, was to give reassurance in the same way that a horseman soothes a skittish colt with his voice. It was part of Dr. Jerome's professional manner.

"Good enough, good enough. Sound. Good shape. Breathe in. Now, out. Good. Hmm-hum. Yes. Good enough."

There's always the question of how much you can believe of what a doctor says—he has one of those ethical problems in how much he can tell you—but I had no reason not to believe Dr. Jerome when he told me I was in perfectly sound shape. I was due for no treatment of any kind before starting Survival Class. I was in first-class condition.

"It's always good to see you, Mia," he said. "I wish

everybody were in as good health. I might have a little more spare time."

He said one other thing. When he took my height and weight, he said, "You've gained three inches since the last time you were here. That's very good."

Three inches. I wasn't sure whether it was Daddy's doing or nature, but I wasn't displeased to hear it.

8

Jimmy and I got off the shuttle at Entry Gate 5 on the Third Level. This was supposedly where our group was to meet at two o'clock. We were about ten minutes early. The shuttle door slid open and we left the car. When we were clear, the car flicked away, responding to a call from another level, much like an elevator. On the cross-level line, a few feet away, there were several cars just sitting and waiting to be called.

The door leading out of the shuttle room was double, with both sides standing open. Above it a sign read: ENTRY GATE 5, THIRD LEVEL: PARK. Through the open door I could see light, grass, dirt and a number of kids about my age, all beyond the gate.

"There they are," Jimmy said.

The Third Level is divided into three distinct and separate types of areas. First there are the areas under cultivation, producing food, oxygen, and fodder for the cattle we raise. Beef is our only on-the-hoof meat, our other meats coming from cultures raised in vats, also here on the Third Level. The second type of area is park. Here there are trees, a lake, flowers, grassland, picnic areas, room to walk, room to ride. This is what you might wish the planets were like. The last type of area is the wilds, which is much like the parks but more dangerous. As the maps might have it, here there are wilde beastes. The terrain is more sudden and the vegetation is left to find its own way. It's designed for hunting, for chance-taking, and for training not-quite-adults. I'd never been in the wilds up to this time, only in the ag and park areas.

"Come on, then," I said.

We went through the doors, then through what amounted to a short tunnel, perhaps ten feet long. The transparent gate dilated and we went through. Outside there were trees and stables, a corral among the trees, and a building that had a wall from about two feet off the ground to about seven feet, and about three feet higher an open-gabled roof. This held lockers and showers.

It was only here on the Third Level that you could appreciate the size of the Ship. Everywhere else there were walls at every hand, but here your view was all but unimpeded. It was fully miles to the nearest point where roof above and ground below met ship-side. The roof was three hundred feet up and it took a sharp eye to pick out sprinklers and such as individual features.

Behind us, the shuttle tube rose out of the station and disappeared blackly into the roof far above. The cross-level shuttle tube went underground from the station so that was not visible.

It was still before two, so the kids who were there already were standing under the trees by the corral and watching the horses. I recognized Venie Morlock among them. I wasn't surprised to see her there since she was only one month older than I and I had expected that we would wind up in the same Trial group.

Others were arriving behind us and coming out of the shuttle station. Jimmy and I moved over to join the others watching the horses. I suppose I might have learned to ride when I was smaller just as I had learned to swim, but for no good reason in particular I hadn't. I wasn't afraid of horses but I was wary of them. There was another girl who wasn't. She was reaching through the fence and teasing one, a red roan mare.

A tall, large-built boy near us looked at her and said, "I can't stand children and that Debbie is such a child."

A moment later there was a metallic toot as somebody blew a whistle. I looked at my watch and saw that it was two exactly. There were two men standing on the single step up to the locker building. One had a whistle. He was young, perhaps forty-five, and smooth-skinned. He was also impatient.

"Come on," he said, and beckoned irritatedly. "Come on over here."

He was about medium height and dark-haired, and he had a list in his hand. He looked like the sort of person who would spend his time with lists of one sort or another. There are people, you know, who find no satisfaction in living unless they can plan ahead and then tick off items as they come.

We gathered around and he rattled his paper. The other man stood there rather quietly. He was also medium height, but slighter, older, considerably more wrinkled, and much less formally dressed.

"Answer when your name is called," said the younger man, and he began reading off our names. He started with Allen, Andersson, and Briney, Robert, who was the large boy who was unenthusiastic about children, and he ended with Wilson, You and Young. There are about thirty names.

"Two missing," he said to the other when he was done. "Send them a second notice."

Then he turned to us and said, "My name is Fosnight. I'm in charge of coordinating all Trial and pre-Trial programs, and that includes survival classes. There are, at present, six classes in training, counting this one, meeting in various areas of the Third Level. This class is scheduled to meet regularly from now on, here at Gate 5, on Monday, Wednesday and Friday afternoons at 12:30. Third Class is here on Tuesday, Thursday and Saturday. If the meeting times conflict with school, tutorial sessions, or anything else, you'll have to find a way out. Reschedule, perhaps—the other, of course, not this—or skip one or the other. That is strictly up to you to settle. It is strictly up to you whether or not you decide to attend, but I can guarantee that almost anyone will find his chances of coming back from Trial alive infinitely improved if he attends Survival Class regularly. Your group is somewhat smaller than the usual one, so you should do very well. You are also lucky to have Mr. Marechal here as your instructor—he's one of our six best chief instructors." He smiled at his little joke.

Mr. Fosnight's manner was brisk and businesslike, as though he were checking his mental items off. Now he turned to Marechal and handed him the whistle. "Whistle," he said. He handed him the list. "List." Then he turned back to us standing in a bunch in front. "Any questions?"

He'd struck us so hard and fast that we just looked blankly up at him. Nobody said anything.

"Good," he said. "Goodbye." And he walked off as though the last item on his list were settled quite satisfactorily, and another tedious but necessary little task were out of the way.

Mr. Marechal looked at the whistle in his hand, and then

after Fosnight as he walked to the shuttle station. He didn't look as though he liked whistles. Then he stuck the whistle in his pocket. He folded the list and put that away, too. When he was finished he looked up and looked us over slowly, perhaps taking our measure. We looked back up at him, taking a good look at the man who was going to have us in charge for a year and a half. It wasn't a case of taking his measure, since the child's scale of an adult-child relationship is pretty ordinarily to assume that the adult knows what he is about. If he doesn't and the child finds out, then things go to pot, but to start with he generally has the benefit of the doubt. I will admit that Mr. Marechal was not an overwhelming figure at first sight.

He said, "Well, Mr. Fosnight forgot something he usually says, so I'll say it for him if I can remember more or less how it goes. There's an anthropological name for Trial. They call it a rite of passage. It's a formal way of passing from one stage of your life to another. All societies have them. The important thing to remember is that it makes being an adult a meaningful sort of thing, because adulthood has been earned when you come back from Trial. That makes Trial worth concentrating on."

He stopped then and looked off to his right. Everybody looked that way. Mr. Fosnight was coming back toward us. Mr. Marechal looked at him and said questioningly, "Rites of passage?"

"Yes."

"Never mind. I just finished going over it for you."

"Oh," Mr. Fosnight said. "Thanks, then." He turned around and went back toward the shuttle station.

He was so dogged about the whole thing that the moment he was out of sight, everybody started laughing. Mr. Marechal let it go on for a moment and then he said, "That's enough. I just want to say a couple of things for myself now. Me and the people who'll be coming in to show you things are going to be doing our best to get you through Trial. If you pay attention, you shouldn't have any trouble. Okay? Now the first thing I'm going to do is assign you horses and show you the first thing about riding."

Mr. Marechal was a slow-speaking sort of person, and didn't have a complete command of grammar, but he did have the sort of personal authority that makes people listen. Without consulting the list in his pocket, he called off people's names and names of horses. I got stuck with something called Nincompoop. That got a laugh. Jimmy's horse was Pet—the final t is written but not pronounced since it comes from the French. Venitia Morlock got a horse named Slats. When Rachel Yung was assigned her horse, we moved over to the corral, where Mr. Marechal perched up on the top rail.

"These horses are yours from here on out," he said. "Don't get sentimental about them. They're just a way to get from one place to another the same as a heli-pac, and you'll be getting practice with both. But you'll have to take care of both, too, and that means especially the horse you have. A horse is an animal and that means he'll break down easier than a machine if he isn't taken care of. You damned well better take care of them."

One of the kids raised his hand. "Yes, Herskovitz?"

Herskovitz was a little surprised to be tagged quite that easily. "If horses are that lousy, why do we have to go to the trouble of learning how to ride them? That's what I want to know."

Even more slowly than usual, Mr. Marechal said, "Well, I could give you reasons, I suppose, but what it all boils down to is that you have to pass a test. The test goes by certain rules and one of those rules is that you have to be able to ride a horse. But don't let it bother you too much, son. You may find that you like horses after a while."

He swung over the fence and landed inside. "Now I'm going to show you the first thing about riding. The first thing about riding is getting a saddle on your animal."

One of the boys said, "Excuse me, but I already know how to ride. Do I have to stick around for this?"

Mr. Marechal said, "No, you don't, Farmer. You can skip anything you want to. Only one thing, though. Before you walk out on anything you'd best be mighty sure you know every blessed thing I'm going to show, 'cause if it's something you walked out on I'll be damned if I'll do it again for you. If you can't help missing I might be generous—if I'm in the right mood. If you fall behind of your own doing, you'll have to catch up on your own, too."

Farmer said that in that case he thought he'd stick around today just to see how things went.

Mr. Marechal caught up one of the three horses in the corral, the red roan mare, and put a bridle on her, showing us what he was doing as he did it. Then he put on the blanket and the double-cinch saddle. He took them off, and then he showed us again from the beginning. When he was done, he said, "All right. Now you people will have to try it. Go collect your tack and lead out your horses."

There was a scramble then to find and get acquainted with your horse, locate your gear, and get both into a position where the second might be strapped onto the first. Nincompoop turned out to be brown—what they call a chestnut—and not terribly large. He was more of a pony than a horse, a pony being less than 56 inches high at the shoulder. It seems to be an arbitrary cutoff point. His size pleased me, since a larger animal would probably have intimidated me more than this one did. As it was, I hardly had time to be intimidated, just time to get in line with everybody else, our animals more or less in a row with gear on the left side. Mr. Marechal stood out in front and told us what to do.

The first time went badly. I got everything where I thought it should go, but when I stood back, the saddle didn't stay in place. It seemed to be in place for a moment and I looked up feeling pleased, but when I looked back, it was tipped. It seemed to be on tightly, but it was tipped.

I figured I'd better try again. I undid the cinch, the strap that goes under the belly of the horse to tie the saddle on, straightened the saddle, and restrapped it.

Mr. Marechal was walking down the line inspecting and offering advice. He got to me as I was hauling the cinch tight.

"Let me show you something," he said. He walked up to Nincompoop, lifted his knee and rammed him a hard one in the belly. The horse gave a *whoof* of expelled air, and he yanked the cinch tight. The horse looked at him reproachfully as he notched it.

"This one will swell up on you every time if you let him," he said. "You've got to let him know you're sharper than he is."

We spent about an hour with saddling and unsaddling before we quit for the day. On the way home, I asked Jimmy what he thought. We were sharing our shuttle car with half-a-dozen others from our group.

"I like Marechal," he said, "I think he's going to be okay."

One of the girls said, "He doesn't seem to stand still for any nonsense. I like that. It means we won't waste any of our time."

The Farmer boy was in our car. He was the one who already knew how to ride. "My time was wasted," he said. "He didn't go over anything I didn't know already today. That's what I call nonsense."

"It may be nonsense for you," Jimmy said, "but most of the rest of us learned something. If you know everything already, don't come. Just like he said."

The boy shrugged. "Maybe I won't."

On the cross-level shuttle to Geo Quad, I said to Jimmy, "I was a little disappointed, myself."

"With Marechal?"

"No. With the whole afternoon. I expected something more."

"Well, what exactly?"

I shot him a look. "You always like to pin me down, don't you?"

He shrugged. "I just like to know what you mean, or if you mean anything."

"Well, Mr. Smarty, what I meant is that it all seemed so businesslike and ordinary. There's got to be a better word . . . undramatic."

"Well, they say Sixth Class is likely to be pretty dull. In three months or so when we've got some of the basic stuff down, it should be more exciting."

We rode silently for a minute while I thought it over. Then I said, "I don't think so. I'll bet things stay the same whether we're Sixth Class, Fourth Class or whatever. It'll be all the same, businesslike."

"What's the matter with you?" Jimmy asked.

"Nothing. I just don't believe in adventure anymore."

"When did you decide that?"

"Just now."

"Because today wasn't exciting. No—'dramatic.' Wasn't going down to Grainau an adventure? How about that?"

"You think being pushed into a big pool of foul-tasting water is an adventure?" I asked scornfully. "Have you ever had an adventure?"

"I guess not. That doesn't mean they don't exist."

"Doesn't it?"

Jimmy shook his head. "I don't know what's the matter with you. You must be in a bad mood. You were talking about bets—I bet if I try I can work up a legitimate, real adventure."

"How?" I challenged.

He shook his red head doggedly. "All right. I don't know how. All I'm betting is that I can find one."

"Okay," I said. "It's a bet."

There is a certain amount of organization to a Ship's Assembly, as with most mass gatherings—it takes somebody to be there to see that everything is in order, that there are chairs, tables, microphones and all that. Mostly this can be just anybody who gets saddled with the job, but the final decisions devolve on the man who chairs the Assembly, meaning Daddy. I think, too, that he was interested that things go smoothly in this first Assembly after he became Ship's Chairman.

The night the Assembly was to meet to consider the case of Alicia MacReady, Daddy finished dinner early and left for the Second Level. Zena Andrus came over to eat with me that night. I had found that in the right circumstances I could like her. She had a tendency to whine at times, but that's not the worst fault in the world. And she did have courage.

As we were finishing dinner, but before dessert, there was a signal at the door. It was Mr. Tubman.

"You said to be here at six-thirty," he said apologetically, seeing that we were not finished as yet.

"That's quite all right, Henry," Daddy said. "I think I'm about finished. You know where the dessert is, Mia. Clean things up and dispose of the dishes when you're finished."

"You don't have to tell me that," I said.

"I know," he said. "It just isn't so long since I did have to and I still have the habit."

Dessert was a parfait. While we were eating it after Daddy had left, Zena said, "What is this Assembly thing about, anyway? Mum and Daddy are going but they didn't talk about it."

I said, "Everybody's been talking about it. I would have thought you'd know."

"Well, I don't," she said. "I don't pay much attention to things like Assemblies and I bet you never did either before your dad became Ship's Chairman."

Well, I hadn't, but I hadn't been completely unaware of them, either. So I explained what I knew of things to her.

"It doesn't seem like very much," Zena said. "They could always get rid of the baby. She couldn't have gotten away with having it, anyway. It seems like a whole big fuss over not very much at all."

"It's the principle of the thing," I said.

Zena shrugged, and went back to her parfait. It was her second. Things always seemed to be much simpler for her than they were for me.

"Must you make that noise?" asked Zena, after we had adjourned from the table. She was sitting on the floor of my bedroom systematically taking one of my dolls apart. As it happened, this one was meant to be taken apart, carefully of course since it was old and worn. The doll was originally Russian and had been in the family since before we'd left Earth. It was wooden and came apart. Inside was a smaller doll which came apart. Altogether there were a total of twelve dolls nested one inside the next. It's the sort of thing you can spend a lot of time with.

I was sitting cross-legged on my bed and playing on the pennywhistle I had discovered a couple of months before. I was playing a very simple little tune, mainly because I couldn't finger fast enough for anything more complicated. Still, it didn't sound half bad to me.

I said, " 'The man that hath no music in himself, nor is not moved with concord of sweet sounds, is fit for . . .' " I shut my eyes trying to remember. " '. . . for treasons, stratagems and something-or-other.' "

"What is that supposed to mean?"

"It's a quotation. From Shakespeare."

"If you're talking about me," Zena said, "I like music well enough."

I held up the pennywhistle. "Well, this is music."

"You ought to practice it in private until you can play it better."

I bounced up, put the pennywhistle away, then hopped over Zena on the floor to get to the vid. "It's time for the Assembly anyway." I turned on the general channel of the vid.

Zena gave a sour look. "Do we have to watch that old thing?"

"Jimmy and I are supposed to," I said.

"Is that Jimmy Dentremont?"

"Yes."

"You spend a lot of time with him, don't you?"

"We've got the same tutor and we're in the same Survival Class," I said.

"Oh," Zena said. She began stacking the dolls together. "Do you like him? He always seemed too full of himself to me."

"I don't know," I said. "He is bright. I guess I can take him or leave him alone."

I flopped on the floor and leaned my back against the bed. The vid showed the Assembly about ready to be called to order.

"If the Assembly doesn't turn out to be interesting we can always turn it off," I said.

We watched the Assembly for the next two hours. It seemed that just about everybody had a firm grasp of the basic questions beforehand. It remained for spokesmen for both sides to state their cases, for questions to be put from the floor, for witnesses to be called, more questions to be put, and a final vote. Daddy, as Chairman, didn't involve himself in the argument.

Mr. Tubman put the case for the Ship. Another member of the Council, Mr. Persson, made the plea for the other side. Witnesses included the Ship's Eugenist, a lawyer giving the point of law at stake, Alicia MacReady speaking in her own behalf, and a number of character witnesses who spoke for her.

The Council and witnesses sat at a table at the base of the amphitheatre. Every adult presently aboard Ship had an assigned seat in the circle above and could speak if he so desired. Potentially the Assembly could have dragged on for hours, but it didn't. This was Daddy's job. He conducted the Assembly, putting witnesses through their paces briskly, cutting the garrulous off, giving both sides an equal share of time. As Ship's Chairman, it was his job to be fair and impartial, and as nearly as I could see he was, though I did know in this case what his real opinions were. Mr. Tubman was speaking for him.

In truth, the MacReady side had no case. All they could do was make a plea for leniency. Alicia MacReady cried when it was her turn to speak, until Daddy made her stop.

Mr. Persson said, "Once we all agree that it was a stupid thing to do, what more is there to say? Alicia MacReady is a citizen of this Ship. She survived Trial. She has as much right to live here as anyone else. Granted that she did a foolish thing, it's a very simple thing to abort the child. You all watched her crawl for you. There isn't any question of this sort of thing happening again. It was a mistake made in a wild moment and heartily repented of. Can't we say that this public humiliation is punishment enough and drop the whole matter?"

When Mr. Tubman had his chance to speak, he said, more crisply than I was used to hearing him speak, "If nothing else, there are a few corrections I would like to make. If what Mr. Persson chooses to call 'this public humiliation' is a punishment, it is a self-inflicted one—discount it. Miss MacReady's case could have been settled before the Council. Bringing it before an Assembly was her own choice. Secondly, her so-called repentance. Repentance when you are found out is much too easy—discount it. 'A mistake made in a wild moment'? Hardly. It took more than a month of deliberate dodging of her APPs for Miss MacReady to become pregnant. That is hardly a single wild moment—discount it. Corrections aside, there is something else. There is a matter of basic principle. We are a tiny precarious island floating in a hostile sea. We have worked out ways of living that observed exactly allow us to survive and go on living. If they are not observed exactly, we cannot survive. Alicia MacReady made a choice. She chose to have a fifth child that the Ship's Eugenist had not given her permission to have. It was a choice between the Ship and the baby. The choice made, there are certain inevitable consequences of which Alicia MacReady was aware when she made her choice. Would we be fair either to her or ourselves if we didn't face and help her to face the consequences? We are not barbarians. We don't propose to kill either Miss MacReady or her unborn child. What we do propose is to give her what she has elected, her baby and not the Ship. I say we should drop her on the nearest Colony planet. And good luck to her."

Which was a nice way of pronouncing a probable death sentence. But then Mr. Tubman wasn't wrong—she had asked for it.

Soon after they held the vote. 7,923 people voted to let her stay. 18,401 voted to expel her.

Alicia MacReady fainted, the reaction of an hysteric. Mr. Persson and some of her friends gathered around.

The other people began to file out of the great room, the business of the evening behind them.

I got up and switched off the vid. "How would you have voted?" I asked.

"I don't know that much about things like this," Zena said looking up. She'd only been half paying attention. "They don't give her anything, a horse or weapons or a heli-pac or anything, when they put her off on a Colony planet?"

"I don't think so."

"Well, isn't that pretty harsh?"

"It's like Mr. Tubman said, we've got rules that have to be followed. If people don't follow the rules they can't stay here. They were doing her a favor by even letting the Assembly vote on the question."

Zena looked sour and said, "What will your father do if he comes home and finds that you haven't thrown out the dinner things?"

"Oh, heavens," I said. "I'd forgotten about that."

I'm likely to put off little bits of drudgery, even when they wouldn't take long to settle. I had managed to put the dinner remains completely out of mind.

As I was collecting the dishes and throwing them in the incinerator, Zena, standing by, said, "Why are you so strong on rules?"

"What do you mean?"

"Well, you're so set on the rules that you won't allow any mistakes at all. And that MacReady woman is going to die now."

I stopped stacking dishes. I looked at her. "I didn't even vote. I had nothing to do with what was decided."

"That isn't the point," she said, but she didn't say what the point was.

Daddy came home about ten minutes later. I asked him if things had gone as he had expected them to, and he said yes.

"I cleared up the dishes," I said.

Daddy said, "I never doubted you would for a minute."

At our next meeting I asked Mr. Mbele if he'd expected the decision to go the way it had.

"I wasn't surprised," he said. "Your father's point of view is widely shared in the Ship. That is why he's Chairman."

9

It may sound like an anachronism to speak of seasons on a Ship, but we always did: that is, July, August and September were "summer," as an example. This never struck me as odd until I was fifteen or sixteen when I was going into the factors responsible for planetary weather, and one day I really *thought* about the meaning of the terms we used so casually. It was obvious that through time they had lost their weatherly connotations and now simply referred to quarters of the year—well, for that matter, the fact that we use the Old Earth Year at all is an anachronism, but we do it anyway.

At the time I was doing my puzzling about this, I mentioned it to a friend of mine. (Since he appears in this book several times, I won't mention his name—he has enough burdens without being made to sound stupid here.) I said, "Do you realize that our calling November 'fall' means that most of the people on the Ship probably came originally from the Northern Temperate Zone on Earth?"

He said, "Well, if you wanted to know that, all you have to do is call for the original Ship Lists from the library."

I said, "But don't you think this is interesting?"

He said, "No."

Perhaps stupid is not the word I intended. Perhaps contentious.

In any case, the summer when I was twelve passed. I think of it as a busy block with a whole number of items, and I'm not sure in what exact order any of them happened. I could invent an order, but since none of them is central, I won't. For instance, during that summer, I had my first menstrual period—that's important insofar as I took it as a sign that I was growing up, but that's about all you can say for it. Then there were dancing lessons. You might well wonder what we were doing with dancing lessons, but they were actually a part of our Survival Class training.

Mr. Marechal said, "This isn't meant to be fun and it isn't meant to be funny. It is deadly serious. You stumble over your own feet. You don't know what to do with your hands. When you are in a position where you have to do the exact right thing in an instant, deft movement is the most important element. You want your body to work for you, not against you. Not only, by God, am I going to give you dancing lessons, but I'm going to start you on needlepoint."

We not only got needlepoint, dancing lessons, hand-to-hand combat training, and weapon instruction, but Mr. Marechal was our tutor in all of them. He showed us films of people drawing hand-guns and dropping them, of people falling off horses (I did that a couple of times myself), of people in a blue funk. The films were taken on an obstacle course where, for instance, if you didn't watch out, the ground might suddenly fall out from underneath your feet. There might be a rope to grab, or you might simply have to land without breaking your ankle. At the end of the summer, when we moved up from Sixth Class to Fifth, we started going through obstacle courses ourselves. The primary aim was not to teach us any individual skill, but how to react smoothly and intelligently in difficult situations. We were shown how to do individual things, but that wasn't the primary aim of the instruction.

All of this adds up to the fact that I had been wrong in thinking it would be simply businesslike first to last. Survival Class was earnest, it was businesslike, but it was intelligent and interesting, too. What it was not was an adventure, but since I had my desire for an adventure settled very shortly it no longer bothered me that Survival Class was not an adventure.

Survival Class gave me a whole new set of friends, and they began taking up enough of my time that I saw less of people like Zena Andrus. I did see Mary Carpentier once more, but we found that we didn't have a great deal to say to one another and we never seemed to call each other again.

Most important, though, out of the thirty-one of us in the Survival Class, there drew together a nuclear group of six. This was hardly pure friendship since some of my best friends were not in it and Venie Morlock was. It was just . . . the group. We drew together originally through a non-adventure. At Jimmy's urging, I took a group of kids up to the Sixth Level and we spent the day exploring. The six of us who went were me and Venie and Jimmy, Helen Pak, Riggy Allen and Attila Szabody. Attila and Helen, and, I guess, Jimmy were my particular friends. Riggy was a good friend of Attila's, and Helen and Riggy both saw something in Venie. That was the way the group hung together, and the trip to the Sixth Level—I guess it was something of an adventure for some of the others and it was fun for me—provided another bond. We usually saw each other for an hour or two after each Survival Class and sometimes on weekends. There were a few others who joined us from time to time, but they were just comers-and-goers.

After Survival Class one day, five of us were sitting in the snackery of the Common Room of Lev Quad on the Fifth Level. By shuttle this wasn't really far from Entry Gate 5, and it was the most convenient central point for all of us. A few changes on the shuttle and we were all home. We didn't know anybody in Lev Quad and we couldn't have found our way around it very well, but still we had our place here, our regular corner, and after a little while we no longer felt so much like intruders.

The missing number was Jimmy. He'd been hurrying off one place and another during the past week after class, mumbling and chuckling around as though he had his little business and would be damned if he'd tell it, and in the meantime was enjoying it thoroughly.

I was doodling on a piece of paper, working out an idea I had in mind. We were sitting at the table with food and drink, but not a lot of it. We were mostly taking up table space and talking. Our regular table was this one, a red-topped affair set in a corner on the left in the under-fourteen area.

We were talking of a prospective soccer game to be played on Saturday morning in Attila's home quad, Roth Quad on the Fourth Level, if we could raise the necessary players. I was thinking that I'd certainly come a long way from the time—not that long ago—when all that it took to page me was a simple call on my home-quad speaker system. I was no longer quite the stick-at-home I'd been then.

"Will Jimmy play?" Attila asked. He was the biggest

amongst us, but a quiet boy for all that. He generally didn't say a lot, but would just sit back and then from time to time come out with some comment that was completely surprising, and all the more surprising because he wasn't the person you'd pick as likely to say anything bright or clever or knowledgeable.

"Mia can ask him," Helen said.

"All right," I said. "I'll have him call you. Unless he's too busy with this whatever-it-is of his, I think he'll want to play. He's a good halfback." I turned my attention back to my scribble.

"What is that you're doing there?" Riggy asked, and snatched it away. Riggy is somebody I have to describe as a meatball—he was hardly my favorite person in the world. He's one of those people who have no governor, who'll do the first thing that pops into their heads whether or not it makes a lick of sense—and then, if necessary, be heartily sorry afterward. He wasn't stupid, or clumsy, or incompetent—he simply had no sense of proportion at all.

"And what's that supposed to be?" he asked, pointing at the paper. Venie and Helen on his side of the table both looked at it, too.

After several tries, I had drawn what was reasonably recognizable as a fist seen palm on, holding a long, clean arrow. I'm no artist and I'd had to keep sneaking looks at my own hand to get even a moderately accurate picture. The arrow I'd managed to draw without benefit of a model.

I made a grab for it, but Riggy held it out of reach. "Uh-uh," he said, passing it on to Venie farther down the table. She looked at it with a frown, making sure at the same time that I wasn't able to grab it back.

I shrugged and said, "It's a picture with a meaning, if you must know. It's sort of a pictorial pun."

"A rebus?" Attila suggested.

"I guess it is."

"Let me see it," he said, and took it from Venie.

"I don't get it," Venie said. "An arrow held in a hand."

"A fist," Riggy said. "The hand's closed."

Tiredly I said, "It's my *name*. 'Have arrow'—Havero."

"Oh, no," Venie said. "That's pretty poor."

Helen said, "I don't think it's too bad. I think it's a pretty clever idea."

"'An ill-favoured thing, but mine own,'" I quoted tartly.

Venie gave me a disgusted look. "You are a show-off, aren't you? What was that supposed to be?"

"Mia's reading Shakespeare for her tutor," Helen said. "That's all. She's been memorizing lines."

Riggy took the doodle back and gave it another look. "You know, this is a good idea. I wonder if I could work my name out somehow."

We spent some time trying, working on all our names. It didn't come out terribly well. By stretching we got "pack," a little knapsack for Helen—but that wasn't truly homonymous. "Szabody" and "Allen" were pretty well unworkable.

"I've got one," Riggy said, after some moments of concentration during which he wouldn't show anybody what he was doing. Triumphantly he held up a sheet with a series of locks drawn on it. " 'More-lock,' " he said. "Get it?"

We got it, but we didn't like it. He had covered the whole sheet with his drawings, which is hardly what you'd call concise.

I'd been working on the same name myself. I came up with a fair-to-middling troglodyte.

"What's that?" Attila asked.

"It's Morlock again."

Venie didn't look pleased, and Riggy immediately challenged, "How do you get Morlock out of that thing?"

"It's from an old novel called *The Time Machine*. There's a group of underground monsters in it called Morlocks."

"You're making that up," Venie said.

"I'm not either," I said. "You can look the book up for yourself. I read it when I was in Alfing, so all you have to do is call for the facsimile."

Venie looked at the drawing again. Then she said, "All right, I'll look it up. I may even use it."

I almost liked her for saying that, since I hadn't been very kind in bringing the subject up. If my name had been Morlock, I might have used the troglodyte idea myself, but I hadn't really expected Venie to stomach the idea. It took more . . . not quite objectivity—but detachment from herself—than I thought she had.

Just then Attila said, "Here comes Jim."

Jimmy Dentremont came between the tables, snaked

up a free chair from the next table over and plunked it down beside me.

"Hi," he said.

"Where have you been?" Helen asked for all of us. Helen is a very striking girl. She has blond hair and oriental eyes—eyes with an epicanthic fold—and it's a wild combination.

Jimmy just shrugged and pointed at our various little doodles. "What's all this?"

We explained it to him.

"Oh," he said. "That's easy. I can get one for me with no trouble." He picked up a pencil and sketched two mountains, and then put a little stick figure man between them.

I looked blankly at him and so did the others.

"My name means 'between mountains,'" he explained.

"It does?" Riggy asked.

"In French."

"I didn't know you knew French," I said.

"I don't. I just looked my name up because I knew it was originally French."

"How about that?" Attila said. "I wonder if my name means something in Hungarian."

Jimmy cleared his throat, looked around at us, and then said to me, "Mia, do you remember our bet about my finding an adventure?"

"Yes."

"Well, I've found one. That's what I've been working on the past few days."

Helen immediately asked for an explanation of what we were talking about, and I had to wait to ask Jimmy just what it was that I was in for until he had finished explaining.

"If this was a bet, what were the stakes involved?" Riggy asked.

Jimmy looked at me questioningly. Then he said, "I don't think we settled that. I assumed it was that if I found an adventure, Mia would have to go along."

Everybody looked at me, and I said, "All right. I guess so."

"Okay," Jimmy said. "This is it: we're going to go outside the Ship. *On* the outside of the Ship."

"Isn't that dangerous?" Helen asked.

"It's an adventure," Jimmy said. "Adventures are supposed to have an element of danger, be fraught with peril and all that."

"Is it dangerous outside the Ship?" I asked.

"I don't know," Jimmy admitted. "I don't know what it's like out there. I couldn't find out. I did try. Finding out should be part of the fun. Besides, even if that's easy, there are some hard parts. We've got to have suits to go outside, and we've got to get ourselves outside. Neither of those will be easy."

"I want to go, too," Riggy said.

Jimmy shook his head. "This is just Mia and me. We are going to need help, though, and if you want to help us you're welcome."

The kids looked at each other around the table, and then they all nodded. We were a group, after all, and this was just too good to miss.

The six of us walked in a body through a corridor on the First Level. Jimmy walked a step or two ahead of us, leading the way. There is something to being a part of a group busy on purposes of its own, something exciting. Even if it is melodramatic, even if it is 90% hokum, it is fun. I was enjoying myself, and so were the others. I could hardly restrain myself from practicing surreptitious glances behind us, simply because they seemed in keeping with the part we were playing.

Jimmy turned half around and pointed ahead and to the left. "It's around here."

There was a little foyer there a couple of feet deep, and then a blank black door, completely featureless. In our world that is unusual—people ordinarily lavish considerable care in making their surroundings lively and personal. Consequently the Ship is quite a colorful place to live in. A black door like this with neither design nor decoration was obviously meant to say "Stay Out" to anybody who came by.

"The air lock to the outside is in the room behind the door there," Jimmy said.

The door had no obvious button, knob, slide, latch or handle, only a single hole for an electronic key—this sort of key when inserted would emit an irregular signal of an established frequency and the door would open.

Attila and Jimmy were the two of us that knew something about electronics and they looked the door over carefully together.

After a moment Attila said, "It's just a token lock."

"What's that?" I asked. We were standing in a half-circle around the two boys and the door.

He said, "This lock is just to keep the door closed and to let people know the door is supposed to be closed, and that's about all. I'll have to work on it a couple of times and I can get through."

Jimmy said, "Can you be through by next Saturday—a week from tomorrow?"

"Oh, sure."

"Let's plan to go then. Helen? You work with Attila. You be his lookout and make sure he doesn't get caught fooling around here and ruin everything."

Then he turned to the other three of us. "All right, let's go see about getting the suits."

Helen said, "But can't I go? I don't want to miss out."

It was interesting—of the six of us, Jimmy was the next-to-smallest and yet he dominated the group when he wanted to. There is something to the idea of natural leadership ability.

Jimmy said, "We have to have somebody be lookout. Besides, you'll be here when we go outside. The only thing you're going to miss is swiping the suits."

To get to Salvage, our next stop, we cut through Engineers. That saved us a long trip around. The four of us must have made considerable noise because as we were passing down the main hall of offices, an elderly woman popped out of one of them behind us.

"Hold on there!" she said.

We turned around. She *was* elderly—short, squarely-built, white-haired and obviously well over a hundred, perhaps even as old as Mr. Mbele. She also looked thoroughly sour.

"Well, what is it you're doing here, making all this noise? Perhaps you don't realize it, but there is important work being done here."

Uneasily Jimmy said that we were just passing through on our way to Salvage and that we meant no harm.

"This is not a public highway," she said. "If you have no business in Engineers, you shouldn't be here. You children have no sense of fitness. Why are you going to Salvage?"

Jimmy and I were standing just behind Venie and Riggy, and her question was addressed to Jimmy.

"It's a school assignment," Jimmy said.

"That's right," I chimed in.

Her glance shifted to the other two of us. "What about you?"

Instead of saying the obvious thing, Riggy said, "We're with them."

"All right," the old lady snapped. "You first two go on, but don't come through here again. The other two of you go on home."

Venie and Riggy looked helplessly at us, but then they turned and went reluctantly the other way. The old lady really had no right to chase them out, but she was so fierce and unarguable-with that we just couldn't say a thing. Jimmy and I scooted on our way before she could add anything more, and she watched until both sets of us had definitely done as she said. Some people get a feeling of power from being unpleasant.

Most of all, Salvage smelled interesting. Salvage and Repair are really little enclaves almost surrounded by the much larger Engineers. There are offices and large machines and large projects a-building in Engineers. Salvage and Repair are just the tail end of the dog, without the personnel, resources or neatness of Engineers. Salvage was a crowded room, full of aisles and racks and benches and tables all in a pleasing state of disarray. It looked like the sort of place that you could poke around in for weeks or even months and always turn up something new and interesting. And hanging over it all was the most intriguing and unidentifiable odor I'd come upon. The smell alone was enough to make you want to spend your spare time here.

We peeked cautiously in. There were a couple of technicians working and moving around.

"Come on," Jimmy said. "I know they have suits here somewhere, probably locked away. We'll have to poke around."

We looked around as inconspicuously as possible, Jimmy taking one aisle and me taking the next. I was lost in a pile of broken toys when Jimmy grabbed at my elbow. I jumped.

"Sorry," he said. "I've found them. They're two rows over and they're not locked away or anything. They're just in a rack."

"How do you know they're safe to use?" I said. I nudged

a broken doll with my toe. "If they're like that, we might as well forget it."

"These aren't in for repair," Jimmy said. "These are the ones they'd use themselves if they had to go outside. They've got seals on from after the last time they were used. The important thing is how we're going to sneak them out. Oh-oh, watch out."

I turned to look. Just down the aisle a pleasant-looking technician was coming toward us. He was a short youngish man with mouse-colored hair.

"Well, what can I do for you kids?" he asked.

"I'm Mia Havero." I said. "This is Jimmy Dentremont."

"Hello," he said. "My name is Mitchell." And waited with eyebrows raised.

I reached into my pocket and took out a couple of folded sheets of paper. Uncertainly I said, "I don't know if you can help us. Maybe this isn't the right place."

Jimmy stayed silent, watching my lead.

Mr. Mitchell said, "Well, we'll see. What is it that you've got?"

I showed him the sketches, Jimmy's and mine, that I'd taken from the table in Lev Quad, and explained how our names were involved.

"These are just rough," I said. "What we wanted to do was draw them a little better and then work up pins to wear with these as designs."

"Hmm," Mr. Mitchell said. "Yes. I don't see why not. It may not fall strictly in our province, but it seems a worthwhile idea. I think I can help you. How does ceramic jewelry sound?'

"Great," Jimmy said. "Could we come down on a Saturday morning?"

Mr. Mitchell said, "There's usually only one technician on duty on Saturdays, but I suppose . . ."

I said, "Could we make it a week from tomorrow? We have this big soccer game in the quad tomorrow and we really ought to be there."

"Oh, sure," Mr. Mitchell said. "I'll even arrange to have the duty a week from tomorrow and help you myself."

After we had thanked him and walked away, Jimmy said, "You certainly can lie. How did you think that one up?"

"Which?"

"About the soccer game."

"I didn't make that up," I said. "I was supposed to tell you. The kids want to play soccer tomorrow."

"Oh," Jimmy said. "Maybe you aren't such a good liar, then."

10

The score in the soccer game in Roth Quad was 5 to 3. Attila and Venie and I were on the losing side.

During the next week we set our plans. With some practice, Attila had that door so well trained that it would practically pop open when he told it to, at least according to Helen. Att looked pleased and didn't deny it. We had borrowing the suits set up pretty well, too. Jimmy sketched the location of the suits for Venie and Riggy.

"There'll be just one technician working on Saturday," Jimmy said, "and he'll be busy helping Mia and me. All you two have to do is sneak easy. As soon as we can, we'll join you in the air lock room."

I had some spare time and Jimmy didn't, so I took Venie and Riggy down to Salvage for a quick scout around. Mr. Mitchell was in the back, but I made sure we didn't attract his attention. We were in, I pointed to the suits, and we were out again in no more than twenty seconds. On our way back, though, the same old woman stopped us in Engineers and lectured us again. She had her desk placed so that she could see everybody who passed in the hall—and, I guess, come out to exterminate anyone who she thought had no business being there. Her name, displayed on her desk, was Keithley. She more than awed me. She scared me. As soon as she turned away, we three scooted.

"You'd better not come this way when you have the suits," I said. "Think what would happen if she caught you."

Riggy paled and shook his head.

"She shouldn't have stopped us," Venie said. "We weren't making any noise this time." She agreed to make a detour when they had the suits, however.

Things aren't always fair, I guess.

Actually, the old lady wasn't the only thing I was afraid

of. I didn't really like the idea of going outside the Ship, and the more I thought about it the less I liked it. The Ship goes faster than the speed of light (the old Einstein barrier) by becoming discontinuous (the Kaufmann-Chambers Discontinuity Equations). I know the thought of standing on the outside of the Ship and looking at the inside of nothing excited Jimmy, but it did not excite me. It seems to be my nature to have second thoughts, and they came to me all through the week. Since it was far too late to back out without looking foolish, I didn't tell any of the others, but I began to regret ever having mentioned the word adventure.

Perhaps the answer is that if you're going to do something impulsive, you should do it the way Riggy does. Act while the impulse is clear and fresh and don't allow any time for second thought.

"Who won that soccer game of yours?" Mr. Mitchell said as he led the way through the maze of unrepaired, half-repaired, and repaired whatnot in Salvage.

"Jimmy's side did," I said. "Mine lost. We really appreciate your helping us like this."

"Oh, it's nothing at all," he said. "Here we are. This is the kiln where we bake the finished pieces. Copper—that's for the base. Then an enamel and a surface painting on that. We can try it a couple of times until it comes out right."

He pointed at each item and, in fact, seemed more than than pleased to help us. I think part of it was the chance to help out eager kiddies, partly he liked me because I was a cute little girl, and part was the sheer joy of operating the bake oven and making the jewelry. The pins were just an excuse for me, though I did find the idea of making them intriguing and the process interesting. I am not a tinkerer, however. Jimmy and Mr. Mitchell both were. They belonged to the let's-putter-around-and-see-what-happens school and they got on very well together.

We started by picking the copper backing, refining our sketches, and planning the colors we wanted to use. Gradually, I became relegated to the position of observer while Jimmy took over the planning and execution of the jewelry with Mr. Mitchell serving as over-his-shoulder adviser. That was after the first try, particularly mine, turned out badly.

The first I ever saw Jimmy Dentremont he was tinkering, or if he wasn't at least that's the way I remember it. He was good at it, too, and that combined with enthusiasm, mild mental myopia, and desire to dominate sometimes carried him away. It wasn't the first time I'd gotten elbowed to the side by him. I didn't care for it particularly, either. It was one of the things that made me wonder, our necessary association aside, if I really *liked* Jimmy.

It wasn't really an important enough thing to get more than slightly irritated about today, since we had larger goals in mind, but I did resent mildly being put in a position where I had to work just to see enough over Jimmy's other shoulder to know what was going on. But, at least, having been put in the role of an observer, I did make an effort to observe and I saw more than either Jimmy or Mr. Mitchell.

When our second tries were in the oven, I poked Jimmy and said, "Mr. Mitchell, it's about lunch time."

"Hmm?" Jimmy said, turning his attention from the oven to me. It was actually something on the early side for lunch, as Jimmy was perceptive enough to be aware. In his concentration on the job of the moment, our larger purposes had escaped him. I gave him another prod to restore his memory.

I said, "We can go and eat and then come back to see how the pins turned out."

Jimmy had the good sense to nod.

Mr. Mitchell seemed a little bewildered, mostly I think because he and Jimmy had been in rapport, working together to do the job, and now, all of a sudden, Jimmy was just dropping things and dashing off. But he said, "Oh. All right. Sure."

When we were in the hall on beyond, Jimmy said, "What I said last week about lies—I was wrong. Boy, did that sound weak: 'Have to go to lunch.' "

"Well, I didn't notice you thinking up anything better," I said, quite tartly. I was walking determinedly enough that before Jimmy saw how fast I was going, I was a good bit ahead and he had to push to catch up. It's my I-mean-business-and-I'm-more-than-just-an-ounce-irked pace.

"What's the matter with you?" Jimmy asked. "I didn't mean anything."

"It's not that," I said.

"Well, what is it?"

"Nothing," I said. Then, "They got the suits about half an hour ago. Venie waved at me. You two had your heads down over the table."

"I hope they got the smallest there were," Jimmy said.

Suddenly, I put my hand on his elbow and stopped. "Hold on there. We'd better go back and go around." I gestured at the hall ahead. "I don't want to get bawled out by that old witch again."

Jimmy looked at me with an impish expression. It's the sort of expression his face, topped by red hair and set between prominent ears, is really fitted for.

"Let's take a chance," he said. "Let's just run for it, and if she comes out we won't stop at all."

Maybe it was my moment to be impulsive. The hall stretched before us like a gauntlet. The door to old Mrs. Keithley's office was open and we were far enough out of her line of sight to allow us a running start. We had to go about thirty yards beyond it, turn a corner left, and then we'd be out of sight and out of practical reach.

"All right," I said. Feeling like little blond-haired Susy Dangerfield running between the lines of hostile Iroquois braves, I took off. Jimmy was right with me, on my left, and we pounded along. As we passed the old lady's office, I shot a glance right, but didn't see her.

Jimmy out-accelerated me, and as we made for the corner, he was a step or two ahead.

"Hey, slow down," I said. "She isn't even there."

He turned his head to look back as he reached the corner, and still moving at considerable speed crashed blindly into someone. Jimmy bounced off and into the wall, but didn't fall down. I skidded to a stop at the corner and looked down. It was Mrs. Keithley, white hair and all, sitting flat on her bottom with an expression of affronted dignity on her face. She looked up at me.

"Hello," I said. "Nice day, isn't it?" I stepped over her and walked at a very sedate pace down the hall.

Jimmy was stunned momentarily, but then he made the best of things. "It was nice to see you again," he said politely to the dear old lady, and then walked after me. I shot a glance back at her and then Jimmy caught up with me and we both broke into a run and left her looking speechlessly after us.

When we were out of breath and out of sight, we stopped running and flung ourselves down panting on a flight of stairs. Then we started laughing, partly because it seemed terribly funny and partly from sheer relief.

When I'd caught my breath and stopped laughing, I looked soberly at Jimmy and said, "I don't know about you, but I'm going to take the long way around from now on."

"That's a pretty obvious thing to say," Jimmy said.

"Well, I'm not a very brave person."

"Oh, I'm not blaming you. I'm going to be careful, too."

When we got to the lock room, Helen was waiting in the hallway. All of us looked in both directions, and then Helen stepped up to the black door and gave a knock that was recognizably a signal and not a casual rapping by some passerby with an unaccountable desire to tap on black doors. The door swung open immediately and we all piled inside. Att, standing behind the door, gave us just time enough to get completely in and then shut the door behind us.

The room was green-colored, small and bare. The lock door was directly opposite the door we'd come in. The suits had been hung on racks that apparently were designed to hold them.

Jimmy looked around in satisfaction. "Ah," he said. "Very, very good. Let's get the suits on, Mia."

I looked around at Venie and Helen and Att and said, "Where's Riggy?"

Att said, "I couldn't talk him out of it. He brought along an extra suit. You know how he wanted to go outside, too. Well, he went."

Looking very unhappy, Jimmy said, "Well, couldn't you stop him, Venie? You could have kept him from taking an extra suit."

Venie said defensively, "If you only wanted one suit between the two of you, I could have made him leave one behind. He said he had as much right to go out as you two did."

Att said, "You know how mad he can get. We told him it wasn't a good idea but he wouldn't have it any other way."

"Oh, well," I said.

Helen said, "He's going to 'surprise' you."

"I guess so," Jimmy said, somewhat sourly. "Well, let's go ahead with what's left of this adventure."

He was obviously quite disgruntled, but trying not to let it show. Or, perhaps, trying to let it show just enough so that he could be a good sport about it all. I've not been above that one myself.

We put on the suits. They were about as similar to the old-time pressure suits described in the novels I liked to read as the Ship is to that silly sailboat I once got so sick in. (In passing, I want to say that it used to strike me as odd the way nobody in the Ship wrote novels at all; nobody had for years and years and years, so that what I read dated from before the Population Wars. Right now I'm not even sure why I liked to read them. Most of them weren't very good by any objective standard. Escapism, maybe. . . .) Anyway, our suits were an adaptation of the basic discontinuity principle that the Ship used, too. To be analogous (and thereby inaccurate), remember that old saw about reaching inside a cat, grabbing it by the tail, and turning it inside out? The discontinuity effect, as far as the Ship is concerned, grabs the universe by the tail and turns it inside out so as to get at it better. Strictly a local effect, but in the process getting from *here* to *there* becomes a relatively simple matter instead of an intensely difficult one. The discontinuity effect doesn't work the same way in the suits—they are more of a self-contained little universe of their own. They were originally invented, my reading tells me, to fight battles in—part of a continuing effort to render individual soldiers invulnerable—and hence were light in weight, carried their own air, heat, air-conditioning, light, etc., plus being proof against just about everything from concentrated light beams to projectiles to any of the unpleasant battery of gases that had been invented. Turned out, of course, that the suits were far more useful for constructive purposes (building the Ships) than they had ever been in wartime. Militarily, of course, they were a bust—everybody on Old Earth who fought in one was long dead—but in their peaceful adaptations they were still useful and still in use, as witness.

Working the lock to the great outside was a simple matter. You began by pushing a priority button, since there was no sense in being embarrassed halfway in or out by somebody trying to come the other way. Going out, you let air into the lock, entered the lock yourself, let air out, and then went outside. Coming in, you let air out of the lock (if there was any), entered the lock, filled it with air, and then passed into the Ship. Since Riggy had let the air out of the lock in order to pass out of it, we locked the controls (which also insured the farther lock door was completely closed) and filled the air lock with air.

As we went in, Att said, "Don't be too mad with Riggy. At least wait until you're all safely back here."

Jimmy nodded, and with everybody saying "Good luck" to us we went into the air lock. Quite frankly, my nerves felt they could use all the good luck they could get. That was the biggest reason that I was, unnaturally for me, saying little or nothing. The door closed behind us and with it the sight of that cheery bare little room and our friends.

As the air silently slipped away around us in response to button-pushing by Jimmy, he said, "When Riggy comes up and goes 'Boo' or whatever stupid thing he has in mind, just pretend you don't see him at all. Ignore him completely."

I didn't like Riggy's butting in, so I nodded. "All right."

Then the air was all out, and Jimmy opened the door at our feet. Since we were on the First Level, which was "down" as far as you could go by the Ship's internal orientation, we had to go further "down" to go out. Jimmy motioned at the ladder, which reminded me of something, I wasn't exactly sure what.

"Go ahead," he said.

I grabbed the ladder and began to climb down. Then I remembered—two other ladders, one to the Sixth Level and another down to a boat. That's what it was. Damned ladders. Halfway down the tube, which was only seven or eight feet long, I suddenly felt dizzy and my stomach turned topsy-turvy and then I found that I was much lighter and standing on my head. It was the point where the internal gravity of the Ship cut out and normal gravity of a small asteroid, no longer blanked out, took over. "Down" in the ship and "down" outside were just opposite, and I was passing from one to the other. So now I was pointed head down, but my feet were outside the tube, and with a little effort and the light gravity, I managed to scramble out. I stood up with a motion that left me with a whirling head and looked around. Overhead there was a sharp, eye-blurring silver-grayness marked by streaks and pinpoints of a black that almost edged over into purple. It hurt my eyes to look at it and I was reminded of a photographic negative, even though this had a tone to it that no photograph ever had. It made you want to squint your eyes and look away, but there was no other place to look. The rocky surface of the Ship had an eerie, washed-out silver look to it, too. The rocks looked sterile and completely dead, as though no one had ever been here before or would ever be here again. A playground for the never-was only a few feet away from the living, breathing, warm real world I was used to, but effectively in another dimension.

Almost as confirmation of the other-dimensionality, Jimmy's legs suddenly stuck out of the hole beside me as he came *down*. I helped him out. He sat beside the edge of the tube as though to right his senses, and then looked around, just as I had.

Beside us, apparently to mark the location of the lock, was an eight-foot pylon. On it were lock controls, a location number, and a crude sign—the joke, I suspect, of somebody long dead—that said in hand-written capitals, KEEP OFF THE GRASS! It gave me a shivery feeling to read it. I don't know if it was the probable age of the sign, the weird tone of its surroundings, the whirling of my head, or some combination.

We looked around us silently, and then Jimmy said, "What are those?"

Beyond the pylon, in the distance, were a long row of giant tubes projecting above the uneven rocky surface like great guns pointed at the universe. They could not have been too far, since for all the irregularity of the Ship's surface the distance to the horizon was not great.

"Scoutship tubes, I think. I didn't realize that we were this close to the scout bay."

"Yes, I guess," Jimmy said.

The distortion that affected everything around us touched him, too. "You don't look very well," I said, peering at what I could see of him in his suit.

"I don't feel very well. I'm getting sick to my stomach. You don't look very well yourself."

"It's just the light," I said, but that wasn't true. My dizziness was making me sick to my stomach, too. I was almost afraid I was going to vomit and out here in a suit was the worst possible place. So I said, "Where's Riggy? Shouldn't he have surprised us by now?"

Jimmy slowly looked around. "There are other locks.

Maybe he went down one of them to leave us wondering."

"Maybe," I said. "I think we'd better look for him, though."

"What if he's hiding? Maybe that's his surprise."

There were so many tumbled rocks around us that if Riggy was hiding it would be no simple thing to find him. He would be just another lump among many.

Then our questions were answered for us.

Jimmy said, "What was that?"

"What?" The noise came again and I heard it this time —a horrible retching sound. I had both send and receive controls on my suit turned low, but in spite of this the sound was almost too much for me. My stomach heaved and I had to fight to keep from throwing up, too. My head continued to spin.

"Where are you, Riggy?" Jimmy asked.

"I don't see him," I said.

Riggy said nothing, just made that awful vomiting sound again. It didn't recommend him to me. Jimmy crouched then and jumped straight up in the "air." In the light gravity he went up a tremendous distance, perhaps forty feet or more and then down. He landed lightly. But then he said, "I couldn't see him at all, I couldn't see a thing. Mia, go out about one hundred or a hundred and fifty feet toward the middle one of those big tubes and look for Riggy. I'll go in the other direction. We'll both make a half-circle clockwise."

I stumbled away over the rocks toward the scout bay tubes, bouncing unevenly, slipping a couple of times, and not helped at all by the sound of Riggy and his vomiturition. I wanted to turn him off, but I didn't because then I couldn't hear Jimmy. When I was about the right distance from the pylon, I started making my half-circle.

Then Jimmy said, "Are you ready, Mia?"

"I've already started," I said.

"Riggy," Jimmy said. "If you don't want to be left out here, you'd better get to your feet and do your best to be found."

What I wanted most was to shut my eyes against the silver, just sit down and try to ease my spinning head (my eyes were beginning to ache and my ears to ring) and concentrate on quelling the nausea I felt. It reminded me of my sailing experience, but this was much worse. It was all I could do to keep walking and my feet were not going where I wanted them to. I didn't go exactly in a half-circle, either. I tried to check on my position, to look for Riggy, and just to keep going, and I wasn't doing very well at any of them. I am completely convinced that the ultimate weapon is one that you can hold in your hand, point at a person, and thereby completely disrupt his sense of balance. All that he could do is lie in a puddled heap and puke. It would probably destroy the concept of heroics for all time.

As light as the gravity was here, I had some trouble with my traction. In jumping from one rock to another, my foot slipped, my feet tangled, and then there wasn't a rock where I thought there was, and I took a header. Under normal gravity and without the protection of a suit, I would probably have been pretty badly hurt. As it was, I just fell. Unless you did some quiet practice first, without the distraction of this unsettling dizziness, I doubted the tremendous bounds that would be possible out here would be worth making. I lay there, fetched up against a rock that resembled nothing so much as a particularly hideous sculpture my mother once made—a distorted bust of old Lemuel Carpentier himself. The only thing that was in proper proportion was his nose, and that was his worst feature. He hadn't been pleased. Lying still, my head didn't clear, so I forced myself to stand up again.

Then I saw Riggy. He was on his knees, if not on his feet. He was hidden completely from the pylon by a tent-like conglomeration of rocks which had pitched together to form a sheltered area. He was still retching.

I said to Jimmy, "I've found him." Then, because it didn't matter anymore and I wanted to save my stomach if I could, I shut off my receive line.

I hardly looked at Riggy. I didn't want to. I got him on his feet and then found that if I was careful about where I put my own feet as I walked, I could carry him. I kept my mind on reaching the pylon and then Jimmy was beside us and helping me.

We set Riggy down by the lock and Jimmy pushed the lock controls on the pylon so that we could make our way inside.

I said, "Go on through. I'll push him inside to you."

Jimmy went ahead. He went head first down the hole and then was gone. I waited a minute and then I fed Riggy down the hole, too. I held him by the ankles. For a moment there was a feeling exactly like that feeling of invisible force when you push the similar poles of two magnets together and Riggy was neither here nor there, but then Jimmy had him and pulled him through. I went through after.

When we were in the lock, Jimmy fed the air in. When the air was all in, the door to the lock room opened. By that time I had the headpiece of my suit off. Just in time, too. When the door opened, I took two steps forward and then threw up. It was, in a way, a considerable relief.

Jimmy and I had been outside for twenty minutes, Riggy for forty. We recovered our equilibrium in a bare few minutes, but Riggy could do nothing but sit and look miserable and hold his head.

When I threw up, Venie looked down at it and then up at me. "You're going to have to clean that up," she said. "I'm not." Apparently she felt she'd had enough of the dirty work on this little adventure. I didn't really blame her. I didn't have the strength. All I did was just sit down and close my eyes and give blessings that I was back in the real world again, even including Venie.

Jimmy and Riggy and I just sat around and the other three threw questions at us. Jimmy told them how it was.

Riggy said weakly, "If anybody wants to go, I'll give them this suit."

"It's hardly in shape for anybody to wear," Helen said, and that was true. For all that he had stopped being racked by heaves, Riggy and the inside of his suit were in impossible shape.

Jimmy said, "We'd best get these things cleaned up and returned."

We got Riggy out of his suit and Venie was delegated to see that he got home. Helen and Att took Riggy's suit off to clean it up, and Jimmy and I cleaned up the lock room. I don't know how Jimmy was able to keep his stomach from first to last, but he did. His iron constitution, I guess.

When everything was cleaned up, we left Att and Helen to close the lock room and go home. I had never realized before that adventures took so much *doing,* so much preparation and so much cleaning up afterward. That's something you don't see in stories. Who buys the food and cooks it, washes the dishes, minds the baby, rubs down the horses, swabs out the guns, buries the bodies, mends the clothes, ties that rope in place so the hero can conveniently find it there to swing from, blows fanfares, polishes medals, and dies beautifully, all so that the hero can *be* a hero? Who finances him? I'm not saying I don't believe in heroes—I'm just saying that they are either parasites or they spend the bulk of their time in making their little adventures possible, not in enjoying them.

Cleaning up after ourselves coupled with the left-handed direction everything had gone took the sparkle out of us. Jimmy and I just tossed the suits over our arms and said goodbye to Helen and Att and went off toward Salvage. Things had gone so unswimmingly that I suppose I should have expected that they would continue that way. On our way, we ran into George Fuhonin. It was again a case of coming around a corner and not being able to avoid someone, though in this case we didn't stumble over him. We simply turned the corner and found him close enough that we couldn't ditch the suits or manage to go unseen.

"Hi, Mia," he said from down the hall.

"Hello," I said. "What are you doing down here?"

Jimmy looked up at the giant so uncertainly that I said, "It's George Fuhonin. He pilots a scoutship—for my dad sometimes," in an undertone.

"Oh," Jimmy said.

"I was looking for you, I think," George said as he came up. "I'm on constable call today and I had a complaint from a Mrs. Keithley in Engineers about two young cubs, a red-headed boy with ears that stick out—and I take it that's you"—pointing at Jimmy—"and a black-haired little girl with bad manners. I'm not even making a guess as to who that is," he said, looking meaningfully at me. "So perhaps we'd better go where we can talk, and while you're about it, you might explain what you're doing with those suits."

"We were returning them," I said.

George looked at us quizzically.

The aftermath I don't care to go into detail about. Mr. Mitchell was quite genuinely hurt to think he had been used. I could tell that he was hurt when he handed each of us our pins, both of which turned out very nicely indeed.

That was at a meeting in Daddy's office with Daddy, Mr. Mitchell, Miss Brancusik who was Jimmy's dorm mother, and Mr. Mbele. They sat on one side of the room and Jimmy and I sat on the other. Mrs. Keithley wasn't there, thank Heaven. The meeting was uncomfortable enough without her, too.

She entered the meeting—we were told to avoid her strictly from now on. I could see that Mr. Mitchell had been hurt, but I didn't really understand why. It was spelled out for us. I had been looking at it from my point of view, that he was in our way and might have stopped us if we had just tried to ask for the suits. I hadn't seen things from his angle at all. That we had used him the way you use a handkerchief. I've always thought more in terms of things than of people, and I'm sometimes slow to put myself in somebody else's shoes. When I did, I wasn't happy about what I'd done—which I think was Daddy's intention.

They didn't question us about who used the third suit, but they did point out how stupid and dangerous it had been for us to go outside.

"I suppose I ought to be pleased by your initiative," Daddy said, "but what I think about is the permanent damage to your sense of balance that might well have resulted if you two hadn't come back inside in time. You might never have been able to move again without suffering vertigo."

The thought alone was enough to make me queasy.

Daddy finished by setting a punishment of not being able to go anywhere for a month. For a month, after class with Mr. Mbele or Survival Class, I had to come straight home and stay there. Miss Brancusik then and there meted out the same restriction to Jimmy.

In some ways, that was the hardest month I ever spent, cooped up in the apartment and not able to go anywhere. Sitting at home when other people were free to come and go, free to play soccer, to go folk dancing at night, or to sit around the Common Room while Jimmy and I had to go check in. In other ways, it wasn't entirely a loss. For one thing, it gave me time to think about my character deficiencies. I didn't think of them in exactly those terms, but I did determine not to be any more stupid than was absolutely necessary, which is much the same thing. Also, since we were both stuck in our own homes, Jimmy and I did quite a lot of talking and I got to know him better.

11

We received our automatic promotions from Sixth Class to Fifth in the fall when First Class went off on Trial and another group of younger kids began training. Through the fall, as we approached the end of our first six months of training, we one-by-one turned thirteen. Not only was I the smallest one in the class—not that I minded, since being cute little black-haired Mia Havero never hurt anything—but my birthday was last. It came, as always, on Saturday, November 29. One of the advantages of a permanent calendar is that it gives you something to count on.

On my birthday, Mother made a special trip to see us—well, she spent the day with Daddy. She presented me with one of her sculptures and I thanked her politely. She didn't like being thanked, for some reason—and I assure you that I was nice—and left the room.

Daddy, who isn't always as single-minded or as busy as you might think, had done something that I would never have thought of. He'd called the library and they made a search of all their recordings and sent him a fair copy of no less than five pennywhistle records. I once, believe it or not, went through a stage of thinking the Andrew Johnson books were all mine and nobody else knew about them, and it was something of a shock to learn that they did. The pennywhistle records that Daddy gave me didn't produce quite the same feeling of losing something private, but I would never have dreamed that anyone would ever have recorded pennywhistle music. I thanked Daddy and kissed his cheek. I had never been able to be demonstrative when I was younger, but since we had moved to Geo Quad somehow it came easier, like a lot of things.

The biggest surprise of my birthday was Jimmy D. He asked me to go to the theatre with him. I think he was a little frightened when he did and that surprised me. I'd always thought that he saw me as, at best, a brother-in-arms, and not as a girl at all.

The play was put on in the amphitheatre where they hold Ship's Assembly and we actually went to it instead of watching it on the vid. It was Richard B. Sheridan's *School for Scandal* and except that I got a little sweaty in the palms of my hands, something that had never happened at home and that I can only attribute to my being excited, I enjoyed myself thoroughly.

I was excited all evening, too. When we got home, Jimmy took my hand and touched the palm with his finger.

"Your hand is sweaty," he said.

I looked up at him and I nodded.

He said, "So is mine," and he showed me, and it was.

Jimmy kissed me then. In spite of what they say, I was a little surprised. I had no idea that he wanted to, though I'd been hoping he would. It shows you what secret passions you can arouse. It was the first time anybody had ever kissed me like that and it made my heart pound and my hands sweat even more. Whatever I've forgotten, I've remembered that birthday.

It was almost as though Jimmy and I had invested something of ourselves because after that we had an unspoken understanding. Instead of carping at each other all the time, we only fought when we were mad. You can't squabble in public with somebody you sometimes kiss privately, or at least I found I couldn't. Of course I didn't tell anybody. I wouldn't want them to think I was changing.

Since I was now thirteen, Trial was less than a year away, but somehow I wasn't quite as awed by the thought as I once had been. It no longer seemed as deadly a thing as it once had—though I did know that far from everyone returned. Survival Class gave me an amazing amount of confidence. For one thing, it made what we had to face more of a known quantity, and the unknown, unnameable, might-be-anything is always more frightening than the known. Trial was beginning to look more and more like thirty days amongst the Mudeaters—soonest begun, soonest done—and not much more, though there were some moments when I was surer of this than others. The moments when I wasn't quite so sure that Trial would be a waltz usually came after one of the afternoons we spent watching various white-fanged this-and-thats come charging efficiently across the projection screen to slice down some galumping creature three times their size, *wham!* But Survival Class also taught us to deal with completely strange things. Many didn't seem to have much to do with Trial, either. Dancing, needlepoint, parachuting. The thing is that once you've discovered that you can do a lot of strange and demanding things, and sometimes even do them well, then coping with the unknown doesn't seem quite as hard. When they ask you to raise a log cabin, you don't object that you never expect the opportunity to come up during Trial. You do it. You learn that you can do it. And you even learn one or two things that might come in handy.

In December, forty-two kids who were exactly a year older than we were, were scattered across the Western Hemisphere of New Dalmatia. They were dropped one at a time with horses and packs and no clear idea of where they were or what planet they were on, then got waved goodbye to. Also in December, about one week later, thirty-one of us kids went on a three-day field trip with Mr. Marechal and an assistant named Pizarro, also to New Dalmatia. The differences, of course, were that we knew where we were going, what we would find there, how long we were going to stay, and a few other nonessentials like that.

Four horses were taken, large draft animals. All of us kids came down to the scout bay with good shoes on our feet, heavy clothing, and back packs. We'd been issued these when we started Survival Class. I'd outgrown my shoes, however, and been issued new pairs, and I was almost ready to ask for a larger set of clothes. As we went on board, I saw Mr. Pizarro and Mr. Marechal counting us off. They weren't too obvious about it because there was that set idea of the voluntary nature of Survival Class and they make a point of not checking up. Still, they wanted to know how many they were taking—somebody would be bound to say *something* if they came back a half-dozen short.

Mr. Pizarro was our pilot. When everybody was aboard —everybody meaning all thirty-one of us, nobody missing; I happen to know that Robert Briney got out of bed with a cracked rib (his horse kicked him) to come along—they raised the ramp and took off. There was some nervous talking and joke telling. Mr. Marechal was even tolerant enough not to tell everybody to be quiet.

I picked a chair against the partition that separated the walk-around from the bull-pen where we were sitting. I've never been at my best in groups like that—where there are only a few people that I know well I talk, but where there are crowds I fade into the background. Besides, I had something to do. Att and Jimmy did come over, though.

"What are you writing?" Att asked.

I put down my notebook. "Ethics notes," I said. "I'm organizing my ideas for a paper Jimmy and I have to do for Mr. Mbele."

Jimmy asked, "How are you doing it?"

I took his hand and ran a finger across the back of it. "I'm not asking *you* that. You'll see when I'm done."

Big Att sat down then and said, "What sort of thing does it have to be?"

Jimmy mussed my hair lightly and said, "No one particular thing. It has to be on the subject of ethics."

I ducked my head away from Jimmy's hand and said, "You seem nervous, Att."

"A little, I guess," he said. "I've never been down on a planet. I don't see how you can be so calm and just sit here and write."

"Scribble," Jimmy said.

"It's not so new for me," I said. "I've been down before."

"Her dad takes her when he goes," Jimmy said.

After a few more minutes, Jimmy and Att broke out a pocket chess set and began to play and I turned back to my notes. I finished off utilitarianism before we landed.

Ethics is the branch of philosophy that concerns itself with conduct, questions of good and evil, right and wrong. Almost every ethical system—and there are a great many of them, because even people who supposedly belong to the same school don't agree a good share of the time and have to be considered separately—can be looked at as a description and as a prescription. Is this what people actually do? Is this what people ought to do?

Skipping the history and development of utilitarianism, the most popular expression of the doctrine is "the greatest good for the greatest number," which makes it sound like its relative, the economic philosophy communism which, in a sense, is what we live with in the Ship. The common expression of utilitarian good is "the presence of pleasure and the absence of pain."

Speaking descriptively, utilitarianism doesn't hold true, though the utilitarian claims that it does. People *do* act self-destructively at times—they know the pleasureful and choose the painful instead. The only way that what people do and what utilitarianism says they do can be matched is by distorting the ordinary meanings of the words "pleasure" and "pain." Besides, notions of what is pleasurable are subject to training and manipulation. The standard is too shifting to be a good one.

I don't like utilitarianism as a prescription, either. Treating pleasure and pain as quantities by which good can be measured seems very mechanical, and people become just another factor to adjust in the equation. Pragmatically, it seems to make sense to say *One hundred lives saved at the cost of one?—go ahead!* The utilitarian would say it every time—he would *have* to say it. But who gave him the right to say it? What if the one doesn't have any choice in the matter, but is blindly sacrificed for, say, one hundred Mudeaters whose very existence he is unaware of? Say the choice was between Daddy or Jimmy and a hundred Mudeaters. I wouldn't make a utilitarian choice and I don't think I could be easily convinced that the answer *should* be made by use of the number of pounds of human flesh involved. People are not objects.

We set down in a great nest of trees in bright morning sunshine. The air was clear and brisk. The season was early summer and things were in bloom. The gravity was enough less than normal that it was noticeable, but not enough less to cause discomfort. We landed in a valley by a quiet river. Our side of the river was gentle with great trees rising from a springy floor, but the other side of the river was a sixty-foot bluff, rough-edged, marked by protrusions of rock, ledges and occasional bits of greenery.

I grabbed up my pack by the straps, slung it over my shoulder and went trooping outside with everybody else, down the ramp and into the sun and the cool air. In my pack were a change of clothes, a change of shoes, manual toothbrush, hairbrush, bedroll, and some odds and ends. We had bubble tents, but we had been told not to bring them. I had a heavy shirt and a light shirt underneath, and since the pocket in the outer shirt was small and the shirt was beginning to be tight through the shoulders and across the breast, I dropped my notebook down my shirt front. It would stay as long as I stayed buttoned and tucked. I squinted as I came into the sun.

The trees stretched serenely upward as though nothing

could ever ruffle their composure, the river moved silently past and then curved away, and the light made patches of light and dark as it cut through the trees, alleys in which dust motes could be seen swimming. The chatter of a bird was the only counterpoint to the noise we made. Most of the kids had never been on a planet before and this was a gentle, pleasant introduction. The wind blew lightly, toying with my hair and sleeve, and died again. The horses were led out after us along with harnesses, ropes and chains.

Mr. Marechal called for us to gather around.

"The first fifteen of you will be with Mr. Pizarro," he said. "That's through Mathur. From Morlock on you'll be with me. We're going to build cabins today, and tomorrow, too, if it takes that long. Mr. Pizarro thinks that his group can build a cabin faster than my group can. We're going to see about that."

That was an obvious sort of appeal, but it sounded like fun, so I didn't even giggle. Jimmy, Riggy, Robert Briney, that Farmer boy and the Herskovitz boy were all in my group. Venie and Helen and Att were in Mr. Marechal's group. Jimmy yanked at my sleeve and we followed Mr. Pizarro away from Mr. Marechal to a place of our own. He sat down on a rock and motioned us to take places on the springy ground around him. Mr. Pizarro was a young man with a narrow face and a brushy red moustache.

"All right," he said. "What we are going to build is a log cabin, fifteen by twenty feet. We're going to need about sixty logs. I want all of you kids to get some experience in felling trees, but the boys will do most of it. This is what the cabin will look like."

He sketched in the dirt with a stick. "This is going to be as good a cabin as we can make in this short a time. We're going to have floors, and doors and windows. But this isn't going to be as good a cabin as it might be—any guesses why?"

Somebody raised his hand and Mr. Pizarro called on him. "Well, if we cut them down, the logs are going to be green. They won't dry evenly and the walls will let air in."

"Right," Mr. Pizarro said. "We'll chink the walls as best we can now."

After we had discussed the cabin for a few minutes, Mr. Pizarro led the way down the hill to a level place near the river. Here the cabin outlines had already been marked, and two saw pits had been dug in the ground. Mr. Marechal's group was already down here.

Mr. Pizarro said, "Mr. Marechal and I came down here last Saturday to mark our spots, blaze our trees, and make the saw pits. This is just to make the work faster. When you cut a tree, try to decide why we picked it rather than some of the others around."

Then he assigned us to jobs: tree-felling, horse-handling and log-hauling, log-peeling, and so on. Jack Fernandez-Fragoso and I were put on sill-laying and lunch. Mr. Pizarro gave us a quick sketch of what we were to do and then took the rest of the people off to get them started on their jobs. Mr. Marechal left two people like us behind on the other cabin, and we took a look at them already at work, and started on our own job.

The side base logs, the long base of the cabin, are the most important because the cabin rests on them. They have to be solidly fitted. The best way to do this is to half-sink them into the ground.

Jack and I got shovels and started digging shallow trenches down the long sides of the cabin outlines. We had pegs and string to keep our trenches straight, level and the same depth. The physical part wasn't too bad, since we had been using hand tools for several months in practice and our hands were not as blister-prone as they once had been. It was somewhat painstaking, involving a good bit of measuring to keep things even. When we were done, we leveled the interior floor of the cabin. As we worked, we could hear axes ringing in the woods, voices, and sometimes the fall of a tree.

Before we had finished the floor, Mr. Pizarro, the two horses and the two base logs were all present. The logs were dragged in along the river bank. We came out almost in a tie with the peeling of the logs. Then Jack and I watched as the top quarters of the ends of the logs were cut off. Across these ends would be laid the similarly cut tenons of the base logs of the cabin's short walls, these logs lying on the ground. After that, logs would be laid in alternate rows—long sides of the cabin then short sides, the tenons allowing the logs to rest on those just below them.

Jack and I went off to gather wood, then, and start lunch. By the time lunch was ready, all four base logs were in place, the long ones sitting half in the ground, the short ones standing higher, and a number of other logs had been brought up by the saw pit. Mr. Marechal's people had done about the same amount here, but I had no idea how much had been done out in the woods.

Jack and I ate before everybody else and then served. I went over and sat with Jimmy and Riggy while they ate. Jimmy had been felling trees, Riggy cutting poles, and they and I were both pleased to have the free hour after lunch that Mr. Pizarro allowed us. There is nothing like doing physical labor to give you reason to *think*, if only to pass the time, so I had more thoughts for my ethics paper on the subject of stoicism. I got out my notebook and wrote them down. Jimmy and Riggy just rested.

The trouble with stoicism, it seems to me, is that it is a soporific. It affirms the *status quo* and thereby puts an end to all ambition, all change. It says, as Christianity did a thousand years ago, that kings should be kings and slaves should be slaves, and it seems to me that that is a philosophy infinitely more attractive to the king than the slave.

It is much the same as the question of determination and free will. Whether or not your actions are determined, you have to act on the assumption that you have free will. If you are determined, your attempt at free will loses you nothing. However, if you are not determined and you act on the assumption that you are, you will never attempt anything. You will simply be a passive blob that things happen to.

I am not a passive blob. I have changed and I think at least some of it is my own doing. As long as I have any hope, I could not possibly be a stoic.

In the afternoon, I walked with Jimmy behind Mr. Pizarro to chop down my tree. We followed the skid marks of previous logs along the edge of the river bank. The sun was bright and the air a little warmer now. I couldn't help thinking that this was very pleasant although it was nothing like home. After a few hundred yards we cut away from the river and up a ridge line. The underbrush was very thin and there was a rust brown carpet of shed tree leaves over the ground.

The boys who had been chopping trees before went back to work. There were several trees down and cut into logs waiting to be dragged away. Mr. Pizarro pointed at a gray tree trunk with a white mark on it.

"That's your tree," he said, as the cling of axes and the whirr-whirr of saws started around us.

I walked around the tree and looked up at it. Finally, just as we had been told and shown, I picked the direction I wanted it to fall. I didn't want it to fall on anybody, and I wanted it to fall where it could be cut and hauled away.

Then I braced my feet, lifted my axe and started my undercut. This is a small cut in the tree on the side you wish it to fall. The axe struck the tree and made a gash. Once again and a big chip flew. When I had my undercut, I stopped to rest.

"Very good," Mr. Pizarro said. "When you are done, send Sonja up here. You know what you are doing this afternoon, don't you?"

"Yes," I said.

He nodded and walked away then. He was overseeing all the different jobs that we were doing, plus doing a good bit of the heaviest work himself. You could expect him to be at your elbow one minute and then gone the next—he had come and tasted a spoonful of the soup while I was making it that morning. As he walked away, somebody yelled, "Stand clear," and we all looked up.

One of the trees was ready to fall. There was a ravine between us and both of our trees were aimed to fall there, this one about thirty feet closer to the river than mine. Mr. Pizarro moved up the hill away from it. The boy, seeing everyone clear, pushed the tree and stepped back. It wasn't cut completely through, but the undercut projected beneath the major cut and the push was enough to break through the bit of wood between and the tree wavered and then with majestic slowness toppled forward. In the silence left by the quieted axes, there was the sound of wood breaking, of branches crashing and then a great splintering rack as it smashed against the ground, raising dirt. Then the axes started again.

I moved around to the uphill side of my tree and started my major cut. I stopped from time to time to catch my breath and kick damp aromatic chips. At last it was beginning to waver and I knew it was ready to fall.

I yelled, "Everybody stand clear," and checked to see that everybody was.

Then I pushed the tree and stepped back. My foot skidded on a chip and I sat down hard, looking up at the tree. At first I thought I was wrong and it wasn't going to fall at all, but then it slowly tottered away from me. It fell and when it hit the ground, the butt, snapped clean from the stump, leapt high and then smacked back against the ground only a few feet away. The tree top that had been high over my head was now fifty feet below me in the gully. The tree, landing on the slope, slid forward a few feet and then came to a stop.

I looked down at it with a great deal of satisfaction. Then I got to my feet, dusted off the seat of my pants, picked up my axe and started back to where the cabin was going up. I waved at Jimmy as I passed.

Of the fifteen of us, seven were girls. Five had cut down their trees in the morning, the only ones who hadn't being me and Sonja. So I found her making a door for the cabin with Riggy. The saw pit was now turning out slabs from medium-sized logs—the slabs being really half-logs, flat on one side, round on the other. The slabs were to be used for shutters, doors, roof and cabin floor. In the case of the door, the poles cut in the morning were being nailed to the flat sides of slabs about six feet long. I gave Sonja my axe and sent her along to find Mr. Pizarro, looked at the saw pit in operation for a minute, and then turned to my afternoon job. In the pit, one person gets down in it, one person stands on the ground above, and the log is sawed between them. The only disadvantage is that the person on the bottom gets sawdust in his hair, but if you switch off this evens out.

My afternoon job was taking the mud and moss brought by the mud-and-moss detail (Juanita) and chinking the cracks between the logs. By the time I got back, the two boys on the walls were working on their third tier of logs. They had skids in place and were now looping ropes around the logs and pulling them up the skids and into place. I happily went along, pushing my mud and moss in place, thinking of ethics, and whiling the afternoon away as the walls rose.

After Riggy finished the door and shutters, Mr. Pizarro showed up and they stopped putting up walls for awhile. By that time the walls were high enough that I felt surrounded, tall enough that I had to stand on a cut block to do my chinking. Where I had yet to chink the light slanted through to cut across the shadowed floor.

Mr. Pizarro climbed over the logs then, needing a little boost, and borrowed my block to stand on. Then he and

Riggy cut through the solid logs to make the windows. They made two cuts for each window and removed the sections of log. It was then easier to get in and out, which was good because the logs were becoming harder to raise into place. Riggy came inside, and instead of two boys raising logs, there were now three boys and Mr. Pizarro, plus me when Juanita didn't have enough mud and moss for me and they needed a hand.

When there were two more rows of logs in place, they cut the door in the same way as the window and suddenly the cabin wasn't a tight little box anymore. Everybody was coming in from the woods then, and I went out of the cabin through the hole that was a doorway. Juanita and I made one last trip for mud together while they were raising the last log into place over the door. When we came back with the mud, everybody pitched in and we finished the outside chinking. It was great fun and at the end we just took mud and threw it at each other. I caught Jimmy a great gob across the back and he returned the favor. All fifteen of us were running around throwing mud while Mr. Pizarro stayed out of range and watched us.

When we were all out of mud, he said, "What are you going to do? You only have one spare change of clothes."

Jimmy looked at the river, gave an *onward ho* point of the finger, and said, "There we are."

He sat down, pulled off his shoes, and then made a dash, fully clothed, for the river, plopped through the shallows and made a plunge into the water. I had my shoes kicked off in an instant, and my notebook out of my shirt, and followed right after. The water was clear and cold, not too swift, and just fine for swimming. It was much better than my one previous planetary swimming experience. We all splashed and made grampus noises in the late afternoon sun, flipped water at each other, and had a real old-fashioned time. Very quickly we were joined by Mr. Marechal's group, who were not mud-covered but most of whom had gotten reasonably dirty or sawdust covered in the course of the day and knew a good thing when they saw it. We stayed in until we were called out, and then we came out soggy.

Our leaders were willing to make one concession to the good usages of civilization, and we took our clothes to the scoutship to be quickly dried. The rest of our weekend—sleeping arrangements, hand-done work, hand-prepared d—was simple enough to please Thoreau, who I am convinced was a nice fellow who confused rustic vacations with life. We did get this one concession, though.

After dinner, freshly dressed, full of food and a warm glow, and thoroughly tired, I wandered over to look at the other cabin along with Jimmy. It was about as far toward completion as ours—that is, the walls were in place and chinked, and the door and window holes were cut—but it looked odd. One of the long walls was higher than the other, and higher than any of our walls. It gave the cabin an odd unfinished look, a hunch-backed look.

We had been issued bubble tents, which can be folded to pocket size and are proof against almost anything, but we had been told not to bring them. Instead we unrolled our beds near the fire and took our chances in the open. I was one of those who drew guard duty, but I was lucky enough to get second hour. I stayed awake, relieved Stu Herskovitz, who hadn't seen anything, and walked for an hour around the camp. I didn't see anything except people ready to go to sleep. I yawned my way through the hour, then got Vishwa Mathur up and went to sleep myself.

There were clouds over the sky in the morning and it was gray through breakfast and cold, but then the clouds began to break into white pieces and move apart and then the sky was clear again and it was bright.

We raised the gable ends of the roof into place and fit the doors and shutters. Then all of us working, we raised the three roof logs into place, the ridgepole on top, the other two below on either side, forming a slope. As we were finishing, somebody looked over at the Marechal cabin and saw what they were doing. They were slanting a roof from the tall wall across the short one. "That's not fair," I yelled. "You're building a shed, not a cabin."

"Ho, ho—too bad," Venie called back. We booed.

We laid the poles that Riggy and Sonja had collected the day before over fitted slabs to make the roof. I was inside the cabin helping to lay the floor. The slabs of wood were laid rounded side down, side by side, to make a reasonably flat floor, what is called a puncheon floor. If we had had the time, we would have smoothed the flat sides, but as it was, we couldn't. The result was a floor that I wouldn't recommend walking on in bare feet unless you have a genuine affection for splinters, but it was a good solid floor. Jimmy was on the roof laying slabs, stuffing moss, and placing poles. A little of the moss filtered through as they worked, but the roof closed in quickly over our heads and when they were done it looked as solid as our floor.

We were clearly beaten by Mr. Marechal's group, which finished almost an hour before we did and then came over and made comments, but we were done before noon, too. I looked over the other building when we were done along with some curious friends and I'll have to honestly say that I preferred our cabin to their shed—better workmanship.

In the afternoon we relaxed with an easy hike and then a swim, this one in suits, not in our clothes. After that, I got out my notebook again and made some more ethics notes—these about an easy one, the philosophy of power.

In effect, the philosophy of power says that you should do anything you can get away with. If you don't get away with it, you were wrong.

You really can't argue with this, you know. It is a self-contained system, logically self-consistent. It makes no appeal to outside authority and it doesn't stumble over its own definitions.

But I don't like it. For one thing, it isn't a very discriminating standard. There doesn't seem to be any possible difference between "ethically good" and "ethically better." More important, however, stoics strap themselves in ethically so that their actions have as few results as possible. The adherents of the philosophy of power simply say that the results of actions have no importance—the philosophy of a two-year-old throwing a tantrum.

We slept that night in the cabin with the door latched, and there was a certain comfort and solidity in sleeping in what we had built. I can also say that the puncheon floor was much harder than the ground had been. Or perhaps I wasn't as tired.

The next day was our last of the excursion and we celebrated it by jumping off the bluff across the river. Then we cleaned up the camp and came home.

It was foggy in the morning, and though the fog lifted, the clouds stayed low and gray over our heads. We set out in one big group this morning with Mr. Marechal leading and Mr. Pizarro bringing up the rear and carrying ropes. Looking at the river, our cabin was on the left and the shed on the right. We had gone upriver for our logs, and Mr. Marechal's group the other way. We went down-river along the river bank, past the point where their skid tracks went uphill away from the river, and then around the long slow bend where the river curved out of sight of the camp. It was a gloomy day but we were in good spirits, chattering as we walked. Our group of six, reunited, walked together.

We picked our way along for more than a mile, sometimes having to leave the river edge and move inland, but making a pretty good pace of it. At last we came out on a sand shoal and looked across at an easy bank on the other side of the river and a broken and easily climbed bluff.

"We're going to have to swim," Mr. Marechal said. He waded out into the water until he was standing in water to his waist about one-quarter of the way across.

Then we were started across with both of our leaders standing guard. The water was cold and it wasn't half as much fun to get soaked as it had been the first time. Our clothes are dirt and water resistant and dry quickly, but believe me, it is far nicer to have them dry off you than to have them dry while you are wearing them. On the far bank I dripped and shivered.

We all gathered on the grassy bank and then Mr. Pizarro and Mr. Marechal splashed and swam across to join us. We climbed through the underbrush and tumbled rock and by the time we reached the top of the bluff, if I wasn't fully dry at least I wasn't shivering.

The bluff was covered with forest, too, but standing on the edge we could see the easy, forest-covered slope on the other side from above, a dark green rising carpet. Then we turned into the woods and didn't come out again until we were standing on the bluff edge opposite our camp.

I didn't like standing on the edge, so I came to the lip on my knees and looked down at the river. It looked a long way down—a drop big enough to kill you, and after that distances are academic. At the base, there looked to be just room to stand and no more. As it had been explained to us, the two ropes would be tied in place here at the top of the bluff and then each of us would whip the ropes around our waists and step off the cliff backward. Looking down, I didn't exactly relish the idea. I moved back from the edge and then got to my feet.

"Well," Mr. Marechal said, "who's going to be the first to try it?"

Jimmy said, "Mia and I will."

Mr. Marechal looked at me and I said, "Yes." I didn't like the thought of doing it, but if it was something expected of everybody and I was going to have to do it eventually, I didn't mind doing it first and getting it over with.

The ropes were tied to trees and then passed around our waists, around the main ropes, and then back around the waists again. Mr. Pizarro and Mr. Marechal demonstrated for everybody how this worked. The ends were finally dropped back between our legs and over the edge of the cliff to dangle just above the river. In effect, what we were doing was putting ourselves in a running loop that slid freely on the rope and then moving down the rope to the river.

At the signal, we stood with our backs to the river, the rope taut between us and our trees. I looked down at the river and sighed, then stepped backward off the edge. I let line pay out for a moment and then stopped it and swung in to come to a halt with my feet against the cliff-face, my body hanging in the loop from the tree on the cliff above. I was almost surprised that it worked. Then I pushed off again and went down another six or seven feet. This was not hard at all, and rather fun. I looked over at Jimmy and laughed. Then, almost before I knew it, I was at the bottom. The bank here was wider than it looked from above, four or five feet wide, and Jimmy and I landed at almost the same moment.

We pulled the ropes free and waved up at the people on top.

"It's easy," Jimmy called.

"It's fun," I said.

The ropes were snaked up again to the top of the bluff as we watched.

Jimmy said, "There's no sense in staying down here. Let's go across the river."

We swam across again and then watched while the next pair rappelled down the cliff. We sat on the last completed part of the cabin, a slab doorstep.

As we watched, I said, "Thank you for volunteering me, by the way."

"I know," Jimmy said. "You're a reluctant daredevil. Aren't you the person who used to crawl around in the air ducts?"

"That was different," I said. "That was my idea."

12

At the end of December, just in time for Year's End, the kids on Trial on New Dalmatia were brought home. Of the forty-two kids who were dropped, seven didn't signal for Pickup and didn't come home. One of the seven was Jack Brophy, whom I'd known slightly in Alfing Quad. I thought about that, and I couldn't help wondering whether I would come back to the Ship in a year. I didn't dwell on the thought, though. Year's End is the sort of holiday that takes your mind off the unpleasant, and besides I discovered something else that occupied my thoughts and gave me something of a new perspective on my mother.

Year's End is a five or six day bash—five days in 2198, which wasn't a Leap Year. In one of the old novels I read, I discovered that before the calendar was reformed, the extra day of Leap Year was tacked onto February. (This was as part of a mnemonic that was supposed to help you remember how many days there were in each month. My adaptation of it for our calendar would go: "Thirty days hath January, February, March, April, May, June, July, August, September, October, November and December." I have a pack rat memory—I even know what a "pack rat" was.) Under our system, the extra day gets tacked onto Year's End.

I was in charge of fixing up our apartment for Year's End. Jimmy and I made a trip down to the Ship's Store on Second Level and picked out a piñata in the shape of a giant chicken and painted it in red, green and yellow. Jimmy's dorm had a piñata, of course, but the impersonality of the dorm took a lot of fun out of Year's End and I had arranged with Daddy for Jimmy to share ours. Between the two of us, Jimmy and I fixed the apartment very nicely and planned the parties we were having on Day Two (for our group of six and some of our other friends) and the big party on New Year's Eve, more or less an open house for anybody who cared to walk in. Since that ticked off an obligation for Daddy, who has no patience for things like party arranging, he was just as glad to have us do it.

In Alfing Quad I had had my friends, but I had almost never brought them home. These days, having people around the place, particularly Jimmy, who lived in Geo Quad, was a regular thing. Daddy has his own patterns of living—in some ways he lives in a private world—and you would have thought that he would object to having strange kids permanently underfoot. I'm sure his life was disturbed but he never objected. In fact, he even went out of his way to make it clear that he approved of Jimmy.

"He's a good boy," Daddy said. "I'm glad you're seeing a lot of him."

Of course, this wasn't too surprising since I had a distinct impression that Jimmy was one of the reasons that we were living in Geo Quad. It certainly wasn't an accident that we had been assigned Mr. Mbele as a tutor at the same time. I even had an impression (partly confirmed) that a talk with the Ship's Eugenist would have shown that Jimmy's and my meeting was even less of an accident, but this didn't bother me particularly because there were moments when I distinctly liked Jimmy and moments when just looking at him made me feel all funny inside.

The partial confirmation as well as another discovery came when I was prowling through the Ship's Records. Every Common Room has a library and there is a certain satisfaction in using them because there is something unique about the size, and shape, and feel of a real physical book, and there is real discovery about running your eye along a line of books and picking one out because it somehow *looks* right. But simple space limitations make a physical collection of all the books that the Ship holds out of the question. So standard practice is to look over titles and contents by vid and then to order a facsimile, a physical copy, if you really want or need one. There are, of course, certain things that most people don't ordinarily look at without some special reason, like Ship's Records, and while I had no special reason beyond curiosity, I was quite willing to look and quite willing to presume upon Daddy's position in the Ship to make it possible for me to look.

"Are you sure?" the librarian said. "They're not very interesting, you know, and I'm not sure that you really ought to be allowed . . ."

I swear that I didn't exactly *say* that Daddy, Miles Havero, Ship's Chairman, had told me that I could and was willing to discuss the point at length with the librarian if he insisted, but I think if you talked to him, the librarian might have had an *impression* that I had said it. In any case, I got to look at the Records.

As I've said, I found some twenty-year-old eugenics recommendations that gave me pause, but it wasn't until I looked up me, or more properly, Mother and Daddy, that I discovered something that really rocked me. I had a brother!

That was a shock. I switched off the vid and it faded away, and then I turned to my bed and just lay huddled there for a long while, thinking. I didn't know why I hadn't been told. I remembered that somebody had once asked me or talked to me or tickled me into wondering about brothers and sisters, but I couldn't place the memory and I never had done anything about it.

Finally I went back to the vid and I found out about my brother. His name had been Joe—José. He had been nearly forty years older than I and dead for more than fifteen years.

I dug around and found out more. Apparently he had been as conscious as I of the lack of creative writing within the Ship. He had written a novel, something I would never do, particularly after I read his. It was not just bad, it was terrible, and it gave me some reason to think that perhaps the Ship just isn't a viable topic for fiction.

In other respects, Joe was much more competent. He'd been regarded as quite a comer in his branch of physics. His death had been the result of a grotesque and totally unnecessary accident not of his own making. He had not been discovered immediately, and when he was it was too late to revive him. His death had apparently bothered my mother greatly.

Now that I knew, I didn't know what to do about it. Finally, in a quiet moment, I approached Daddy and as impersonally as I could I asked him about it.

He looked puzzled. "You knew all about Joe," he said. "You haven't asked about him in a long time, but I've told you twenty times."

I said, "I didn't even know he existed until a week ago."

"Mia," he said seriously, "when you were three you used to beg for stories about Joe."

"Well, I don't remember now," I said. "Will you tell me?"

So Daddy told me about my brother. He even said that we were a lot alike in looks and personality.

I didn't talk to Mother because I didn't know what I could say about it. I cannot really talk to her. The only person besides Daddy that I talked to was Jimmy and he made a comment that was very perceptive, whether or not it was accurate. He said that maybe I hadn't remembered because I hadn't wanted to, at least until now, and that "finding" the record of my brother wasn't as much of an accident as I thought. To tell you the truth, that got me mad at first, and it was my getting mad that later made me think that there might have been some truth to it. The cost was that Jimmy and I didn't speak for two days.

Thinking in psychological terms got me to thinking about my mother, about her keeping me at arm's length and about her becoming unhappy when I was nice to her. I finally came to the conclusion that maybe it wasn't me, Mia, the individual, that bothered her, but just me, the physical fact, and I proceeded on that basis. I can't say that I liked her any better, but we did manage to deal together more pleasantly after that.

Something else changed that winter—what I thought I wanted from life. It came as a direct result of the papers on ethics that Jimmy and I did.

We met in Mr. Mbele's apartment and talked about our conclusions over the usual refreshments provided by Mrs. Mbele. She was a very comfortable person to have around. Very nice. It was our regular Friday night meeting.

My paper was a direct discussion and comparison of half-a-dozen ethical systems, concentrating on what seemed to me to be their flaws. I finished by saying that it struck me that all the ethical systems I was discussing were after the fact. That is, that people act as they are disposed to, but they like to feel afterward that they were *right* and so they invent systems that approve of their dispositions. This was to say that while I found things like "So act as to treat humanity, whether in your person or in that of another, in every case as an end and not as a means merely," quite attractive principles, I hadn't run onto any system that exactly fitted my disposition.

In his discussion, Jimmy took another tack entirely. Instead of criticizing ethical systems, he attempted to formulate one. It was humanistic, not completely unlike some of the others that I had considered. Jimmy started by saying that true humanity was an achievement, not an automatic inheritance. There were things that you could pick at in what he had to say, but his system did have one advantage and that was that he spoke in terms of a general attitude toward living rather than in terms of exact principles. It is too easy to find exceptions to principles.

As I listened, I became increasingly bothered, not by what he was saying, which fit Jimmy's disposition quite closely, but by the sort of paper he was giving. I was the one who was supposed to be intending to be a synthesist, assembling castles from mortar and bricks, only that wasn't what I had done. It came to me then that I had never done it—making pins or building cabins, putting things together, none of this was really in my line, and I should have seen it long since.

I am not a builder, I thought. *I am not a tinkerer.* It was a moment of pure, unheralded revelation.

When Jimmy was done, Mr. Mbele said, "Let's have a discussion. What comments occur to you? Mia?"

"All right," I said. I turned to Jimmy. "Why do you want to be an ordinologist?"

He shrugged. "Why do you want to be a synthesist?"

I shook my head. "I'm serious. I want an answer."

"I don't see the point. What does this have to do with ethics or what we've just said?"

"Nothing to do with ethics," I said. "It has a lot to do with your paper. You didn't listen to yourself."

"Do you mind explaining yourself a little more fully?" Mr. Mbele said. "I'm not sure I follow you."

"After a while," I said, "I wasn't listening to Jimmy's points. I got thinking about what sort of paper he had put together and about what sort of paper I'd put together. We had our own choice. It just struck me that if Jimmy really wanted to be an ordinologist, he would have written a paper like mine, a critical paper. And if I were really cut out to be a synthesist, I would have written a paper like Jimmy's, a creative paper. But neither of us did."

"I see," Mr. Mbele said. "As a matter of fact, I think you're right."

Jimmy said, "But I want to be an ordinologist."

"That's just because of your grandfather," I said.

Mr. Mbele agreed with me almost immediately, but Jimmy had had his aims too long set on ordinology to change his mind easily. It took some time before the sense of it got through to him, but then he doesn't have a critical mind, and that, of course, was the point. I just made it clear that I now intended to be an ordinologist, and Mr. Mbele accepted that. It was easier for me to change, because when I had thought of the future, I had thought of synthesis, but with parentheses and a question mark after. This change of direction was *right* for me, and now when I thought of ordinology there was no question of any kind in my mind, particularly when Mr. Mbele told me that I had the equipment to make a success at it.

And after Jimmy got used to the idea, he finally changed his direction, too. Because, after all, he was creative.

I said, "You're the one who is always thinking up crazy things for us to do. I'm the one who should be thinking why they won't work."

"All right," Jimmy said. "You be the ordinologist and I'll be the synthesist."

I kissed his cheek. "Good. Then we can still be partners."

My change in direction may have been part of growing up. Nearly everything was, or so it seemed these days. I certainly didn't lack for signs of change. One came while Helen Pak and I were down in the Ship's Store looking for clothes.

There is a constant problem of stimulation in living in the Ship—if life were too easy, we would all become vegetables. The response has been to make some things more difficult than they might be. This means that shopping is something you do in person and not by vid.

Helen and I were in the Ship's Store not because our clothes had worn out, but because we'd outgrown them. I'd been growing steadily for the last year, but I hadn't caught up with anybody because they had all been growing, too. I was now having to wear a bra, which was something new and uncomfortable, and my taste in clothes had developed beyond light shirts, shorts, and sandals. That was partly Helen's doing. She had a good eye for clothes and she insisted I make more of myself than I had been.

"You're pretty enough," she said, "but who's going to know it the way you dress?"

For myself, I didn't care—I would just as soon have lived naturally—and I had no great desire to overwhelm the world. However, there were a few people I wanted to be attractive to, so I put myself in Helen's hands, and by God I did come out looking better. Among other things, she got me to wearing pink, which went well with my black hair, and which I wouldn't have chosen myself. It all came as a pleasant surprise.

Helen said, "It's a matter of emphasizing your best points." She was quite modest about it, but she had reason to be proud. Even Daddy noticed, and Jimmy did, too. No compliments, of course, from Jimmy, though I did get them from Daddy.

We were down in the Ship's Store, picking things out, trying them on, piling things up, giggling, rejecting, posing, approving and disapproving. I even found something for Helen that she looked good in—that blond hair and those oriental eyes. She generally knows what looks good on her—it was pleasant to find something for her that she liked.

We were thumbing through the racks when I saw somebody I knew and I said, "Just a second." I waved.

It was Zena Andrus, who wasn't quite as plump as she once had been. She was looking quite excited and apparently trying to find someone. She saw me wave and she came over.

"Hi, Mia," she said. "Have you seen my mother?"

"No," I said. "Is something the matter?"

"Oh, no," she said. "It's nothing bad. I just got my notice. I start Survival Class next week."

"Oh, that's fine," I said.

After she'd gone off after her mother again, Helen and I looked at each other. Time does pass. It was only yesterday.

13

The culmination of Survival Class came when we were Class One and went on a tiger hunt on the Third Level. It, like so much else, was designed to give us confidence in ourselves. There is nothing like hunting a tiger almost bare-handed to give you a feeling of real confidence in yourself. If you manage to survive the experience.

Come to think about it, though, we did manage to survive, so maybe there was a point to it.

By that time, going down to the Third Level with packs was a commonplace. Jimmy and I went down from Geo Quad in the shuttle. I was not in the best of spirits, because I never am before something like that, and I was playing somewhat morosely on the pennywhistle.

Jimmy said, "You're not going to bring that along, are you?"

"Why not?"

"I have to admit that you play fairly well now, but if you play like that you're just going to depress everybody."

I said, "I've got Campfire Entertainment tonight." That was something we had instituted after our second expedition in order to liven camping evenings.

"You're not going to play the pennywhistle, are you?"

"No," I said. "I was going to tell a story. You almost make me change my mind, though."

"Are you afraid?" He wasn't talking about the Campfire Entertainment.

"I can't say I relish the thought of throwing rocks at a tiger," I said, "but I guess I'll get used to it. How about you?"

"I'm always scared beforehand," Jimmy said. "That's why I like to talk or play chess."

We got off at familiar Gate 5 and joined everybody else in getting our heli-pacs. Mr. Marechal was there with a couple of dogs, and he was being assisted again by Mr.

Pizarro, who had grown a red beard to go along with his brushy moustache. They were loading the dogs and food into a carrier. Before we left, Mr. Marechal lined us up and looked us over.

"You understand," he said, "that nobody has to come along."

We all nodded, but nobody made a move to leave.

"Do you have your knives?"

"Yes," we said. That was it, the only weapons we had.

"I want you to understand that at least one of you's going to get hurt, maybe killed. You're going to chase down a tiger, which is about as mean and rough an animal as you're liable to meet anywhere you get dropped on Trial. On Trial, I hope you'll have the sense to avoid anything like that. This time, though, we're going to pick one out, track it down and kill it by hand. You can do it because you're rougher and meaner than it is—at least as a group. I can guarantee you that some one of you is going to get hurt, but when you're done, that tiger's going to be dead. You'll be surprised to find how satisfying you're going to find that. All right?"

The wild areas of the Third Level are about as unpleasant as any you'll find on a planet. The terrain is perhaps not as rugged as you'll find in places on planets, but the wildlife is fully as unpleasant, and that's the major factor. On this final jaunt we were going without the bubble tents and sonic pistols that we would be allowed to carry on Trial and we were deliberately seeking out the most dangerous animal that we have on board the Ship. Something like this is not only a preview of Trial, it brings home to you what is real and what is not, and quite designedly shows you that death is real. You may call it backhanded, but as I say, the point is to lend confidence.

We lifted like a flock of great birds away from the Training Center toward the roof above, and then swept away. We moved across the parkland, looking down on the trees and bridle paths, and then finally across the thorn hedge wall that marked the edge of wild country. At first it did not look greatly different, but then we passed over a herd of broom-tails, our noise and shadows frightening them and sending them careening over the grassland.

Mr. Marechal led the way and Mr. Pizarro brought up the rear with the carrier. We buzzed along in about the same relation to the roof, the ground rising and falling beneath us. With the ground in small hills covered by scrub and occasional trees, and the grassland behind us, we set down at a signal from Mr. Marechal.

When the dogs were released from the carrier, they yapped and strained at their leads, but Mr. Pizarro simply tied them up. We put guards around immediately and then started to make camp. We had just about time to gather wood and set up fires before the great lights in the roof began to fade, the air currents to die, and the temperature to fall. The temperature didn't fall far, but the fire was not for that—it was for cooking and for security.

After dinner, everybody gathered around the fire, including Mr. Pizarro and Mr. Marechal, and I was privileged to give my Campfire Entertainment. For Jimmy's sake, I forbore the pennywhistle and instead told the story that I had prepared and had intended to tell. It's an old, old story called "The Lady of Carlisle."

I waited until everybody was quiet. I stood in front of the sitting people in the wavering light of the fire and began:

This happened a long time ago in a place called Carlisle where they had wild lions. Tigers, as you know, stick to themselves, but these lions lived together in bunches and terrorized the country.

There was a lady living in Carlisle without a bit of family who had been filled with strange ideas by her long-dead mama. She was very beautiful and courted by all the bachelors in the district, who reckoned her a great prize on account of her looks and her money. However, her mama had taught her that to be beautiful was to be special and therefore she shouldn't throw herself away on the first, or even the second, young man who came along. She should wait instead for a man of good family, wealth, honor and courage. "Test 'em," her mama said.

Now since her papa had made a fortune selling stale bread crumbs . . .

"Oh, come on, Mia," somebody said. "Who'd want to buy stale bread crumbs?"

"I'll tell you exactly, Stu," I said. "It was to children to make trails behind them when they went into the woods so they could find their way out again."

* * *

Anyway, her papa had left her enough money that she could afford to sit year after year waiting for her regular Sunday afternoons and her suitors to come calling. She always disqualified them, however, if not on one ground than on another. She spent a good many years this way, sitting in her parlor getting odder and odder, and having great fun turning down suitors on Sunday afternoons. In time, there wasn't a single eligible man in forty miles that she hadn't said "no" to at least once. In fact, it finally got so that when a stranger was in town on a Sunday afternoon, the local fellows would send him out to be turned down. The town was small and this provided them with at least one consistent amusement.

Finally, however, it happened that on one particular Sunday there were two young men drinking in town. One was a lieutenant with a plumed hat and a fancy coat with several shiny medals. The other was a sea captain who had sailed around the world no less than three times, for all that he was young. Both were of quite unexceptionable families, were more than full in the pocket, were men of honor and had medals or other testimony to their courage —and both were single. They were, in point of fact, by a good margin the two likeliest candidates that had ever been in Carlisle. The local fellows didn't even try to choose between them. They simply laid the situation straight out, and both young men had drunk enough to find the idea appealing as well as a quite sensible method of settling the age-old rivalry between the Army and the Navy. So they went off to pay court.

They found the lady at home and quite disposed to receive them. In fact, it put her in quite a flutter. And she turned out to be, even after all these years, as fine looking a woman as either of these well-traveled young men had ever seen. She, on her side, found them both to be exactly the sort of men that her mother had told her to watch and wait for, for she quizzed them quite closely. That they had both shown up on the very same day, however, gave her quite a problem to resolve, and she finally determined to settle it by her mama's method. "I will set you both a test," she said, "and the man that passes it will be the man I wed."

She had a span, which means a pair, of horses and a carriage brought around, and they all climbed in. The young bloods who had sent them in were all waiting in the yard and they followed the carriage down the road, sporting and making bets. The carriage went over the hill and down the road, and in time it came to the den of those lions that had been offending the local people, and there the fair young lady brought the horses to a stop. She'd no sooner done that than she fell rigid to the ground. They picked her up and dusted her off, but she didn't say a word to anybody for upward of a quarter hour. The two young fellows asked the local boys about that and they were told that it was the sort of thing she was likely to do from time to time.

"Well, what happened to her?"

"That's the way the original story goes," I said. "I wouldn't be surprised if it meant that she was a hysteric."

"Now, hush," somebody said, "and let her get on with it."

When the lady came to her senses again, after a manner of speaking, she threw her fan down in the den amongst the lions. That stirred them up, as you can imagine, and they began growling and prowling around. Then, quite satisfied with herself, the young lady said, "Now which of you gentlemen will win my hand by returning my fan to me?"

That really got the local boys to laying bets. The two young men looked down at the lions' den and then at her, back and forth, mulling the situation over and trying to come to a good, fair decision. Finally the lieutenant, who deserved every one of the medals he wore but who'd been taught a thing or two about good sense by his own mama, shook his head and said he thought he'd go back to town and have another pint of beer. He walked off down the road muttering under his breath about women and their silly notions.

Then everybody looked at the sea captain, wondering what he would do. Finally he took off his coat so that it wouldn't get mussed, straightened his collar so that he would look at his best in spite of not being dressed properly, and said, "I'll do it." And he climbed down to the entrance to the lions' den. There were some who said that he had more courage than brains, and there were some who said he'd just had too much to drink. In any case, he disappeared inside the den, and there wasn't anybody who thought he'd ever come back out again.

They strained to see, but it was dark inside the den. They could hear the lions grumbling among themselves. And then the sea captain emerged, looking slightly rumpled, with the fan in his hand.

Well, when the lady saw him coming, she said, "Here I am," and prepared to throw herself into his arms.

The sea captain just looked her in the eye and said, "If you want your fan, you can get it yourself," and threw it back to the lions.

Then he walked back to town and stood the lieutenant the price of a beer, after which each of them went his own way. I don't know if the lady ever got her fan back.

When he had a chance to speak to me privately, Jimmy said, "Isn't it lucky we're out here for a *good* reason?"

In the morning, with the fires out, the lights high and the heli-pacs protected by a bubble tent, we set out casting for tracks behind the leashed dogs. We followed behind in anticipation.

As we walked, I picked up hand-sized rocks and practiced throwing. Att and Jimmy offered criticism.

"Not like that," Jimmy said. "Like this." He threw. It looked smooth and more effective, but I didn't see what was different about it.

"I don't know quite what you're doing wrong," Att said, "but you twitch your whole body when you throw."

"I think I see," Jimmy said. "You keep your forearm stiff and throw with your shoulder. You ought to be using your wrist and your forearm more. Snap them forward."

Venie edged over toward us and said, "Being all sweet and helpless again, Mia?"

I picked up another rock and threw it.

"That's better," Jimmy said.

I turned to Venie and was about to make a sharp comment when the dogs began to yelp. It wasn't their ordinary yapping. It was a more musical note as though they felt they had something to sing about.

"Come on over here," Mr. Pizarro said, and we gathered around.

Mr. Marechal was kneeling by a pug-mark that was a full four inches across and more than that long. He pointed to it.

"There we are," he said. "Look at the grains of sand

in the track. It's not more than two hours old. Probably less," he added as he tested the breeze.

Mr. Pizarro brought the dogs forward and unsnapped their leashes. They sniffed and quivered over the tracks. It was an exciting moment as they poised and then sprang forward, bugling as they went. Now that they were at their business, the noise they made was more businesslike. We set out, trotting after them, up and down the sand hills. I was glad that I was wearing sandals that emptied of sand as fast as they filled.

It is amazing what differences in terrain and vegetation can be produced by slight variances in breeze, temperature and above all moisture. We ran through gullies between sand shoulders, through scrub and around it when we could, going farther from the grassland all the time. The tiger, in all probability, came down to the grassland to hunt, and then returned to the scrub where it had its lair.

There were times when we lost sight of the dogs and kept on their track only by following their sound. Once the dogs lost their scent and had to cast back to find it. Running became an effort. Finally, the dogs' voices lifted and it was clear that they had caught sight of the tiger. We came over the hillside behind them to see the purple hindquarters of the tiger sliding behind a rock projection and the dogs winding around the base of the rocks to find their way up.

If making the Third Level as it is had been a matter of filling an empty volume with rock and dirt, the job would hardly have been worth attempting. Just take a slide rule and figure the number of scoutship loads it would take. The amount of effort is ridiculous. But in point of fact, the Ship is nothing more than a great rock, partly honeycombed, and making the Third Level as it is required nothing more than blasting and chipping rock loose and then pulverizing it to a desired consistency. The great rock jumble into which the tiger was disappearing was nothing more than a giant rain of rock left where it had fallen. It sat there, a red tumble, and the dogs followed the tiger into it.

We pelted down the slope, yelling, and followed the noise of the dogs. There was a trail into the rocks, and then it split, one branch going up and apparently away from the noise ahead, one going directly toward the noise.

Mr. Marechal waved breathlessly at the high trail and said, "Take some of them that way."

I followed him straight ahead. In a moment we came to an opening in the rocks and there, at bay, snarling and striking at the dogs, was the tiger. It was purple, with high-set black shoulders and a wicked wedge-shaped head. Its teeth seemed too large for its narrow face. It was as essentially useless as a soccer professional and as ornamental, elegant and entertaining. We spread around in a circle. The dogs were yapping at its flanks and then darting out of reach as it spun to strike at them. It had been trying to break for the far side of the rock opening, but the dogs never let it get a chance. As we encircled it, one of the dogs was too slow in anticipating the tiger and was knocked into a broken, bloody heap where it kicked slowly.

Then on the rocks above the tiger appeared Mr. Pizarro and four of the kids. They looked down at the noise, blood and dust.

One of them was David Farmer, who was almost as much of a goof as Riggy Allen. He posed picturesquely at the top of the red rock face and, I have no doubt, was about to yell to be looked at, and then he lost his footing. One of his legs doubled beneath him and he went skidding down the face of the rock and landed heavily on the flanks of the startled tiger. It sprang forward and went charging right over the one cringing dog.

The tiger snarled and charged at the circle of people. Unfortunately, he picked me to charge at. Without thinking, I heaved the rock in my hand and whether I threw it properly or not, it rapped him in the muzzle. That was the signal that set off the barrage of rocks, and the poor bewildered tiger spun away again back toward the rock face. Those above threw rocks down at him.

The circle started closing on him, nobody quite daring to dash in and face him alone, but gathering courage from those who moved in beside them. Then working almost like the dogs, Jimmy waved his knife in the tiger's face and it snarled and slapped at it. And then, with the tiger's attention held, Att, whom I'd never have expected to do it, jumped on the tiger's back and slid his knife between its ribs.

The tiger hunched its shoulders and threw Att off, making a wounded cry. Then it was swarmed under by all of us knife-wielding, screaming kids. In just a few seconds it was dead. When we drew away, it lay there in a hot, limp pile, its purple streaked with streams of blood.

David Farmer came out with a badly broken leg. Bill Nieman had a clawed and broken shoulder, the tiger having struck him almost as it died. I had one tiny scratch and a moderately-serious knife gash, not from my own knife.

They were right, too. It gives you a feeling of power to know that you can kill something as alive, as beautiful and as dangerous as a tiger. But the feeling of power can come from pushing a button at the range of five hundred yards. We killed the tiger on his own terms. We chased him on foot, we caught him, and we killed him. That makes you feel able.

You also learn about yourself. You learn about the sight of a claw a foot from your face. You learn about blood. And you learn that a tiger hunt can give you a sore throat.

For whatever positive effects on our minds that the tiger hunt held, nonetheless it cannot be denied that the month of November was a time of growing uneasiness and tension. I was not at my most cheerful. Though my mind told me, as it had for months, that Trial would be the simplest sort of waltz, my viscera refused to be convinced. I tried to act decently to people, but by the end of the month I could hardly bring myself to talk to anybody at all, let alone nicely, and I was sleeping badly. I woke myself screaming one night, something I hadn't done in years.

The worst thing about it was waiting. If I had had a choice, by the middle of November I would have elected to go then, rather than later, simply to have it begun. Instead, I just got more and more edgy.

I even managed to get on bad terms with Jimmy, and that wasn't easy, partly because Jimmy is very good-natured, partly because we were close. Though you are dropped separately, one at a time, after landing you can join forces. I had been intending to go partners with Jimmy, and I'm sure he had the same thought in mind, but our quarrel ended that.

It started with an intransigent remark by me about the Mudeaters. I said what I thought, but I may have overstated my ideas for the sake of emphasis. In any case, Mr. Mbele was moved to comment.

"I thought you'd gotten over that, Mia," he said. "This is a point that's important to me. I don't like this oversimple categorizing. Some of my ancestors were persecuted during one period and held to be inferior simply because their skins were dark."

That was plain silly, because my skin happens to be darker than Mr. Mbele's and I don't feel inferior to anybody.

"But that's not an essential difference," I said. "This is. They just aren't as good as we are."

On the way home, Jimmy tried to argue with me. "Do you remember those ethics papers we did last winter?"

"Yes."

"It seemed to me that you approved of Kant's proposition that we should treat all humans as both ends and means."

"I didn't attack it."

"Well, then, how can you talk this way about the Colons?"

I said, "Well, really, what makes you think that the Mudeaters are *people?*"

"Oh, you sound just like your father," Jimmy said.

That's where the fight started. Jimmy never physically fights anybody, at least he hasn't since I've known him, and I hadn't been in a swinging fight with anybody in more than a year, but we came very close to it then. We ended by going separate ways and not speaking to each other. And I gave Jimmy back his "between mountains" pin. That was Friday night, the night before my birthday.

Jimmy didn't show up on my birthday. That day, when I turned fourteen, was completely flat. So was Sunday. On Monday, we left for Trial.

Part III

A Universal Education

14

There are basically two ways of facing Trial—the turtle method and the tiger method. The turtle method means that you dig yourself a hole and stay in it for a month, looking for no trouble, looking for nothing, simply sitting. The tiger method means that you prowl, investigating, seeing what there is to see. There is no doubt that the tiger method is more dangerous. On the other hand, there is also no doubt that it is more lively. None of our instructors was ever presumptuous enough to recommend one course or the other, and there was no official stigma attached to being a turtle, but certainly there was more prestige in being a tiger. We used to talk about it sometimes. Riggy was determined to be a turtle.

"I want to come home again," he said, "and I've got a better chance if I'm a turtle." It just shows you what happens when a rash boy starts thinking.

Att wouldn't talk about his plans, but Jimmy said that *he* was going to be a tiger. When I was thinking in terms of going with Jimmy, I was thinking of being a tiger. When I decided that I was going by myself, I toned my projected tigerhood down by about sixty percent. Call me a reluctant tiger.

I got up early on the morning of the first of December and went out to get myself breakfast. I found both Daddy and breakfast waiting for me. We ate a subdued meal.

When I was ready to go, Daddy said, "Goodbye, Mia. Your mother and I will be there waving when you come home."

I kissed him and said, "Goodbye, Daddy."

Then I took the shuttle down to Gate 5 on the Third Level. I was wearing sturdy shoes, pants, light and heavy shirt. I had my knife and my handgun, my bubble tent, my bedroll, some personal things, changes of clothes, a green, yellow and red cloth coat, food, and, most important, my pickup signal. This, a little block three inches by two, was my contact with the scoutship. Without it, without a signal from me at the proper time, I might as well be dead, and as far as the Ship was concerned I would be. Silent or dead—either way you didn't come home.

I collected Ninc, my stalwart and stupid pony, and his gear and loaded them on a transport shuttle. Then I helped Rachel Yung do the same, and we went down together to First Level and the scoutship bay. We loaded our stuff and went outside to wait.

There were no bands playing. There were just the scoutships standing quietly over their tubes, men working in a businesslike fashion in the great rock gallery, and us. We were ignored—we might not come back, you know.

One by one the kids came, loaded their stuff aboard, and then came outside to join us in standing around. We weren't making much noise, except for Riggy, who told a joke and then laughed at it, his voice echoing. Nobody else laughed.

We were to leave at eight. At quarter to eight, Mr. Marechal came in, wished us luck, and went on his way. His new class was to have its first meeting that afternoon and I think he was probably already memorizing names.

There were sixteen of us girls, and thirteen boys. David Farmer and Bill Nieman were missing, still recovering from the tiger hunt. They would have another chance in three months, though I didn't envy them the wait at all. Especially after we came back and were adults, and they weren't.

Just before eight, George Fuhonin and Mr. Pizarro arrived. George was quite bright and cheerful in spite of the early hour. I was standing near the ramp and he stopped.

"Well, the big day at last," he said. "I'd wish you luck if I thought you needed it, Mia, but I don't think I have to worry about you."

I don't know whether I appreciated his confidence or not.

Mr. Pizarro went about halfway up the ramp and then turned and waved for attention. "All right," he called. "Everybody aboard."

We took our seats in the bull-pen. Before I went in, I paused at the head of the ramp and took a good long look at home, possibly the last look I would ever have. After we were settled, George raised the ramps.

"Here we go," he said over the speaker. "Ten seconds to drop."

The air bled out of the tubes, the rim bars pulled back, and then we just . . . dropped. George didn't have to do that. He would never have dared to do that with Daddy aboard. My stomach flipped a little and then settled again. George has an odd sense of humor and I think he thinks it's fun to be a hot pilot when he can get away with it.

Att was sitting near me and he turned then as though he had finally gotten up the nerve to say something difficult.

"Mia," he said, "I wondered—do you think you might want to go partners?"

After a moment I said, "I'm sorry, Att, but I guess not."

"Jimmy?"

"No. I think I'll just go by myself."

"Oh," he said, and after a few minutes he got up and moved off.

I guess it was my day to be popular, because Jimmy came over, too, a little later. I was busy thinking and I didn't see him come up. He cleared his throat and I looked up.

Almost apologetically, he said, "Mia, I always thought we'd join up after we were dropped. If you want to, I will."

I still had that final crack of his in mind, the one about being a snob, so I simply said, "No," and he went away. That bothered me. If he cared, he would have tried to argue, and if he'd argued I might have changed my mind.

That crack of his continued to rankle. He had to bring Daddy into it, but Daddy never convinced me. People who live on planets *can't* be people. They don't have any chance to learn how to be, so they grow up to be like those characters I met the first time I was on a planet. And I heard lots of other stories at home. If both you and your father come to an inevitable conclusion based on facts, that doesn't mean he convinced you. I'd made up my own mind. And tell me, is it being a snob not to like people who aren't people?"

The planet that we were being dropped on was called Tintera. Daddy told me that one thing at breakfast, sailing a little close to the edge of the rules. But it was hardly much of an admission on his part since he well knew that I had never heard of the place. Our last contact with the planet, and we were aware of none recently, had been almost 150 years before. We knew the colony was still extant, but that was all. The Council always discusses Trial drops before they are made, and this much time out of contact had given them something to talk about. But the planet was conveniently at hand, so in the end they went ahead. Actually, for them not to, Daddy would have had to make some objection, and speaking practically, he couldn't object because of me.

When we reached Tintera, George began dropping us. We swung over the sea from the morning side and then dropped low over gray-green forested hills. George spotted a clear area and swung down to it. When we came to a stop, he lowered the ramp.

"Okay," he said over the speaker. "First one out."

The order in leaving the scoutship is purely personal. As long as somebody goes, they don't care who it is. Jimmy had all his gear together before we set down. As soon as the ramp was lowered, he signaled to Mr. Pizarro that he was going, and led his horse down the ramp. It was what you would expect Jimmy to do. Mr. Pizarro checked him off, and in a minute we were airborne again.

I began to check my gear out then, making sure I had everything. I'd checked it all before and I had no way to replace anything missing, but I couldn't help myself.

At the next landing, I said to Mr. Pizarro, "I'll go now," cutting out Venie, who sat down again. I grabbed Ninc's reins. I didn't lash my gear on, but just slung it over the saddle, and then walked down the ramp with Ninc. It had nothing to do with Jimmy. I just wanted to go. I didn't want to wait any longer.

I waved at George to show him I was clear, and that I was going, and he waved back as he lifted the ramp. Then the scout rose impersonally away as I held Ninc tightly to keep him from doing something foolish. In just a moment it was gone. Its gray-blue color was almost the color of the overcast sky, so I was never sure when I saw it last.

It left me there, the Compleat Young Girl, hell on wheels. I could build one-fifteenth of a log cabin, kill one-thirty-first of a tiger, kiss, do needlepoint, pass through an obstacle course, and come pretty close (in theory) to killing somebody with my bare hands. What did I have to worry about?

I lived through that first day—the first of my thirty. It was cool, so the very first thing I did was put on my colored coat. Then I slung Ninc's saddle bags, strapped my bedroll on, and swung aboard. I didn't push things, but just rode easily through the forest making a list of priorities in my mind, the things I had to do and the order I should do them in. My list ran like this:

The first thing was to stay alive. Find food beyond the little supply I had. Any shelter better than a bubble tent—locate, or if necessary, build.

Second—look over the territory. See what the scenery and people looked like.

Third—see some of the other kids if things should happen to go that way. I hadn't been dropped a great distance from Jimmy, after all, and Venie or somebody wouldn't be terribly far the other way.

The gravity of Tintera was a shade on the light side, which I didn't mind at all. It is better, after all, to be light on your feet than to be heavy. Or worse—to have a horse with sore feet. The country under the forest top was rugged. There were times when I had to get off and walk, picking my way through the trees or around a rock formation.

I stopped fairly early in the day. Being alone and lonely, feeling a little set at odds by the change from warm, comfortable Geo Quad to this cold, gray, forested world, I was ready to make a fire, eat and go to bed at a time I would have found unreasonably early at home.

I located a little hollow with a spring and set up my bubble tent there. I finished eating by the time dark fell and went into the tent, but I didn't turn on the light. Even in the shelter I felt unaccountably cold, something like the way I had felt in the week after I got my general protection shot. I ached all over. If it weren't the wrong time of the month, I would have thought I was having my period. If it weren't so unlikely, I would have thought I was sick. But I wasn't having my period and I wasn't sick—I was just miserable.

I huddled and I cried, curled up in my bedroll. I hated this wretched planet, I was mad at Jimmy for letting me be alone like this, and I wasn't any too happy with myself. I hadn't expected Trial to be like this. So lonely, so strange. As I'd been riding during the afternoon, I had scared up some large animals. They were ungainly things with knobby knees and square, lumpy heads. When they noticed Ninc and me, they threw up their heads and stared at us. They had the kind of horns that sprout—antlers. After a moment, they bolted in a wobble-legged gallop that carried them crashing into the brush and then out of sight. They knew an outsider when they saw one, and I knew I didn't belong. I didn't get to sleep easily.

The sun was up in the morning. The morning was cold, but the day was brighter. As I moved around and as the sun rose higher, it became almost warm, the heat of the sun and the cold of the breeze balancing each other.

I wasn't feeling much better, but I did keep busy and that took my mind off my troubles. I was recognizing a disadvantage to being a turtle that I hadn't previously reckoned on. It gave me far too much time to appreciate the awfulness of planets in general and the specific failings of this particular place, not to mention the misery of being alone and deserted. I couldn't stand that. I had to be a tiger to occupy my mind, if for no other reason.

So I packed up early in the morning, and I started Ninc in a great widening circle, the most efficient sort of search pattern. The country continued to be rough. If I had been following the line of the land, it wouldn't have been so bad, but trying to go in a spiral was difficult. There were any number of times that I had to get off Ninc and lead him.

At one of these times, a small animal came bounding across my path. I'd seen other small ground animals and gliders in the trees once or twice, but never this close. I pulled my gun the instant I saw it. My first shot with the sonic pistol missed, the sighting beam slapping left, because Ninc chose that moment to toss his silly brown head. I shot again and dropped it this time. A sonic pistol is a nice short range weapon.

I led Ninc over and as I bent to pick it up, there was a loud noise of something moving in the bushes. I turned to look. The thing that stood poised there was nothing short of startling. It stood on two legs and was covered with gray-green hair. It had a square, flat animal mask for a face. I had a feeling that I had just killed its intended dinner.

We looked at each other. Ninc snorted and started backing away. I dropped the reins and hoped Ninc wouldn't run. I took a deep breath to quiet my pounding heart, and then I walked straight at it with my pistol in hand. I yelled, "Shoo. Get out of here," and waved my arms. I yelled again, and after an uncertain moment, the thing shook its head and plunged away.

I turned back and grabbed Ninc, feeling surprisingly good. I'd been thinking about my general misery, my feeling I'd just had a shot. It struck me that if I had a choice, I'd be better off without a gun than without immunization. I'll bet more explorers on old Earth died from the galloping whatdoyoucallits than were killed by animals, accidents and aborigines put together.

I kept going until the light began to fade. The animal I shot turned out to be edible. It's all a matter of luck. In the course of Survival Training I'd had occasion to eat things that were so gruey that I wonder how anybody could choke them down (the point under demonstration, of course, being that the most astounding guck will keep you alive). I'd done better than just find something that would keep me alive, so I hadn't done badly at all. By the time I had eaten, I was thoroughly tired, and I had no trouble at all in falling asleep.

It was the next day that I found the road. I was riding along and singing. I don't like the idea of people who don't sing to themselves when they're all alone. They're too sober for me. At least hum—anybody can do that. So I was riding and singing as I came to the crest of a hill. I looked down and through the trees I saw the road.

I brought Ninc down the hill, losing sight of the road for a time in the trees and rocks, and then coming clear of the welter of brown and gray and green to find the road. It curved before and behind, following the roll of the land with no attempt made to cut the land for a straighter, more even way. It was a narrow dirt road with marks of wagons and horses and other tracks I couldn't identify. There were droppings, too, that weren't horse droppings.

We had come in over the ocean from the west and I knew we weren't terribly far from it now. It seemed likely that one of the ends of this road was the ocean. I, of course, had no intention of going in that direction since I had already seen one ocean and counted that sufficient. My quota of oceans had been filled. It is an axiom that roads lead somewhere, so I oriented myself and headed eastward —inland.

I came on my first travelers three hours later. I rounded a tree-lined bend, and pulled Ninc to a stop. Ahead of me on the road, going in the same direction that I was, were five men on horseback herding a bunch of the ugliest creatures alive. The creatures were making a wordless, chilling, lowing sound as they milled and plodded along.

I looked after them, my heart suddenly fluttering. For a brief moment I wanted to turn and head back the way I had come. But I knew I had to face these locals sometime if I was going to be a tiger, and after all, they were only Mudeaters. Only Mudeaters.

Ninc set into a walk as I kicked him. I got a better look at the creatures as we approached, and it seemed likely to me that they were brothers of the thing I had encountered in the woods the day before. They were quite unhuman. They were green and grotesque with squat bodies, knobby joints, long limbs and square heads. But they did walk on their hind legs and had paws that were prehensile —hands—and that was enough to give an impression of humanity. A caricature.

All the men on horseback had guns in saddle boots and looked as nervous as cats with kittens. One of them had a string of packhorses on a line, and he saw me and called to another who seemed to be the leader. That one wheeled his black horse and rode back toward me.

He was a middle-aged man, whatever middle age was here. He was a large man and he had a hard face. It was a normal enough face, but it was hard. He pulled to a halt when we reached each other, but I didn't. I kept riding and he had to come around and follow me.

I believe in judging people by their faces, myself. A man can't help the face he owns, but he can help the expression he wears on it. If a man looks mean, I generally believe he is unless I have reason to change my mind. This one looked mean, and that was why I kept riding. He made me feel nervous.

He said, "What be you doing out here, boy? Be you out of your head? There be escaped Losels in these woods."

I had short-cut hair and I was wearing my cloth coat against the bite in the air, but still I wondered. I wasn't ready to dispute the point with him, though. I had no desire to linger around him. I didn't say anything. I believe I said once that I don't talk easily in strange company or large crowds.

"Where be you from?" he asked.

I pointed to the road behind us.

"And where be you going?"

I pointed ahead. No other way to go except cross-country. He seemed exasperated. I have that effect sometimes.

We had caught up to the others and the animals by then, and the man said, "Maybe you'd better ride on from here with us. For protection."

He had an odd way of twisting his sounds, almost as though he had a mouthful of mush. It was imprecise, but I could understand him well enough. He wanted me to do something I didn't want to.

One of the other outriders came easing by then. I suppose they'd been watching us all the while. He called to the hard man.

"He be awfully small, Horst. I doubt me a Losel'd even notice him at all. We mought as well throw him back again."

The rider looked at me. When I didn't dissolve in obvious terror—I was frightened, but I wasn't about to show it—he shrugged and one of the other men laughed.

The hard man said to the others, "This boy will be riding along with us to Midland for protection." He smiled, and the impression I had of a cat, a predatory cat, was increased.

I looked down at the plodding, unhappy creatures they were driving along. One of them looked back at me with dull, expressionless golden eyes. I felt uncomfortable to look at it.

I shook my head. "I don't think so."

What the man did then surprised me. He said, "I do think so," and reached for the gun in his saddle boot.

I whipped my sonic pistol out from under my coat so fast that he was caught leaning over with the rifle half out. His jaw dropped. He recognized the pistol for what it was and he had no desire to be fried.

I said, "Ease your guns out and drop them gently to the ground."

They did, watching me all the while with wary expressions. When all the rifles were on the ground, I said, "All right, let's go."

They didn't want to move. They didn't want to leave the rifles. I could see that. Horst didn't say anything. He just watched me with narrowed eyes and made me anxious to be done and gone.

One of the others held up a hand and in wheedling tones said, "Look here, kid . . ."

"Shut up," I said in as mean a voice as I could muster, and he did. It surprised me a little. I didn't think I sounded that mean. Perhaps he just didn't trust that crazy kid not to shoot him if he prodded too hard.

After twenty minutes of easy riding for us and harder walking for the creatures, I said, "If you want your rifles, you can go back and get them now."

I dug my heels into Ninc's sides and rode on. At the next bend I looked back and saw four of them holding the packhorses and creatures, while the last beat a dust-raising retreat down the road.

I put this episode in the "file and hold for analysis" section of my mind and rode on, feeling good. I think I even giggled once. Sometimes I even convince myself that I'm hell on wheels.

15

I was nine when Daddy gave me a family heirloom, the painted wooden doll that my great-grandmother brought from Earth, the one with eleven smaller dolls inside it. The first time I opened it, I was completely amazed, and I like to watch other people when they open it for the first time. My face must have been like that as I rode along the road.

First there were fields. As I traveled along the road and the day wore on, the country leveled into a wide valley and the trees gave way to fields. In the fields, working under guard and supervision, were some of the green hairy creatures. That surprised me a little because the ones I'd seen earlier had seemed frightened and unhappy and certainly had given no sign of the ability to count to one, let alone do any work, even with somebody directing them. It relieved my mind a little, though. I'd thought they might be meat animals and they were too humanoid for that to seem acceptable.

The road widened in the valley and was cut twice by smaller crossroads. I overtook more people and was passed once by a fast-stepping pair of horses and a carriage. I met wagons and horses and people on foot. I passed what seemed to be a roadside camp set between road and field. There was a wagon there and a tent with a woman hanging laundry outside. There was a well and a great empty roofless wooden structure. As I traveled, nobody questioned me. I overtook a wagon loaded heavily, covered bales in the back, driven by the oldest man I'd ever seen. He had white hair and a seamed red face. As I trotted past on Ninc he raised a rough old hand and waved.

"Hello," he said.

I waved back, "Hello." He smiled.

Then, in the afternoon, I came to the town. It was just an uncertain dot at first, but at last I came to it, one final doll. I came down the brown dirt road and rode into the town of stone and brick and wood. By the time I came out on the other side, I felt thoroughly shaken. My hands weren't happily sweaty. They were cold and sweaty and my head was spinning.

There was a sign at the edge of the town that said MIDLAND. The town looked handmade, cobbled together. Out of date. Out of time, really, as though nothing but the simplest machines had been heard of here.

I passed some boys playing tag in the dirt of the street and saw that one of the buildings was a newspaper. There was a large strip of paper in the window with the word INVASION! in great letters. A man in rough clothes was standing outside puzzling the word out.

I looked at everything as I rode through the town, but I looked most closely at the people. There were boys playing, but I saw only a couple of little girls and they were walking primly with their families.

There are a number of things that I'm not fond of, as you know. Wearing pants is one. I'd been glad to have them here because they kept my legs warm and protected, but I wouldn't wear them except from necessity. The men and boys that I saw here were wearing pants. The women and girls weren't. They were wearing clothes that struck my eye as odd, but flattering. However, they were as hampering as bound feet and I wouldn't have undertaken to walk a hundred yards in them. Riding would have been a complete impossibility. I decided then that pants might be preferable to some hypothetical alternatives.

The number of kids that I saw was overwhelming. They swarmed. They played in the street by squads and bunches. And these were just boys.

The only girls I saw were a troop wearing uniforms and hobbling along under the eyes of a pack of guardians. School girls, I guessed.

More than half of the people were kids—far more than half. When I saw a family together, the answer hit me. There was a father, a mother, and a whole brigade of children—eight of them. The family resemblance was unmistakable.

These people were Free Birthers! The idea struck me hard. The very first thing you learn as a child is the consequences of a Free Birth policy. We couldn't last a generation if we bred like animals. A planet is just an oversized Ship and these people, as much as we, were the heirs of a planet destroyed by Free Birth. They ought to know better.

A planet is different enough from a Ship that we wouldn't expect population to be restricted as tightly as ours, but some planning is necessary. There is no excuse for eight children in one family—and this just counted those present and walking. Who knows how many older and younger ones there were? It was sickening immorality.

It frightened me and filled me with revulsion. I was frantic. There were too many things going on that I couldn't like or understand. I held Ninc to a walk to the far edge of town, but when I got there I whomped him a good one and gave him his head.

I let him run a good distance before I pulled him down to a walk again. I couldn't help wishing that I had Jimmy there to talk to. How do you find out what's going on in a strange land like this one? Eavesdrop? That's a lousy method. For one thing, people can't be depended on to talk about the things you want to hear. For another, you're likely to get caught. Ask somebody? Who? You can't afford to be too casual about that, you know. Make the mistake of bracing a man like that Horst and you might wind up with a sore head and an empty pocket. The best thing I could think of was to use a library, and I wasn't any too sure that they had anything as civilized as that here. I hadn't seen anything in Midland that looked like a library to me—only a stone building with a carved motto over the door that said, "Equal Justice under the Law," or "Truth Our Shield and Justice Our Sword," or something stuffy like that. Hardly a help.

There were signs along the road that said how far it was to one place and another. One of the names, Forton, was in larger letters than the rest. I hesitated for a long moment, caught between the sudden desire to become a turtle and the thought of continuing as a tiger. You know, turtles on old Earth sometimes lived for a hundred years or more—tigers nowhere near that long. But after a moment I kicked Ninc and continued along the road. What I wanted was a town large enough for me to find out answers without being obvious and a place large enough to get lost in easily if that turned out to be necessary. I've seen days when I was glad I knew of places to get lost in.

In the late afternoon, when the sun was beginning to

sink through its last fast fifth and the cool air was starting to turn colder, one last strange thing happened. I was, by that time, in hills again, though less rugged ones with slopes that had been at least partly cleared. It was then that I saw the scoutship high in the sky. The dying sun colored it a deep red. The only thing I could think of was that something had gone wrong and they had come back to pick us up.

I reached down into my saddle bag and brought out my contact signal. The scoutship swung up in the sky in a movement that would drop the stomach out of anybody aboard. It was the sort of movement you would expect from a very bad pilot, or one who was very good, like George Fuhonin. I triggered the signal, not really feeling sorry.

The ship swung around until it was coming back on a path practically over my head. Then it went into a slip and started bucking so hard that I knew for certain that this wasn't hot piloting at all, but simply plain idiot stutter-fingered stupidity at the controls. As it skidded by me overhead, I got a good look at it and knew that it wasn't one of ours. It wasn't radically different, but the lines were just varied enough that I knew it wasn't ours.

My heart stopped turning flips and I realized that I was aching all over again. Maybe the gravity was heavier here after all. I shouldn't have expected it to be George. I knew as well as anybody that they just didn't come back for you until the month was up.

But this was one more question. Where did the ship come from? Certainly not from here. Even if you have the knowledge—and we wouldn't have given it to any Mudeater—a scoutship is something that takes an advanced technology to build.

A few minutes later, still wondering, I came across a campsite almost identical to the one I'd seen earlier in the day, down to the well and the high-walled log pen. There were several people already in the process of making camp for the night and it looked so tempting that I couldn't resist. There were a number of sites on the slope and a little road led between them. So I turned off the main road. I originally picked a spot near the log structure, but it stank horribly there and so I moved.

I set up camp and ate my dinner. Before I was done, the wagon driven by the old man who had waved hello to me swung into the camp. There was a tent about thirty feet from me with three young children and their parents. The kids stared at me and the bubble tent and one of them looked ready to talk to me, but their father came out, shot me a look sitting there drinking my soup, and hauled them away.

After dinner a joint fire was started up by the old man's wagon and people gathered around it. I was attracted by the singing. It wasn't good but it sounded homey. Everybody in camp was there, so I thought it was all right for me to come, too. The kids from the next camp were given places in front and their mother, poor helpless thing, was given a stump to sit on. I just stayed in the background and drew no attention to myself.

In a little while, the kids' father decided it was time for their mother to take them back and put them to bed, but the kids didn't want to go. The old white-haired man then proposed that he tell a story, after which the children would go with their mother. In the old man's odd accent, as I sat there in the light of the campfire beyond the circle of people, the story seemed just right.

He said, "This story be told to me by my grandmother and it be told to her by her grandmother before her. Now I tell it to you and when you be old, you may tell it, too."

It was about a nice little girl whose stepmother had iron teeth and unpleasant intentions. The little girl had a handkerchief, a pearl and a comb that she had inherited from her dear dead mother, and her own good heart. As it turned out, these were just enough to find her a better home with a prince, and all were happy except the stepmother, who missed her lunch.

The old man had just finished and the kids were reluctantly allowing themselves to be taken off to bed when there was a commotion on the road at the edge of camp. I turned to look, but my eyes had grown used to the light of the fire and I couldn't see far into the darkness.

A voice there said, "I be damned if I'll take another day like this one, Horst. We should have been here two hours ago. It be your fault, and that be truth."

Horst said, "You signed on for good and bad. If you want to keep your teeth, you'll quit your bitching and shut up!"

I had a good idea then what the pen was used for. I decided that it was time for me to leave the campfire, too. I got up and eased away as Horst and his men herded their animals past the fire toward the stockade. I cut back to where I had Ninc parked for the night. I threw my bedroll out of the bubble tent and knocked the tent down.

There seemed to be just one thing to do, everything considered. That was to get out of there as fast as possible.

I never got the chance.

I was just heaving the saddle up on Ninc when I felt a hand on my shoulder and I swung around.

"Well, well. Horst, look who we have here," he called. It was the one who had made the joke about me being beneath the notice of a Losel. He was the only one there, but with that call the others would be up fast.

I brought the saddle around as hard as I could and then up, and he fell down. He got up again, though, so I dropped the saddle and reached for my gun under my coat. The saddle bounced off him and he went down again, but somebody caught me from behind and pinned my arms to my sides.

I opened my mouth to scream—I have a good scream—but a rough, smelly hand clamped down over it before I had a chance to get more than a lungful of air. I bit down hard—5,000 lbs. per square inch, or some such figure, in a good hard bite—but he didn't let go. I started to kick, but it did me no good. One arm around me, right hand over my mouth, Horst dragged me off, my feet trailing behind.

When we were behind the pen and out of earshot of the fire, he stopped dragging me and dropped me in a heap. "Make any noise," he said, "and I'll hurt you."

That was a silly way to put it, but somehow it said more than if he'd threatened to break my arm or my head. It left him a latitude of things to do if he pleased. There was enough moonlight for him to see by and he examined his hand.

"I ought to club you anyway," he said. "There be no blood, at least."

The one I'd dropped the saddle on came up then, shaking his head to clear it. He'd been hurt the second time and had gone down hard. When he saw me, he brought his booted foot back to kick me. Horst gave me a shove that laid me out flat and grabbed the other one.

"No," he said. "You go look through the kid's stuff and see how much of it we can use and bring it all back with the horse."

The other one didn't move. He just stood glaring. The

last three men were putting the animals in the pen, so it was a private moment.

"Get going, Jack," Horst said in a menacing tone and finally Jack turned away. It seemed to me somehow that Horst wasn't objecting so much to me being kicked, but was rather establishing who it was that did the kicking around here.

But I wasn't out of things yet. In spite of my theoretical training, I wasn't any too sure that I could handle Horst, but I still had my pistol under my coat and Horst hadn't relieved me of it yet.

He turned back to me, and I said, "You can't do this. You can't get away with it."

It was a stupid thing to say, I admit, but I had to say something.

He said, "Look, boy. You may not know it, but you be in a lot of trouble. So don't give me a hard time."

He still thought I was a boy. It was no time to correct him, but it was very unflattering of him at a time when I was finally getting some notice from people to make a mistake like that.

"I'll take you to court."

He laughed. A genuine laugh, not a phony, curl-my-moustaches laugh, so I knew I hadn't said the right thing.

"Boy, boy. Don't talk about the courts. I be doing you a favor. I be taking what I can use of your gear and letting you go. You go to court and they'll take everything from you and lock you up besides. I be leaving you your freedom."

"Why? Why would they do that?" I asked. I slipped my hand under my coat slowly. I could feel the hard handle of the sonic pistol.

"Every time you open your mouth you shout that you be off of the Ships," Horst said. "That be enough. They already have one of your brats in jail in Forton."

I was about to bring my gun out when Jack came up leading Ninc. I mentally thanked him.

He said, "The kid's got good equipment. But I can't make out what this be for." He held out my pickup signal.

Horst looked at it, then handed it back. "Junk," he decided. "Throw it away." He handed it back.

I leveled my gun at them. (Hell on wheels strikes again!) I said, "Hand that over to me carefully."

They looked at me and Horst made a disgusted sound.

"Don't make any noise," I said. "Now hand it over to me."

Jack eased it into my hand and I stowed it away. Then I paused with one hand on the horn of the saddle.

"What's the name of the kid in jail in Forton?"

"They told us about it in Midland," Horst said. "I don't remember the name."

"Think!" I said.

"It's coming to me. Hold on."

I waited. Then suddenly my arm was hit a numbing blow from behind and the gun went flying. Jack pounced after it, and Horst said, "Good enough," to the others behind me.

I felt like a fool.

Horst stalked over, reached in my pocket and brought out my signal, my only contact with the Ship and my only hope for pickup. He dropped it on the ground and said in a voice more cold than mine could ever be because it was natural and mine wasn't, "The pieces be yours to keep." He stamped down hard and it didn't break. It didn't even crack. Frustrated, he stamped again, even harder, and then again and again until it finally came to pieces. My pieces.

Then he said, "Pull a gun on me twice. Twice!" He slapped me so hard that my ears rang. "You stupid little punk."

I looked at him and said in a clear, penetrating voice, "And you big bastard."

It was a time I would have done better to keep my mouth shut. All I can remember is a flash of pain as his fist crunched against the side of my face and then nothing more than that.

Brains are no good if you don't use them.

16

I remember pain and sickness and motion dimly, but Hell-on-Wheels' next clear memory came when I woke in bed in a strange house. I had a vague feeling that time had passed, but how much I didn't know. I had a sharp headache and a face that made me wince when I put a tentative finger to my cheek. I didn't know where I was, why I was there, or why I ached so.

Then, as though a bubble had popped, the moment of disassociation was gone and it all came back to me. Horst and being knocked around. I was trying to push my way out of bed when the old man who had told the story came in the room.

"How be you feeling this morning, young lady?" he asked. His face was red, his hair white, and his deep-set eyes a bright blue. It was a good strong face.

"Not very well," I said. "How long has it been?"

"Two days," he said. "The doctor says you'll be well soon enough. I be Daniel Kutsov. And you?"

"I'm Mia Havero," I said.

"I found you dumped by the camp where Horst Fanger left you."

"You know him?"

"I know of him. Everyone knows of him. A very unpleasant man—as I suppose he be bound to be, herding Losels."

"Those green things were Losels? Why are they afraid of them?"

"The ones you saw been drugged. They wouldn't obey otherwise. Once in awhile a few be stronger than the drug and they escape to the woods. The drug cannot be so strong that they cannot work. So the strongest escape. They be some danger to most people, and a great danger to men like Horst Fanger who buy them from the ships who bring them to the coast. Every so often hunters go to kill as many as they can find."

I was tired and my mind was foggy. My head still hurt, and when I yawned involuntarily it was painful.

Sleepily, I said, "It seems like slavery, drugging them and all."

Mr. Kutsov said gently, "Only God can decide a question like that. Be it slavery to use my horses to work for me? I don't know anyone who would say so. A man be a different matter, though. The question be whether a Losel be like a horse, or like a man, and in all truth I can't answer. Now go to sleep again and in awhile I will bring you some food."

He left then, but in spite of my aching tiredness I didn't fall asleep. I didn't like it, being here. The old man was a Mudeater and that made me nervous. He was nice, being kind, and how could I stand for that? I tried to see my way around the problem and I couldn't. My mind wouldn't rest enough to see things clearly. At last I drifted off into a restless sleep.

Mr. Kutsov brought me some food later in the day, and helped me eat when my hands were too unsteady. His hands were wrinkled and bent.

Between mouthfuls, I said, "Why are you doing this for me?"

He said, "Have you ever heard the Parable of the Good Samaritan?"

"Yes," I said. I've always read a lot.

"The point of the story be that at times good will come even from low and evil men. But there be books that say the story been changed. In the true version, the man by the road been the Samaritan, as bad a man as ever been, and the man that rescued him did good even to such a one. You may be of the Ships, but I don't like to see children hurt. So I treat you as the Samaritan been treated."

I didn't know quite what to say. I'm not a bad person. I thought he ought to be able to see that. I didn't understand how he could think so badly of us.

He added then, perhaps seeing my shock, "I be sorry. I don't think as harshly of the Ships as most. Without the Ships we wouldn't be here at all. That be something to remember in these bad times. So be sure that I won't tell that you be a girl or from the Ships, and rest easy. My house be yours."

The next day he suggested that for my own good I learn to speak so that I would not be noticed. That was sensible. My mind wasn't as foggy now and I was starting to worry about things like finding a way to contact the Ship. To do it, I might very well have to pass as a native. And if I didn't do it, I'd definitely have to pass as a native, damn it.

I didn't fully understand Mr. Kutsov. I had the feeling that there was more in his mind than he was saying. Could he just be doing good to a despised Samaritan? No, there was more. For some reason he was interested in *me*.

We worked on my speech for a couple of hours that day. Some of the changes were fairly regular—like shifted vowel sounds and a sort of "b" sound for "p," and saying "be" for "is"—but some of the others seemed without pattern or sense, though a linguist might disagree with me. Mr. Kutsov could only say, "I don't know why. We just don't say it that way, be all."

After he said that once, I just gave up, but he coaxed me into trying again. He coaxed me, and that was the sort of thing that made me wonder what he had in mind. Why did he care?

After awhile, I began to catch on. I couldn't tell you offhand what all the changes were—I think rhythm was a large part of it—but I did have a good ear. I suppose that there was a pattern after all, but it was one I only absorbed subconsciously. I got better after we'd worked for several days.

Mr. Kutsov said once, "Not like that. You sound as though you be talking around a mouthful of gruel." Not surprising, since that was what he was feeding me, but in any case I was only repeating what I heard.

During those hours we talked. You have to have something to correct and with no textbooks at hand it had to be normal speech. As we talked, I made mistakes and he corrected them.

In the course of our talks, I got a fuller picture of the dislike of these colonists—for some reason, Mudeaters wasn't the word that came into my mind anymore, at least, not most of the time—for Ship people.

"It been't a simple thing," he said. "These be bad times. Now and again, when you decide to stop, we see you people from the Ships. You be not poor or backward like us. When we be dropped here, there been no scientists or technicians amongst us. I can understand. Why should they leave the last places where they had a chance to use and develop their knowledge for a place like this where there be no equipment, no opportunity? But what be felt here be that all the men who survived the end of Earth be the equal heirs of man's knowledge and accomplishment. But things be not that way. So when times be good, the Ships be hated and ignored. When times be bad, people from the Ships when known be treated as you have been or worse."

I could understand what he said, but I couldn't *really* understand it.

I said, "But we don't hurt anybody. We just live like anybody else."

"I don't hold you to blame," Mr. Kutsov said slowly, "but I can't help but to feel that you have made a mistake and that it will hurt you in the end."

After I felt better, I had the run of Mr. Kutsov's house. It was a small place near the edge of Forton, a neat little house surrounded by trees and a small garden. Mr. Kutsov lived alone, and when it wasn't raining he worked in his garden. When it was, he came inside to his books. He used his wagon to make a regular trip to the coast and back once every two weeks. It wasn't a very profitable business, but he said that at his age profit was no longer very important. I don't know whether he meant it or not.

He took my clothes away, saying they weren't appropriate for a girl, and in their place he brought me some clothes that were more locally acceptable. They were about the right length, but they were loose under the arms as though they had been meant for somebody who was broader than I.

"There," he said. "That be better." But I had to take them in a little before they fit.

I had the run of the house, but I wasn't allowed outside. In some ways this wasn't so bad because it rained, it seemed, two days in three, and the third day it threatened to. I kept busy. Mr. Kutsov continued to tutor me until he at last decided that if I was careful I could get by in polite society. When Mr. Kutsov was outside, I prowled around the house.

Mr. Kutsov had a good library of books and I looked through them, in the process finding a number of very interesting things. History—the Losels' natural home was on a continent to the west where they had been discovered one hundred years earlier. Since that time they had been brought over by the shipload and used for simple manual labor. There had previously been no native population of Losels on this continent. Now, in addition to those owned and used for work, there was a small but growing number of Losels running wild in the back country. Most of the opinions I read granted them no particular intelligence, citing their inability to do anything beyond the simplest sort of labor, their lack of fire and their lack of language. For my part, I remembered what Mr. Kutsov had said about the ability of the wild ones to recognize their particular enemies and that didn't seem stupid to me at all. In fact, I was relieved that I had come off so well from my encounter with one that second day.

Geography—I oriented myself by Mr. Kutsov's maps and I tentatively tried to copy them.

And I found a book that Mr. Kutsov had written himself. It was an old book, a novel called *The White Way*. It was not completely successful—it tried to do too many things other than tell a story—but it was far better than my brother Joe's book.

When I found it, I showed it to Mr. Kutsov and he admitted that it was his.

"It took me forty years to write it, and I have spent forty-two years since then living with the political repercussions. It has been an interesting forty-two years, but I be not sure that I would do it again. Read the book if you be interested."

There were politics in the book, and from something else Mr. Kutsov said in passing, I got the impression that the simple, physical job he held was in part a result. Politics are funny.

I found two other things. I found my clothes where Mr. Kutsov had hidden them and I found the answer to a question that I didn't ask Mr. Kutsov in one of his newspapers. The last sentence of the story read, "After sentencing, Dentermount been sent to the Territorial Jail in Forton to serve his three-month term."

The charge was Trespassing. I thought Incitement to Riot would have been better, and that the least they could do would be to spell his name correctly. Trust it to be Jimmy.

So when I got the chance, I put on my own clothes and my coat and snuck into town. Before I came home I found out where the jail was. On the way, I passed Horst Fanger's place of business. It was a house, pen, shed, stable and auction block in the worst quarter of town. From what I gathered, it was the worst quarter of town because Horst Fanger and similar people lived there.

When I came back, Mr. Kutsov was very angry with me. "It been't right," he said, "going on the streets dressed like that. It been't right for women." He kept a fairly close eye on me for several days after that until I convinced him that I now knew better.

It was during the next two days, while I was being good, that I found the portrait. It showed Mr. Kutsov and a younger man and woman, and a little girl. The little girl was about my size, but much more stocky. Her hair was dark brown. It was obviously a family picture and I asked him about it.

He looked very grave and the only thing he said was, "They all be dead." That was all. I couldn't help but think that the picture might have something to do with his keeping me, and beyond that to his keeping me close at hand. Mr. Kutsov was a nice and intelligent old man, but there was something that was either unexplainable or irrational about the way he treated me. He expected me to stay in his house, though he should have known that I wouldn't and couldn't stay. When I ran off, he was unhappy, but then it was pathetic how little assurance it took before things were all right again. I think he was telling himself lies. He must have been telling himself lies. He was already preparing to make another wagon trip. His old-fashioned nature wouldn't allow him to take me along, so quite happily he made plans for me to stay alone in the house until he got back. He told me where things were and what to do if I ran out of butter and eggs. I nodded and he was pleased.

When he went off to arrange his wagon load one afternoon, I went off to town again. To reach the jail, I had to walk across most of the town. Although it was the Territorial Capital, it was still a town and not a city, not as I understood the word. It was a raw, unpleasant day, the sort that makes me hate planets, and rain was threatening when I reached the jail. It was a solid, three-story building of great stone blocks, shaped like a fortress and protected by an iron spike fence. All the windows, from the cellar to the top floor, were double-barred. I walked around the building as I had before and looked it over again. It seemed impregnable. Between the fence and the building was a run in which patrolled two large, hairy, and vicious-looking dogs. One of them followed me all the way around the building.

As I was about to start around again, the rain started. It gave me the impetus I needed, and I ran for the front door and dodged into the entrance.

I was standing there, shaking the rain off, when a man in a green uniform came stalking out of one of the offices that lined the first-floor hallway. My heart stopped for a moment, but he barely glanced at me and went right on by and up the stairs to the second floor. That gave me some confidence and so I started poking around.

I looked at the bulletin boards and the offices on one side of the hall when another man in green came into the hall and made straight for me, much like Mrs. Keithley. I didn't wait, but walked toward him, too.

I said, as wide-eyed and innocently as I could, "Can you help me, sir?"

"Well, that depends. What sort of help do you need?"

He was a big, rather slow man with one angled cloth bar on his shirt front over one pocket, and a plate that said "Robards" pinned over the pocket on the other side. He seemed good-natured and un-Keithley-like.

"Well, Jerry had to write about the capitol, and Jimmy had to interview the town manager, and I got *you*."

"Hold on there. First, what be your name?"

"Billy Davidow," I said. I picked the last name out of a newspaper story. "And I don't know what to write, sir, so I thought I'd ask one of you to show me around and tell me things. That be, if you would."

"Any relation to Hobar Davidow?" he asked.

"No, sir," I said.

"That be good. Do you know who Hobar Davidow be?"

I shook my head.

"No, I guess you wouldn't. That would be a little before you. We executed him six, no, seven years ago. Mixed in the wrong politics." Then he said, "Well, I be sorry, son. We be pretty caught up today. Could you come back some afternoon later in the week, or maybe some evening?"

I said slowly, "I have to hand the paper in this week." Then I waited.

After a minute he said, "All right. I'll take you around. But I can't spare you much time. It will have to be a quick tour."

The offices were on the first floor, with a few more on

the third. The arsenal and target range were in the basement. Most of the cells were on the second, and the very rough people were celled on the third.

"If the judge says maximum security, they go on the third, everybody else on the second unless we have an overflow. We have one boy up there now."

My heart sank.

"A real bad actor. He has already killed one man."

My heart came back to normal. That, for certain, wasn't Jimmy and his trespassing.

Maximum security had three sets of barred doors before you got to the cells, as well as armed guards covering the block and the doors from wall stations. The halls were lit with oil lamps and the light was warm and yellow. We didn't go beyond the first door. Sgt. Robards just pointed and told me what things were like.

"By this time next week, it will all be full in here," he said sadly. "The Anti-Redemptionists be getting out of hand again and they be going to cool them off. Uh, don't put that in your paper."

"Oh, I won't," I said, crossing off what I was writing.

The ordinary cells on the second floor were a much simpler affair and I got a guided tour of them. I walked down the corridor between the ranks of cells right beside Sgt. Robards and looked at every prisoner. I stared right at Jimmy Dentremont's face and he didn't even seem to notice me. He's a smart, lovely boy.

Sgt. Robards said, waving a hand at the cells, "These be all short-timers here. Just a week or a month or two to serve." He jingled his keys. "I be letting them out soon enough."

"Do they give you any trouble?" I asked.

"These? Not these. They don't have long enough to serve. They all be on good behavior. Most of the time, anyway."

When we finished, I thanked Sgt. Robards enthusiastically. "It sure has been swell, sir."

He smiled. "Not at all, son," he said. "I enjoyed it myself. If you have time, drop by again when I have the duty. My schedule be on the bulletin board."

"Thank you, sir," I said. "Maybe I will."

I ran back home through the rain and when Mr. Kutsov got home about an hour later I was dry, dressed in proper clothes and reading a book.

17

Before I scouted the jail, I had only vague notions of what I could do to get Jimmy free. I had, for instance, spent an hour or so toying with the idea of forcing the Territorial Governor at the point of a gun to release Jimmy. I spent that much time with it because the idea was fun to think about, but I dropped it because it was stupid.

I finally decided on a very simple course of action. It seemed quite possible that it might go wrong, but I didn't have a great many days left and I had to bring this off by myself. Before I left the jail building, I looked very closely at the duty schedule, just as Sgt. Robards had recommended.

Mr. Kutsov left in the afternoon two days later, his wagon loaded.

"I be back in six days, Mia," he said. "Now you know exactly what to do, don't you?"

I reassured him, and I stood at the back door of the house as he drove off, dressed in pink because I knew he liked it, and waved goodbye. Then I went back into the house. I sat down and wrote a note to Mr. Kutsov. I didn't tell him what I was going to do because I thought it might distress him, but I thanked him for all that he had done for me. I left the note in the library where he would be sure to find it. I was sorry to do it to him because I knew it would make him unhappy, but I couldn't stay.

Then I went into the kitchen and started getting food together. I picked out things I thought we would need like matches, candles, a knife and a hatchet, and I made up a package. Finally, I changed into my own clothes.

I set out just after dark. It was raining lightly in the night and the spray on my face felt surprisingly good. I carried paper and pencil in one pocket as before for protective coverage. In the other pocket of my coat I had a single sock and several stout pieces of line, and matches.

This is the way I had it figured. The jail was a strong place —bars, guards, dogs, guns and spiked fences. These were primarily designed to keep in jail the people who were supposed to be in jail. They weren't designed to keep people out.

In the Western-cowboy stories I used to read in the Ship, people were always breaking into jails to let somebody out. It was a common thing, an expected part of day-to-day life. But I couldn't imagine that people here made any sort of practice of breaking into jails. It wouldn't be expected, and that was one advantage I had. I knew whom I was up against. I knew the layout of the jail. And when I walked into the jail, nobody was going to see a desperate character intent on busting a prisoner out—they were going to see a little eager schoolboy. I think that was the biggest advantage. People do see what they expect to see.

On the other hand, all I had was me, a not-always-effective hell on wheels. If I didn't do things exactly right, if I weren't lucky, I would be in jail right beside Jimmy, probably on the third floor.

Just before I got to the jail, I stopped and knelt on the wet ground. I took out the sock and I filled it with sand until it was about half full.

I didn't hesitate then. I went right into the jail. There were warm oil lights in only two of the main floor offices. I looked in the first and Sgt. Robards was there.

"Hello, Sergeant Robards," I said, going in. "How be you tonight?"

"Hello, Billy," he said. "It be pretty slow tonight down here. Won't be later, though."

"Oh?"

"Yes. They pick up the Anti-Redemptionists tonight. The boys just went out. You won't be able to stay long."

"Oh," I said.

"How did your paper go?"

I had to backtrack for a moment. Then I said, "I finished it this afternoon. I'll turn it in tomorrow."

"Found out everything you want to know?"

"Oh, yes," I said. "I just came by to visit tonight. You know when you showed me the target range? That been neat. I thought if you had time you might shoot for me like you said."

He looked at the clock. Then he said, "Sure. I be local champion, you know."

"Gee," I said. Just like some of the fatuous boys I know.

We went downstairs, Sgt. Robards leading the way with a lamp. He was picking out the key to the target range when I pulled out my sock. I hesitated for a moment because it isn't easy to deliberately set out to hurt somebody, but then he started to turn his head to say something. So I swung as hard as I could and the sand hit him wetly across the back of the neck. He crumpled. He was too heavy for me to catch, but I pushed him against the door and then managed to get him to the floor without dropping him on his face. I left the lamp on the floor where he had set it.

The weapons room was across the hall. I took the keys from the floor by Sgt. Robards's hand and tried the ones on either side of the one he had picked out for the target room door. The door opened on the second try. I left it open and went back to Sgt. Robards, lying on the floor. I grabbed his collar and his coat and heaved him, then heaved him again and eventually got his dead weight across the floor and into the weapons room. I got out my line and tied his elbows and knees. I emptied the sand out of the sock onto the floor, and then shoved the sock into his mouth. My heart was pounding and my breath was coming fast as I went back for the lamp.

Then I turned to the weapons rack. I took a hurried look over them. There was nothing modern, of course, only powder-and-lead antiques like those in the old books. I'd never fired one, but I understood that they didn't hold still when you shot them—for every action there is an equal and opposite reaction, and all that—so I picked out a pair of the smallest guns they had. I tested the ammunition until I found the right kind of bullets, and then I put the guns and a number of the bullets in my pocket.

I swung the door shut and locked it again, leaving Sgt. Robards inside. I stood then for a moment in the hallway with the keys in my hand. There were ten of them, not enough to cover each individual cell, yet Sgt. Robards had clinked his keys and said that he could unlock the cells. Maybe I would have done better to stick up the Territorial Governor.

My heart pounding, I blew out the light and started upstairs. I eased up to the first floor. Nobody was there. Then I went carefully up the wooden stairs to the second floor. It was dark there, but a little light leaked up from the first floor and down from the third. There were voices on the third floor, and somebody laughed up there. I held my breath and moved quietly to Jimmy's cell.

I whispered, "Jimmy!" and he came alert and moved to the door of the cell.

"Am I glad to see you," he whispered back.

I said, "I have the keys. Which one fits?"

"The key marked 'D.' It fits the four cells here in the corner."

I couldn't see well enough there and I didn't want to light a match, so I moved back to the light and fumbled through the keys until I found the key tagged "D." I opened the cell with as little noise as I could manage.

"Come on," I said. "We've got to get out of here in a hurry."

He slipped out and pushed the door shut behind him. We started for the stairs. We were almost there when I heard somebody coming up. Jimmy grabbed my arm and pulled me back. We flattened out as best we could.

The policeman looked around in the dark and said, "Be you up here, Robards?" Then he saw us and started to say, "What the hell?"

I stepped out and pointed one of the pistols at him. I hadn't loaded it. I had just stuck them in my pocket.

I said, "Easy now. I've got nothing to lose by shooting you. If you want to live, put up your hands."

He put up his hands.

"All right. Walk down here."

Jimmy opened the door for him and the policeman stepped inside the cell. While his back was turned, I hit him with the pistol. I probably hurt him worse than I did Sgt. Robards—a gun is a good deal more solid than a sack of sand—but I didn't feel quite so bad about it because I didn't know him. He groaned and fell and I didn't try to break the fall at all. Instead I swung the cell door shut and locked it.

Then I heard the sound of low voices in one of the other cells and somebody said, "Shut up," quite clearly to somebody else.

I turned and said, "Do you want to get shot?"

The voice was collected. "No. No trouble here."

"Do you want to be let out?"

The voice was amused. "I don't think so. Thank you just the same. I be due to be let out tomorrow and I think I'll wait."

Jimmy said, "Come on. Come on. Let's go."

On the stairs, I said, "Where's your signal? We've got to have it."

"It's not here," Jimmy said. "The soldiers took all my gear when I was arrested. All they have here are my clothes."

"We're in trouble," I said. "My signal is broken and lost."

"Oh, no!" Jimmy said. "I was counting on you. Well, we can try to get mine back."

There was no real comfort in that. We collected Jimmy's coat and clothes and headed into the night. When we were three blocks away and on a side street we stopped for a moment and kissed and hugged, and then I handed Jimmy one of the guns and half the ammunition. He loaded the gun immediately.

Then he said, "Tell me something, Mia. Would you really have shot him?"

"I couldn't," I said. "My gun wasn't loaded."

He laughed and then he asked in another tone, "What do we do now?"

"We steal horses," I said. "And I know where, too."

Jimmy said, "Should we?"

I said, "This man stole Ninc and everything else I have. He smashed my signal, and he beat me up."

"He beat you up?" Jimmy said, immediately concerned.

"I'm all right now," I said. "It only hurt for awhile."

There was a fetid, unwashed odor hanging around the entire district and the rain did nothing to carry the smell away. Instead the wetness seemed to hold the odor in place in a damp foggy stink that surrounded and penetrated everything. There were Losel pens all along the street. When we came to Fanger's place, we slipped by the pen and if the Losels heard us, they made no noise. I had marked the stable and we went directly to it and slipped inside. Jimmy closed the door behind us.

"Stand outside and keep watch," I said. "These are mean, unpleasant people. I'll pick out horses."

Jimmy said, "Right," and slipped outside again.

When the door had clicked shut, I struck a match. I found a lamp and lit it. Then I started along the rows. I found Ninc, good old Nincompoop, and my saddle and I saddled up. Then I picked out a fairly small black-and-white horse for Jimmy and quickly saddled it, and added saddle bags.

After that, I took a quick look around. I didn't find my gun, but I found the bubble tent thrown in a corner—apparently they hadn't figured out how it worked. I found my bedroll, too. The rest of my things I wrote off. I decided that I would have to get Jimmy to share his clothes with me.

On impulse, then, I took out my pad and pencil. I wrote, "I'm a *girl,* you Mudeater!" and hung the note on a nail. I blew the light out.

We led the horses to the street and rode. I didn't regret the note, but I was feeling sorry I hadn't picked a better name than Mudeater. On the way, I asked Jimmy how he got caught.

He said, "There's an army encampment north of here. They've got a scout from one of the other Ships there."

"I've seen it," I said.

"Well, I got caught looking the place over," Jimmy said. "That's where my gear is."

"I've got a map," I said. My copying hadn't come out well so I had reluctantly added a map of Mr. Kutsov's to my package. "We'll go that way."

I told Jimmy about Mr. Kutsov. "He left this afternoon. After he left, I gathered things we'll need. All we have to do is pick them up and get going. The sooner we get away from this town, the better."

When we got to the house, we rode to the back.

"Hold the horses," I said. "I'll be out in just a second."

We both dismounted and Jimmy took Ninc's reins from me. I went up the steps and inside.

"Hello, Mia," Mr. Kutsov said as I stepped inside.

I shut the door. "Hello," I said.

"I came back," he said. "I read your note."

"Why did you come back?"

He said sadly, "It didn't seem right to leave you here by yourself. I be sorry. I think I underestimated you. Be that another child from the Ships outside?"

"You're not mad?"

He shook his head slowly. "No. I been't angry. I think I understand. I couldn't keep you. I thought I could, but I be a foolish old man."

For some reason, I started crying and couldn't stop. The tears ran down my face. "I'm sorry," I said. "I'm sorry."

"You see," he said, "you even talk as you did before."

The front door signal, a knocker, sounded then and Mr. Kutsov got up and moved to answer the door. A green-uniformed policeman stood there in the doorway, his face yellowish in the light of the single candle in the front room.

"Daniel Kutsov?" he asked.

Instinctively, I shrank back. I swiped at my face with my sleeve.

The policeman moved one step inside the house and said in a flat voice, "I have a warrant for your arrest."

I watched them both in fear. Mr. Kutsov seemed to have forgotten that I was there. The policeman had a hard, young face, nothing like Sgt. Robards in any way except for the uniform. Sgt. Robards was a kind man, but there was no kindness at all in this one.

"To jail again? For my book?" Mr. Kutsov shook his head. "No."

"It be nothing to do with any book, Kutsov. This be a roundup of all dissidents, ordered by Governor Moray. It be known that you be an Anti-Redemptionist. Come along." He reached out and grasped Mr. Kutsov by the arm.

Mr. Kutsov shook loose. "No. I won't go to jail again. It be no crime to be against stupidity. I won't go."

The policeman said, "You be coming whether you like or not. You be under arrest."

I had known that Mr. Kutsov was *old*, for all that my father had lived several years longer than he had, and I had suspected that his mind was no longer completely firm, but now at last his age seemed to catch up with him. He backed away and said in a voice that shook, "Get out of my house!"

The policeman took another step inside. I was fascinated and frozen. Why exactly, I cannot say, but I couldn't speak or move. I could only watch. It is the only time in my life that this has ever happened and since then I have felt I understood the episode on the ladder with Zena Andrus a little better. But in my case, it wasn't just fear. Events got out of control and rushed past me, something like watching a moving merry-go-round and wanting to jump on, but never quite being able to decide to go.

The policeman lifted his gun from its holster and said, "You be coming if I have to shoot."

Mr. Kutsov hit the policeman and in retaliation the policeman clubbed Mr. Kutsov to death while I watched. The policeman hit Mr. Kutsov once and if he had fallen that would have been the end of it, but he didn't and the policeman hit him again and again until he did fall.

I must have screamed, though I have no memory of it. Jimmy says I did and that's what brought him. In any case, the policeman looked up from Mr. Kutsov and stared right at me. I remember his eyes. He raised the gun he'd hit Mr. Kutsov with so many times and pointed it at me.

Then there were three reports at my elbow, one on the heels of the next. The policeman stood for a moment, balanced, and then the force of life keeping him upright was gone, and he fell to the floor. He never fired his gun. In one instant my life was his to take, and in the next he was dead.

I passed him by without even looking and bent over Mr. Kutsov. As I bent down beside him, his eyes opened and he looked at me.

I was crying again. I held him and cried. "I'm sorry," I said. "I'm sorry."

He smiled and said faintly, but clearly, "It be all right, Natasha." After a minute, he closed his eyes as though he were terribly tired. Then he died.

After another minute, Jimmy touched my arm. I looked up at him. His face was pale and he didn't look at all well.

"There's nothing we can do. Let's leave now, Mia, while we can."

He blew out the candle. As we mounted our horses, it continued to rain.

18

We rode north through the night rain for hours. At first we stuck to the road, but when the ground started to rise and the country to roughen we cut off the road and followed a slow route of our own into the hills and forest. It was a tiring, unpleasant journey. The rain came down steadily until we were wet inside our coats. When we left the road, there were many times when we had to dismount and lead our horses through wet, rough brush that scratched and slapped. The noise of the cold wind was shrill as it blew through the trees and tossed branches. The only satisfaction that we had was knowing that with the rain as it was, following us would be close to impossible. Considering the route we took, following us would have been difficult at the best of times.

At last we decided to stop, feeling ourselves beyond pursuit and knowing ourselves within another day's ride of the military camp where Jimmy's gear might be. We were both tired and bruised by our experience. Jimmy had had no practice in killing people and no stomach for it. The books I used to read made killing seem fun and bodies just a way of keeping score, but death is not like that, not to any normal person. It may seem neat to point a gun, and keen to pull a trigger, but the result is irrevocable. That policeman couldn't get back up again to play the next game, and neither could Mr. Kutsov. They were both dead for now and always. That fact was preying on both Jimmy and me.

I've always wondered what it would be like to be a spear carrier in somebody else's story. A spear carrier is somebody who stands in the hall when Caesar passes, comes to attention and thumps his spear. A spear carrier is the anonymous character cut down by the hero as he advances to save the menaced heroine. A spear carrier is a character put in a story to be used like a piece of disposable tissue. In a story, spear carriers never suddenly assert themselves by throwing their spears aside and saying, "I resign. I don't want to be used." They are there to be used, either for atmosphere or as minor obstacles in the path of the hero. The trouble is that each of us is his own hero, existing in a world of spear carriers. We take no joy in being used and discarded. I was finding then, that wet, chilly, unhappy night, that I took no joy in seeing other people used and discarded. Mr. Kutsov was a spear carrier to the policeman, a spear carrier who asserted himself at the wrong moment, and then was eliminated. Then the policeman suddenly found himself demoted from hero to spear carrier and his story finished. I didn't blame Jimmy at all. If I had been able to act, I would have done as he had, simply in order to stay alive. And Jimmy didn't see the policeman as a spear carrier. Jimmy was always a more humane, open, warmer person than I, and it cost him greatly to shoot the man. I admit that the man was still a spear carrier to me, but nonetheless both deaths bothered me.

If I had the opportunity, I would make the proposal that no man should be killed except by somebody who knows him well enough for the act to have impact. No death should be like nose blowing. Death is important enough that it should affect the person who causes it.

We made our camp at last. We attended to the horses as best we could, sheltering them under the lee of some trees. Then we set up the bubble tent, pitching it on a level spot. Jimmy went after the saddle bags, bedroll and saddles while I finished with the tent. We stowed things away in all the corners and that left just enough room to stretch out the bedroll.

We were soaking wet. The rain made a steady pitter on the bubble and we could hear the rising and falling shrill of the wind outside. We left the light on until we had taken off all our clothes. Undressing was difficult because of the lack of room and a cold saddle is an unpleasant place to put your bare bottom. Jimmy was more hairy than I had ever suspected. Finally we spread our clothes out to dry, turned out the light and got into bed.

The bed was cold and so was I, and I put my arms around Jimmy. His skin was cold too, at first, but he was comfortingly solid. I needed comfort. I think he did, too.

I touched his cheek with my hand. "I'm not mad any more, you know."

"I know," he said. "I didn't think you were. I'm sorry,

anyway. I've got to take you as you are, even when you say stupid things. You can't help what you think."

He kissed me gently. I cooperated with the kiss.

"I'm glad you came for me," Jimmy said. He moved his hand up the length of my back and across my shoulders. It gave me shivers. "Are you cold?" he asked.

"No," I said. "Did you think I'd come?"

"I hoped, I guess. I'm glad you came. I'm glad it was you, Mia."

He shifted and then put his hand on my breast. I put my hand over it.

"You're beautiful," he said.

"Why didn't you ever say that before?" We'd kissed and done some other things, and I'd assumed he *liked* me, our differences aside, but he'd never said he liked the way I looked. I pressed the hand on my breast and I kissed his cheek and his mouth. I felt safer and warmer and more secure than I had in days. Oh, he was good to hold on to.

I let his hand go free and he let it wander. "I never dared," he said. "You'd have used it against me. Hey, you know, that's funny. When I touch this one, I can feel your heart beat and when I touch this one, I can't."

"I can feel yours, too," I said. "Thump, thump, thump, thump, thump."

I kissed my hand and let it touch his face. Kissed his face.

"You do like the way I look?"

"Of course. You are beautiful. I like the way you look. I like your voice—it doesn't squeak. I like the way you feel." He moved his hand. "I like the way you smell." His face moved in my hair.

"It's odd, isn't it?" I said. "I don't think I'd like this if I didn't like the way you smell, and I never thought about it before. What do you mean I'd have used it against you?"

He said slowly, "You'd have said something snippy. I just couldn't take the chance."

I never realized before that he was that vulnerable, that something I might say could hurt him. "I say things sometimes," I said, "but never if you told me that."

He kissed my breast, moved his tongue experimentally over the nipple, and it swelled without my willing it. I thought my heart would become too large and break with the surge it made. We moved tightly into each other's arms and kissed deeply. I held Jimmy to me and my knees moved apart for him.

Sex in the Ship is for adults. If you are an adult, then it doesn't matter particularly whom you do sleep with. Nobody checks. But just as anywhere, people tend to be fairly consistent, fairly discriminating about what they do, at least the people I'm likely to be friends with. I don't think I'd want to know well the sort of person who makes notches on the end of her bed, the sort of person who takes sex wherever he can, the sort of person who takes sex lightly. I can't do any of those things. I'm much too vulnerable. I enjoy making love, but I couldn't do it if I didn't have confidence and trust, liking and respect, beyond the basic fact of physical attraction. I had known Jimmy for nearly two years and been attracted to him for nearly that long, but making love with him was something that I could not have done much sooner than I did.

In a sense, Jimmy and I were intended for each other. Whether we had met or not, whether we had liked each other or not, we still would have had at least one child, and probably more. But that is a mechanical process that has nothing to do with living together and loving. It was nice that knowing each other we could love. The passion of age fourteen is not an ultimate, but age fourteen does not last forever and passions do grow.

Sex in the Ship is for adults. We were not officially adults, but we needed each other then, and I was no longer quite the stickler for rules that I once had been. We needed each other then and it was the proper time. If we didn't make it back to the Ship, who would ever care? And if we made it back to the Ship, we would be officially adults and the question would be irrelevant.

So we made love there in the dark with the rain falling outside, safe in each other's arms. Neither of us knew what we were doing, except theoretically, and we were as clumsy as kittens. It was something of a botch, too, in an extremely pleasant way. At the climax there was simply a hint of something we couldn't reach.

We lay quietly and after a few minutes Jimmy said, "How was that?"

I said, somewhat sleepily, "I think it takes practice."

Just before I fell asleep, I said, "It was comforting, though."

* * *

The next night, we left our horses tied in the trees. We were miles from our camp of the previous night. We had arrived on the hillside in the late afternoon, then crawled through the woods to look over the army complex. Below us, in the gold light, was a town cupped in a bowl between the hills. On our side of the town was an enfenced army base, patrolled like all army bases by regular guards, and on what must have been their parade ground was sitting the scoutship.

"I got curious," Jimmy said. "It seemed strange to me that they should have a scoutship. I snuck out there to take a look and I got careless and got caught."

Buildings framed the parade ground on three sides. The enclosed short side was nearest to our vantage point high above. The open short side was at the far end of the parade ground nearest to the town. There were some few trees mixed among the buildings. The fence was linked iron spikes, and it completely circled the camp. It was perhaps a hundred feet from the fence to the nearest building.

Jimmy pointed through the leaves. "See the two-story building just below there? That's their headquarters. That's where they took me until the police came from the town. That's where we ought to look for my gear."

The building was red brick with a gray slate roof and it dominated the end of the parade ground. Most of the other buildings in the camp were only single story—barracks and stables and the like—and the other two-story buildings were not as large.

We timed the guard on his rounds. It took him twenty minutes to walk from one end of his post to the other in the slow, casual way of guards killing watch hours. Sometimes he reached the end of his post at the same time as the guard from the adjacent post and they stopped and talked.

I said, "We couldn't count on more than twenty minutes if we hit the guard."

"No," Jimmy said. "We'll do best if we can sneak over without being seen."

After we had checked everything, we crawled back out of sight on our knees, and then we went back to our horses, where we ate a cold meal. Jimmy's mistake before had been that he had entered the camp too early, when people were still about and the guards were alert. We were both tired from riding all day and we went to sleep until well after dark. I woke when Jimmy shook me.

"Come on," he said. "It's time to go."

We took our time picking our way down the dark slope, making as little noise as possible. I was glad to be with Jimmy. We did make a team, and with Jimmy along I felt something more of an effective hell on wheels than I did by myself. It was twenty feet from the edge of the brush to the fence, the space cleared. We crouched there in the brush, able to see the fence and barely able to make out the outline of the two-story headquarters building beyond.

"Shh," Jimmy whispered, holding my arm. "There's the guard."

We waited until he had passed and then we ran low to the iron fence. Jimmy gave me a boost and I grasped the spikes, the points sharp under my thumbs. He pushed me up and I got a knee on the top bar between the spikes. I paused there for a brief moment and then I jumped clear on the far side, ripping my pants on one of the spikes. I looked both ways to see if the noise of my landing had alerted anyone, and then I turned back to the fence. I put both hands through the bars and cupped them for Jimmy's foot. He stepped into my hands and I pushed up. He got his other foot on the top bar and then sprang over. He landed on his feet with a thud that was noisier than mine and then without pausing we ran for the nearest tree, where we stopped for a moment before we ran to the shadow of the headquarters building.

There was a partial cloud rack overhead and the light varied from dim to worse as the clouds moved by. We moved to the end of the building, Jimmy preceding, and there we stopped while Jimmy put his head around. Then we went around the corner and I could see the silent and empty parade ground and one or two night lights in the buildings on its edge. I could barely see the scoutship squatting in the dirt. We checked again at the next corner and then we ghosted along the front of the building.

"There should be one man on night duty," Jimmy said. "The office is just to the right inside the door."

He pointed up to a window over our heads. I could see light there and shadows on the ceiling. We went up the steps, flattened in the doorway while Jimmy and I took out our pistols and then we went through the door. The hall was dark and quiet. The door to the room on our right was open and light was streaming out.

Jimmy went through the door, gun in his hand, and said, "Put your hands up."

There was just one man behind the desk and his head had been nodding. He came awake with a start and looked at us.

"You again," he said.

It was a chubby little man, not particularly competent looking, dressed in a green uniform with red markings and red braided epaulets on the shoulders. The room was large and contained a number of desks, one on the side of the door and two on the side opposite. There were several offices behind the desks. The lamp turned low on the officer's desk was the only light.

"Keep your voice down," Jimmy said. "I'll shoot you if I have to. Now where is my gear?"

The officer said, "I don't know," but his voice was uncertain. He was startled and still half asleep.

Jimmy nodded to me to go around the desk. I took out my knife and the man's eyes watched me. He tried to move his chair, but I pushed at the back of it so that he couldn't rise.

"Careful there, boy," he said, his voice rising.

I took the point of the knife and I pricked his ear. It didn't even bring a drop of blood.

"Where is the gear?" I asked.

The man choked and cleared his throat. "Not in any one place. I don't know where everything be."

"Where are my saddle bags?"

He shrugged helplessly. "In the stables, I suppose."

"What about the stuff that was in them?"

Eagerly he said, "They been fooling with that in the mess. Some of the boys."

"Take us to the mess."

"I can't show you," the officer said. "I can't leave my post."

I tickled his epaulet with my knife. "You'll have to."

"Don't cut that!" he said in agitation.

"Show us." I raised the knife.

"Very well," he said helplessly. "It be on the second floor."

I took the lamp from the desk and Jimmy prodded the officer to his feet. He led us out into the corridor and then up the stairs. We walked down another corridor on the second floor, our footsteps echoing hollowly. At last we came to a door and the pudgy little officer unlocked it and threw it open.

"There," he said.

The lamp light showed a silent room with a great long white-cloth covered table surrounded by ranks of chairs. There was a lounge and a great fireplace.

"Show us," Jimmy said.

The officer led the way over to the lounge. There was a dart board there and newspapers and games, and on one of the tables Jimmy's chess board. I recognized it. I don't know who Jimmy had been intending to play with. Some of his other things were scattered about.

"Jimmy," I said, in a voice filled with dread. "I don't see it."

Jimmy took a quick look himself. "No," he said. He turned to the officer. "We're looking for a little block-sized object about so by so. Have you seen it?"

"No," said the officer. "I haven't been playing with your stuff."

I poked him with the knife. "Are you sure?"

With some asperity he said, "I be sure! I don't remember seeing anything like that."

"What are we going to do now?" I said to Jimmy.

"I don't know. It must be somewhere, but I don't know where we could look."

I was really beginning to worry as I hadn't before. We couldn't run loose around this place for very long without being caught, and if we didn't find the signal we would never get home at all.

We went back downstairs and into the office. It was then that I was suddenly struck by an idea.

"There's the scoutship outside," I said. "We could take that! If these people can fly it, we can."

The chubby officer said, "No you won't! You Ship people think you have everything, but we'll show you. We've got a little ship of our own now and we be tougher people than you. You won't take that ship."

"No need," Jimmy said. He picked a paperweight off one of the desks. It was his missing signal. He turned with it to the officer. "I thought you hadn't seen this . . . ?"

"Oh, be that what you wanted? I never noticed it."

The officer's back was turned to me. I took out my

pistol and somewhat squeamishly hit him with it under the ear.

"Come on, Jimmy," I said. "If you've got the signal, let's go."

We went out into the night again. We went around the corner of the building toward the back, but then Jimmy pulled me to a stop. He put his mouth to my ear.

"It's the guard. See?" He pointed.

We crouched there in the lee of the building as the guard paced slowly down the fence toward the other end of the building. Then, all of a sudden, the night was split with a shout.

"Guards! Guards!"

It came from the front of the building. The guard on patrol here swung around at the shout, but like a good soldier he didn't leave his post. He simply cut off our retreat.

"Come on," Jimmy said. We slipped along the buildings parallel to the fence. The shouting continued. Jimmy stopped by a small building at the corner of the square, a building set apart. From there we could see in two directions along the fence.

Jimmy said, "Couldn't you have hit the officer harder?"

"I don't like to hit people."

There was all sorts of hoorah going on. We couldn't see it, but we could hear it.

Then I said, "Jimmy, do you know what this building is?"

"No."

"It's a powder house. See the danger sign? Let's create a diversion. Let's blow up the scoutship."

Jimmy smiled. He reached out and touched my hair for just a second.

We found the door and Jimmy broke the lock with his pistol butt. Whatever noise we made was amply covered. We piled inside and Jimmy swung the door shut behind us. There were small windows in the front of the building and through them we could see soldiers running about on the parade ground and lamps and torches being lit. Guards ran by on their way to reinforce the fences. It began to seem a very good thing to be inside. In the light of the torches we could see the scoutship with its ramp down. Men formed in a line on the parade ground, a formation. Then they were being talked at.

Jimmy said, "They'll probably be searching the buildings soon."

I found a small powder keg and set a fuse about five feet long in it. The principle was simple enough. The only thing I wasn't sure was how long the fuse would take to burn. That was a chance.

Jimmy and I talked about what we would do while the men on the far side of the parade ground were being given their orders. It was almost like playing Paper-Scissors-Rock, where you both decide what you're going to do and then reveal at the same time. We'd make our plans, and they would make theirs, and then we'd see who won. I gave Jimmy my gun and he loaded it. We then slipped out the back door again. I trailed another fuse out the door behind us.

I said, "Start firing in forty seconds."

Jimmy said, "Yes," and he slipped away along the buildings.

I crouched in the dark with my back to the fence and took out a match. I shielded it carefully and scratched it on the lighter board. It didn't light and so I struck it again. It flared into light and I touched it to the fuse end. The fuse began to sputter and I waved out the match, lifted the small powder keg and went around the side of the building.

Then down the way Jimmy opened up over the heads of the men in formation. They fell to the ground and began to fire back. I trusted Jimmy to keep his head down.

I didn't hesitate. I plunged straight out onto the parade ground. The keg was heavy and I concentrated simply on running for the scoutship ramp. I don't know if anybody saw me or if I was shot at. I just concentrated on running. As I got to the ramp, the powder house blew up in a great flash of light and noise. Pieces of the building flew into the air. The concussion knocked me to my knees, but I got up again immediately and dashed up the ramp.

Inside the scoutship, I didn't hesitate but went immediately to the control room. I set the keg on the pilot's seat, right next to the main panel. Through the dome I could see men and confusion everywhere. Nobody was firing now. Fire from the powder house had spread to one of the barracks and men were running for water.

I lit another match and touched this fuse off. Then I went down the stairs as fast as I could. Outside, I looked back at the scoutship. Great shadows and flickerings were reflected on the dull metal.

Somebody ran into me then and said, "Watch out there," and ran on. The parade ground was a crisscrossing of men and nobody even noticed me.

I was beginning to despair, to think I'd have to go back and relight the fuse, when I felt a dull *whump*. These people were not going to use the scoutship again.

I slipped between the buildings, out of the parade ground, and out of the light and noise. The fences were deserted. It took me several difficult minutes to climb over. Then I climbed through the tree- and brush-covered hillside slowly.

At the top, very near the place from which Jimmy and I had made our observations in the afternoon, I looked back at the army compound. The fire had spread to a second building and men like ants rushed around. I watched for a few minutes and then I went on.

Jimmy was waiting by the horses when I got there.

"Are you all right?" I asked.

"Yes. I'm all right. But I dropped the signal."

I gasped.

"I'm just kidding," he said.

I sat down on a rock and spread my torn pant leg. Somewhat gingerly, I touched my leg.

"What's the matter?"

"Oh, I cut myself going over the fence the first time."

"That's too bad," Jimmy said. He took a look himself. "It's not too bad. Do you want me to kiss it and make it well?"

"Would you?"

Jimmy stood up then and looked toward the light-streaked sky. He waved at it. "You know, that's an awful lot of trouble to make simply because you can't bring yourself to hit somebody."

19

The final morning on Tintera was beautiful. We and the horses were in a rock-enclosed aerie high on a mountainside near the coast. In the aerie were grass and a small rock spring, and this day, the final day, was bright with only a few piled clouds riding high in the sky and warm enough that we could put our coats aside. We had eaten breakfast and packed one final time, and now we were just sitting quietly in the sun.

Looking from the top of the rocks, you could see over miles of expanse. On one side, the mountain dropped and beyond it you could see miles of ocean, gray flecked with white, see part of the coast and shore, brown cliff and dark wet rocks and a narrow beach, see occasional birds gliding on the wind and imagine their calls. Turning your gaze inland, you could see upland meadows in the foreground and mountains much like this one beyond, making a line along the coast. Farther inland were lower hills and curving valleys, blending together, all covered with another rolling sea of trees, a sea at close range made of varying shades of gray and green, but at a distance an even olive.

Down there, under that sea, were all sorts of things—wild Losels and men hunting us. We had seen the Losels and they had seen us; they had gone their way and we had gone ours. The men hunting us we hadn't had a glimpse of for four days, and that last time they hadn't even seen us. Also under that sea might be some of the other kids from the Ship, but we hadn't seen them at all.

Early in the morning we triggered the signal. It was six hours before the ship came. We passed the time quietly, keeping one eye on guard, talking. There was a tiny little animal chittering and nipping around the rocks and I tossed it some food.

We went aboard when the scout came, and put our

horses away. Mr. Pizarro was there, checking us back aboard. We were the sixth and seventh.

I said to Jimmy, "I'm going upstairs and talk to George."

"All right," he said. "I'll tell Mr. Pizarro what happened to us."

We thought they ought to know. Certainly things had been more adventurous for us than anything we thought might have been counted on during Trial. So I went upstairs to George.

"Congratulations, Adult," he said when he saw me. "I knew you'd make it."

"Hello, George," I said. "Tell me, have you had any trouble in picking up people so far?"

"No trouble," he said, "but I have been worrying. Look." He waved his hand at the grid he was using as a guide for his pickups. There were nowhere near twenty-nine lights. I counted them and there were twelve.

"The last light came on two hours ago," George said. "I'm afraid a lot of people aren't going to get picked up."

I told him a little of what had happened to us. I stayed upstairs while we dropped down and picked up Venie Morlock, and then another double pickup. Then I went down and sat with Jimmy.

I said, "There are only six more pickups to make. Look how few of us there are."

"Is it that bad?" Jimmy said. "I wonder what the Council will say."

There were only ten of us aboard now. Jimmy and I and Venie were safe, but Att and Helen and Riggy were not yet aboard.

All of a sudden, George called for attention over the speaker. "All right, kids—shut up and listen. One of our people is down there. I didn't get close enough to see who, but whoever it is is being shot at. We're going to have to bust him out. I'll give you two minutes to get your weapons and then I'm going to buzz down and try to get him out. I want all of you outside and laying down a covering fire."

Some of the kids had their weapons with them. Jimmy and I hopped for the gear racks and got out our pistols. I loaded mine for the first time. There were eleven of us, including Mr. Pizarro, and four ramps to the outside. Jimmy and I and Jack Fernandez-Fragoso stood by one ramp. Then George swooped down, touched light as a feather, and dropped all four ramps.

We dived down the ramp. Jack went left, Jimmy center, and I to the right. We were at the top of a wooded slope and my momentum and the slant put me right where I wanted to be—flat on my face. I rolled behind a tree and looked over to see Jimmy almost hidden by a bush.

Here, hundreds of miles from where we had been picked up, it was misting under a familiar rolled gray sky. From the other side of the ship and from below there was the sound of gunfire. Our boy was pinned down fifty yards below us among some rocks that wouldn't have sheltered properly anything larger than the tiny animal I had been feeding earlier in the day. The boy in the rocks was Riggy Allen and he was fighting back. I saw the sighting beam of his sonic pistol slapping out. About thirty feet toward us up the slope was the body of Riggy's horse. Riggy turned his head and looked at us.

Riggy's attackers, the ones that weren't separated now on the far side of our ship, were dug in behind trees and rocks, at least partly hidden from Riggy, as he was partly hidden from them. From where we were, though, they could be seen more clearly.

I took all this in in seconds, and then I raised my pistol and fired, aiming at a man firing a rifle. The distance was greater than I had counted on and the shot plowed earth ten feet short, but the man jerked back.

This was the first time I had fired the pistol. It bucked in my hand and it made a considerable noise. In a sense, there was a certain satisfaction in it, though. A sonic pistol is silent and if you missed the most you could expect was a sere and yellow leaf. This gun made enough noise and impact in your hand that you knew that you were doing something and a miss might raise dirt, or make a whine, or rip a tree—enough to make the steadiest man keep his head down.

I aimed higher and started to loft my shots in. Jimmy was doing the same thing, and the net effect was enough that the firing at Riggy stopped. Riggy got the idea, stood up and began racing up the hill. Then my gun clicked empty and Jimmy's firing stopped, too. Jack continued to fire, but except for one burnt arm, the result was less obvious to those being shot at and as our firing stopped, those heads came back up again and took in the situation. They began firing again immediately. Riggy gave a twitch and a hop and went flat behind the body of his horse.

I reloaded as fast as I could, and then I was firing again. Jimmy started firing, too, and Riggy was up and running again. Then I started thinking clearly and held my fire until Jimmy stopped. The instant he stopped, I started again, a regular squeeze, squeeze, squeeze, not caring whether I hit a thing as long as those heads stayed down.

As I finished, Jimmy opened again and then Riggy was past us and up the ramp. He went flat in the doorway there and started firing himself. I retreated up the ramp, then Jack, then Jimmy. When Jimmy was inside, I yelled for George to lift the ramp. He was either watching or he heard me, and the ramp lifted smoothly up and locked in place.

Shots were still coming from the other sides of the ship, so I yelled at Jimmy to go left. I cut through the middle, tripping and practically breaking my neck on one of the chairs.

In the doorway, I skidded flat on my face again and looked for targets. Then I started firing. The three I was covering for used their heads and slipped aboard one at a time. As the second one came aboard, I heard Jimmy call for his ramp to be raised. My third was Venie Morlock, and as she ran aboard, I couldn't resist tripping her. I yelled to George.

Venie glared at me and demanded, "What was that for?" as the ramp swung up.

"Just making sure you didn't get shot," I said, lying.

A second later, Jack yelled for the last ramp to be raised. My last view of Tintera was of a rain-soaked hillside and men doing their best to kill us, which all seems appropriate somehow.

Riggy had been completely unhurt by the barrage, but he had a great gash on his arm that was just starting to heal. So much for a turtle policy, at least on Tintera. Riggy said that he had been minding his own business in the woods one day when a Losel jumped out from behind a bush and slashed him. That may sound reasonable to you, but you don't know Riggy. My opinion is that it was probably the other way around—the Losel was walking along in the woods one day, minding his own business, when Riggy jumped out from behind a bush and scared him. That is the sort of thing that Riggy is inclined to do.

Riggy said, "Where did you get that gun? Can I see it?"

I handed it over to him. After a minute of inspection,

Riggy said, "You wouldn't want to trade something for it, would you?"

I said, "Riggy, you may have it." I didn't particularly want it anymore. I knew I would never use it again and it held no fascination for me.

Only seventeen of us in all came aboard. Twelve didn't live or trigger their signals. I thought about that on the way back to the Ship. I counted the times I was in some danger of being killed, and I came up with a minimum of five times. If you say the chances of living through any single one of these encounters was nine in ten, the chances of living through five are only six in ten. Fifty-nine in a hundred, actually. If everybody's experience was like mine, it wasn't unreasonable that twelve of us should not come back. The trouble was that Att was among the missing twelve.

When we got to the Ship, people were there to take care of our horses. We went through decontamination quickly and then they led us into the reception room. They had decorations up for Year End on the walls and colored mobiles that twinkled overhead. There was a band and Daddy in his official capacity to welcome the new adults. Daddy shook my hand.

There were parents waiting. There was Mother and I saw Jimmy's mother and her husband and his father and his father's wife. When they saw Jimmy they all waved. And I saw Att's mother.

I said to Jimmy, "I'll see you later."

I went to Att's mother and I said, "I'm sorry, but Att isn't with us." I didn't know how else to say it. I wished I could say it so that it didn't hurt her, but it hurt me, too, to know that he wasn't coming back, and it hurt me to tell her. When she hadn't seen him with us, she must have known. She began to cry and she nodded and touched my shoulder, and then turned away.

I went over to Mother and she smiled and took my hand. "I'm pleased you came home," she said, and then she began to cry, and turned her head.

Daddy came away from giving his congratulations and he hugged me. He put a measuring hand over my head and said, "Mia, I believe you've grown some."

I nodded, because I thought I had, too. It felt very good to be home.

20

I've always resented the word *maturity*, primarily, I think, because it is most often used as a club. If you do something that someone doesn't like, you lack maturity, regardless of the actual merits of your action. Too, it seems to me that what is most often called maturity is nothing more than disengagement from life. If you meet life squarely, you are likely to make mistakes, do things you wish you hadn't, say things you wish you could retract or phrase more felicitously, and, in short, fumble your way along. Those "mature" people whose lives are even without a single sour note or a single mistake, who never fumble, manage only at the cost of original thought and original action. They do without the successes as well as the failures. This has never appealed to me and that is another reason I could never accept the common image of maturity that was presented to me.

It was only after I came back from Trial that I came to a notion of my own as to what maturity consists of. Maturity is the ability to sort the portions of truth from the accepted lies and self-deceptions that you have grown up with. It is easy now to see the irrelevance of the religious wars of the past, to see that capitalism in itself is not evil, to see that honor is most often a silly thing to kill a man for, to see that national patriotism should have meant nothing in the twenty-first century, to see that a correctly-arranged tie has very little to do with true social worth. It is harder to assess critically the insanities of your own time, especially if you have accepted them unquestionably for as long as you can remember, for as long as you have been alive. If you never make the attempt, whatever else you are, you are not mature.

I came to this conclusion after the Ship's Assembly that was held as a result of our experiences on Tintera. Our experiences were shocking to the Ship, and Tintera seemed like a glimpse of the Pit. The Tinterans were Free Birthers beyond a doubt. (I don't like that idea even now.) They might be slavers. They had obtained a scoutship by some low method and had intended to use it against us. Finally, they had killed an unprecedented number of our Trial Group. To die on Trial was one thing—to have children assassinated by Mudeaters was another.

Rumors started to spread almost as soon as we had arrived home. The day after we came home, a Ship's Council Meeting was held, and thereafter an account of what had actually happened was broadcast through the Ship. To most people, it was worse than the rumors.

I sat in on the Council meeting and testified, and I could see that every man on the Council was bothered by what we had to say. The Council concluded that a major decision needed to be made, and made with reasonable promptness, so two days later a Ship's Assembly was called.

The only adults who were not in the amphitheatre for the Assembly were the few hundred people absolutely required to keep our world running. The seventeen of us who had survived, Mr. Pizarro, and George Fuhonin sat with the Council on the stage at the base of the theatre. I had seen plays performed where I was sitting.

Daddy called the Assembly to order on the hour, and began by apologizing for interrupting the holiday with serious business.

"I know, however," he said, "that most of you have caught the vid discussions of Tintera and realize the serious nature of the problem. We dropped a Trial Group on this planet one month ago. We'll have them tell you as they told the Council exactly what they saw and experienced. When they have finished, the floor will be open to questions and debate."

The audience had previously heard the facts. Now they heard them directly from us. I testified about Free Birth. I told exactly what I had seen. Jack Fernandez-Fragoso testified about the Losels. Jimmy told about the captured scoutship. One by one, we told what we knew, led by Daddy's questions, and Mr. Pizarro and George added their testimony to ours. When we were done, the questioning started. Mr. Tubman recognized the signal of a little man sitting high in the left banks and put him on screen. The whispering-gallery amplifiers picked up his question.

"Do I understand that they were using these Losel things as slaves? Is that right?"

Mr. Persson answered that fairly. "We don't know that. They were definitely using them as involuntary labor. The question seems to be whether they are intelligent enough to be called slaves. As you heard from Mr. Fernandez-Fragoso, there are some indications that they are, and some that they aren't. But I think we should bear the possibility in mind."

The little man nodded, and Mr. Tubman passed on to another man who had signaled for recognition.

"Am I right? They actually intended to move against our Ship by force?"

Mr. Persson said, "That's not certain, either. It's another possibility and it was settled by the disabling of the scoutship."

The man said, "Barbaric," half to himself. Then: "I think we ought to offer a vote of thanks to these young people for solving our problem for us." And he sat down.

The next person to gain recognition seconded the idea, and my face got hot. I looked at Jimmy and saw that he was embarrassed, too. I wished that they would pass on. I didn't want any vote of thanks like a stone hung around my neck.

Mr. Persson said, "I think that's a fine idea. I call for a vote on the motion."

One of the others on the Council raised an objecting hand. He said, "I think that's getting away from the purpose of this Assembly. If at some other time the idea seems in order, we can take action on it then."

There was a great deal of commotion. When everything settled down, Daddy made his ruling.

"I think we should continue now."

Knowing what Daddy had in mind to do in this Assembly, I was just as glad not to be thanked.

The next man to speak said, "I think we're missing the main point. These people are Free Birthers! That's the whole question. We all know what that sort of policy leads to. And they've proven it again with this scoutship business—who did they murder to get it?—with throwing our youngsters in jail, and all the rest. They're a menace, and that's the truth."

Mr. Persson started to answer that one, too. "It's their

planet, Mr. Findlay. I wouldn't want to deny them the right to have laws of trespass. And for the . . ."

My father cut him off. "I disagree. I think Mr. Findlay has raised a valid issue. It should be considered seriously."

There was a lot of noise on this, but since the Council members were the only ones on an open circuit outside the controller's direction, Mr. Persson and Daddy were the only ones who could be heard clearly. There were, as I well knew, firmly drawn lines here. Under the politesse and apparent impartiality, Daddy was heading straight for a definite purpose with the aid of Mr. Tubman, and Mr. Persson was trying just as hard to turn the Assembly aside.

When they could be heard, Mr. Persson said, "We're aware. We are aware of the danger these people present. We are aware. But the question has been settled for the moment. They may be Free Birthers, but still there are no more than a few million of them. They are primitive. They are backward. They have no *means* by which to do us harm. At worst, they can be contained. Let's leave the poor devils alone in isolation to work out their own destiny."

Daddy said just as doggedly, "I don't agree!"

Somebody started yelling for debate then, and it spread, more and more people yelling—this is the fun of Assemblies—and then, finally, they got everything quieted down.

The man who was recognized by the controller said, "It's all right for you to sit there and tell us that, Mr. Persson, but can you guarantee that they won't get another scoutship by whatever way they got their first one? Can you guarantee that?"

"If the other Ships are warned," Mr. Persson said, "there won't be any problem. But the real point is being missed here. The real point is not the damage that this backward planet can do to us. The real point is, what is the reason that there is any possibility of damage being done to us? I maintain that it is *because* they are backward!"

"That isn't the question we are considering," my father said. "We're considering a specific case, not general issues. It isn't pertinent. That's my ruling."

"It is pertinent!" Mr. Persson said. "It couldn't be more pertinent. This question is larger than you want to admit, Mr. Havero. You've been avoiding bringing this question of policy, of basic policy for our Ship, out into the open. I say that now is the time."

"You're out of order."

"I am not out of order! I say we should consider the point of general Ship policy. I call for a vote now to decide whether or not we should consider it. I call for a vote, Mr. Havero."

People in the Assembly started yelling again, some calling for a vote and some not. Eventually those calling for a vote got the louder end of it and my father held up a hand.

"All right," he said, when it was quiet enough for him to be heard. "A motion has been made and seconded for a vote on the question of consideration of our planetary policy and carried by acclamation. Controller, record the vote."

"Thank you," Mr. Persson said, and punched his vote button.

I knew that Daddy wanted a vote of no, but I voted yes.

When everybody had voted, the master board showed "Yes" in green, "No" in red. The vote was 20,283 to 6,614. So we considered the question.

Mr. Persson said, "As you all know, our past policy has been to hand only as little technical information out to the planets as possible, and then only in return for material considerations. I say this is a mistake. I've said it before in Council meetings and I've attempted to bring it up before past Assemblies. In testimony that was made before the Council, Mia Havero stated that part of Tintera's great hate for us is their feeling that they have been unfairly dealt out of their inheritance to which they have as much a right as we. I can't say that I really blame them. We had no use for them—they had nothing we felt we could use—and in consequence they live lives of squalor. If there is any blame to assign for the fact that they are Free Birthers, I think it is ours for allowing them to lose contact with the unpleasant facts of history that we know so well. The responsibility was ours and we failed. I don't believe that we should punish them for our failure."

There was a round of applause from the Assembly as he finished. Then my father began to speak.

"I'm sure you all know that I disagree in every respect with Mr. Persson. First, the responsibility for what these people are—Free Birthers, possibly slavers, certainly attempted murderers—belongs to them, and not to us. They are products of the same history that we are, and if they have forgotten that history, it is not our business to teach it to them. We cannot judge them by what they might have been or by what they should have been. We have to take them for what they are and what they themselves intend to be. They are menaces to us and to every other portion of the present human race. I firmly believe that our only course is to destroy them. If we do not, then and only then will we have grounds to lay blame on ourselves. We in the Ships are in a vulnerable position; we live in an uneasy balance and the least mistake will be our ruin. Tintera is backward today, but even contained, tomorrow it may not be. That is the main fact to remember. A cancer cannot be contained and a planet that does not regulate birth is a cancer. A cancer must be destroyed or it will grow and grow until it destroys its host and itself. Tintera is a cancer. It must be destroyed.

"As for our planetary policy, I don't believe that it needs fresh justification. The reasons for it are clear enough and they have not changed. We do live in a precarious balance, but there is reason for our living so. If we were to abandon the Ships and take up life on one or more of the colony planets, inevitably much of the knowledge that we have preserved and expanded would be lost or mutilated. If we were to take up life on one of the colonies, we would be swallowed and lost, a small voice in a population many times our size. In the exigencies of making a living under primitive conditions—and the most advanced of the colonies is still primitive—how much time would be left for art and science and mathematics? These things require time, and time is one thing that is not free on the colonies. Much that is around us could never be transported to a planet and preserved if the Ship were left behind. It could not be reproduced on any planet. It would have to be abandoned.

"We do live in a balance. We use and we re-use, but once we use and re-use we lose something that we cannot replace ourselves. We are dependent on the colonies for our survival. That is à cold fact. We are dependent upon the colonies for our survival. To gain the things we have to have in order to survive, we must give something in return. The only thing we have that we can spare to trade is knowledge—we cannot give it away as Mr. Persson has suggested in the past that we might. We cannot give it away. It is our only barter for the means to continue to exist as we want to exist. The only alternative to our present policy—the only alternative—is to abandon the Ship. I don't want that—do you?"

As Daddy finished, the Assembly applauded again. I wondered if the same people were applauding who had applauded Mr. Persson. When they quieted, Mr. Persson spoke again.

"I deny it. I deny it. I deny it! It is not the only alternative. I agree that we live in a balance. I agree that we fulfill a necessary function and cannot abandon it. But I still believe that the colonies, our fellow heirs, deserve better of us than they have received. Whatever is decided about Tintera, it is a tragedy as it stands today. It is an indictment of our policy. We have other alternatives to this policy. Without even spending time on it, I can think of two, either of which is preferable to our present course. Our dependence on the colonies is artificial. We pride ourselves on our proven ability to survive. We pride ourselves that we have kept ourselves tough, mentally and physically. But what does our toughness prove? We think it proves much—but actually? Nothing! Nothing because it is all a waste. How could we prove our fitness? We could hunt up a planet and produce for ourselves the raw material we need. Or for another, we could actually attempt to apply some of our avowed scientific superiority and devise a method by which we could avoid any dependence on any planet, colony or uninhabited, for raw material. We could devise a method to make the Ship truly self-sufficient. By either of these courses we would lose nothing in doing what we should have been doing from the beginning—sharing knowledge, teaching and helping to make something of the human race as a whole.

"I accuse us. I accuse us of being lazy. We meet no challenges at all. We drift instead on a lazy, leisurely, floating course that takes us from planet to planet, meeting no challenges, fulfilling none of our potential, being less than we could be. To me, that is a sin. It is an affront to God, but more than that, it is an affront to ourselves. I can think of nothing sadder than to know that you might be more than you are, but be unwilling to make the effort. We could be raising our fellow men from the lives of squalor and desperation that they lead. You don't wish this? Then I say it would be better to leave them alone completely than to follow our present meddlesome, paternalistic, repressive course. We have the power to explore the stars. If we were willing to take the chance, we could travel to the end of the Galaxy. That is within our power and it would certainly add to the knowledge we claim to be interested in. But our present life is parasitical. Can we leave things as they now stand?"

The debate went on for two hours. After Mr. Persson and Daddy had spoken, it went to the Assembly. At times, it was extremely bitter. At one point, someone said that a sign of the sterility of our life was that we in the Ship had no art.

Mr. Lemuel Carpentier rose to dispute this. That was the only time during the evening that Mr. Mbele spoke. He bowed to Mr. Carpentier and then he said simply, "Sir, you are wrong," and took his seat again.

In the end, the lines were drawn so plainly that everyone knew where he stood. At the end of two hours, my father rose and called a halt to the debate.

"It all seems clear enough," he said. "Any further argument will simply be recapitulation, so there seems no point in carrying things further. I propose we call this all to a vote. The basic question seems to be, what shall be done with Tintera? That is the purpose of this Assembly. Those who agree with Mr. Persson on a policy of containment, and I don't know what else—re-education perhaps?—will also be voting for a change in our basic way of life along one or more of the lines that Mr. Persson has suggested or some similar alternative. Those who vote with me for the destruction of Tintera will also be voting for a continuation of the policies we have been living by for 160 years. Is that a fair statement of the situation, Mr. Persson?"

Mr. Persson nodded. "I will second the motion for a vote myself."

"Is the motion carried?"

There was an overwhelming response from the Assembly.

"The motion is carried. The vote will be—shall Tintera be destroyed? All those in favor vote 'Yes.' All those opposed vote 'No.' Controller, record the vote."

I pressed my button. Again the master board showed "Yes" in green and "No" in red. The vote was 16,408 to 10,489—and Tintera was to be blown out of existence.

It took just a few more minutes for the meeting to be closed. The amphitheatre began to clear, but I didn't leave immediately and neither did Jimmy. I saw Mr. Mbele making his way down toward us. He walked up to the table and looked at Daddy and for a long moment he didn't say anything. Daddy was putting his papers together.

Mr. Mbele said, "So we've returned to the days of 'moral discipline.' I thought all of that lay behind us."

Daddy said, "You could have made that point, Joseph. In this case, I happen to think 'moral discipline'—if you want to use that tired old phrase . . ."

"Euphemism."

"All right, euphemism. I happen to think it was justified by the circumstances."

"I know you do."

"You could have spoken. Why didn't you?"

Mr. Mbele smiled and shook his head. "It wouldn't have made any difference today," he said. "Change isn't going to come about easily. I'm just going to have to wait for another generation." He nodded at Jimmy. "Ask him how he voted."

He knew Jimmy and there was no question in his mind.

Daddy said, "I don't have to. I already know how they both voted. Mia and I have been talking about this for the past three days—arguing—and I know we don't agree. Was it a mistake to put her in your hands?"

Mr. Mbele was surprised. He looked at me and raised his eyebrows. He said, "I doubt it was me. If it were, you'd have voted against your own motion. I think it's the times that are changing. I hope it is."

Then he turned and walked away.

I said to Daddy, "Jimmy is going to help me pack."

"All right," Daddy said. "I'll see you later."

I was leaving the apartment. That had been decided earlier in the week. It wasn't merely a matter of Daddy's and my complete inability to agree. He'd asked if it was.

I said, "No. I just think it would be better if I left. Besides, Mother will be moving back in."

"How did you know that?"

I smiled. "I just knew she would."

With Mother coming back, I knew it was time for me to leave. In any case, I was an adult now, and it was time for me to stop holding on to Daddy's hand.

I wasn't entirely candid with him, however, as I suspect he knew. We no longer saw things exactly the same way—I didn't like what Daddy was doing—and it would have made a difference in living in the same apartment. I had changed, but it wasn't just Mr. Mbele who had changed me. It was a lot of things—experiences and people—including Daddy himself. If he hadn't moved us to Geo Quad, there is no doubt that I would never have voted the way I did, if I had by some miracle passed Trial.

As Jimmy and I were leaving the amphitheatre, Daddy turned and called to George. "Come along. The Council will want to talk with you before you leave."

I said to Jimmy, "You were sitting next to George. How did he vote?"

"He voted for."

"They're going to send him to do it, you know."

Jimmy nodded.

The thing that I didn't understand was how people who are as fine and as kind as Daddy and George could vote to destroy a whole world of people. The reason that I didn't understand was that it was only in the past few weeks that my world had grown large enough to include Mud-eaters and other patent inferiors and that I had learned to feel pain at their passing. I simply did not want to see Tintera destroyed. Daddy was *wrong.* I had had my moral blindness and now it was gone. I could not understand my former self and I could not understand Daddy and George.

Five years have passed since then and I still don't fully understand. There is a lesson that I learned at twelve—the world does not end at the edge of a quad. There are people outside. The world does not end on the Fourth Level. There are people elsewhere. It took me two years to learn to apply the lesson—that neither does the world end with the Ship. If you want to accept life, you have to accept the whole bloody universe. The universe is filled with *people,* and there is not a single solitary spear carrier among them.

I envy people like Jimmy who knew that all along and didn't have to learn. Jimmy says he had to learn, too, and that I just never noticed, but I don't believe him.

Daddy and George and the other 16,000 had no right to destroy Tintera. If you like, it is never right to kill millions of people that you don't know personally. Intellectually I knew long ago that the ability to do something doesn't necessarily give you the right to do it—that's the old power philosophy, and I never liked it. We might be able to discipline Tintera, but who appointed us to the job? We were doing it anyway and there was no one to stop us, but we were wrong.

New Year's Eve is the final night of Year End, and the biggest night of celebration of them all. There are parties in every corner of the Residential Levels, all designed to wind up the clocks for another year. I was supposed to meet Jimmy at a party being given by Helen Pak, but I didn't show up.

George was out there somewhere in his scoutship, eliminating Tintera, and I didn't feel particularly like going to a party. Happy 2200, everyone.

I was down on the Third Level. I'd gone past Lev Quad and down to Entry Gate 5. I walked for awhile in the park and then they turned on the precipitation and I ran for shelter, the familiar building in which I'd stowed my gear for a year and a half before I had graduated to a more exalted state in which I could participate in decisions to morally discipline all the bad people in the universe.

It was dark except for the light shining at the entry gate. The temperature was cool and pleasant and the rain dripped from the roof in a steady trickle. It was, as much as any I've ever known, a fine night to be alive. That was where Jimmy found me eventually, tunelessly humming to myself. I saw him come out of the entry gate, look around, and then run through the rain, and it struck me how much he had grown.

He sat down next to me. "I finally figured you might be here. Depressed?"

"A little."

"Tomorrow, let's stop in and see Mr. Mbele. He wants to see us, you know, and we have to start planning our advance training."

"All right," I said. Then I said, "I wonder if Att was still alive."

Jimmy said, "Don't . . . dwell on it."

"I'll tell you something . . ." I began with vehemence.

"I *know*. We'll change things."

I nodded. "I hope it doesn't take too long," I said. "What will we be like if it does?" I found the thought horrifying.

Jimmy got up and said, "Come on. Let's go home to bed."

We splashed through the rain, running toward the light over the entry gate.

About the Author

Alexei Panshin was born in Lansing, Michigan, in 1940. He is a mixture of English-American and Russian, and he insists that his name is easy to pronounce. He served in the Army in Texas and Korea, graduated from Michigan State University in 1965 and received an M.A. from the University of Chicago in 1966.

He sold his first story in 1960, and has since appeared in all the major science fiction magazines as well as such diverse markets as *Dapper, motive,* and *Seventeen.* His first full-length critical work, *Heinlein in Dimension,* was published early in 1968 by Advent Publishers, Inc., and he has completed a second, *Science Fiction: A Critical Introduction,* under contract to another hardcover publisher. *Rite of Passage* is his first novel.